A Meeting of Magic

"With one hand, he pulled me up, while at the same time dropping to one knee just like I had done before. Then, he stood up again and he smiled at me. 'Forgive me, lady, for I haven't given you a name. I am Baour and I am honored to meet someone who respects nature as much as you do.' Or something to that effect. Most gracious, isn't it? Of course, that was before I saw him *kill* for the first time. But still...

"I must admit: he played on my vanity. I don't know for sure if he meant it, at least not anymore, but I think he did. Yes... yes, I do think he did. I was enchanted. 'My name is Esmeralda,' I told him, 'and to the people who live here, I am a witch.'

"He just smiled. It wasn't just a courteous smile, but a genuine one. A – dare I say it? – *boyish* one, even. 'I'm sure you are.'

"Baour looked over my shoulder and winked. 'I don't mean to be obtrusive, but as I have said, I have traveled far. May I call upon the King's Law and ask for shelter?'

"It occurred to me that for someone who claims to be a stranger, the necromancer had a good grasp of our customs. He knew it is forbidden to deny a traveler shelter shortly before evening falls if there is no inn nearby. Now that I come to think about it, he speaks our language fluently, as if it's his native tongue. Strange. I've never thought of that. Why didn't it cross my mind before? Ah, well, I guess it doesn't matter, does it?

"I let him in. I know some of you think I shouldn't have, but why not? I wasn't going to break the Law and this stranger had been kinder to me than any of you have in quite a while. He didn't need to, either. He knew I had to welcome him in anyway, as long as no physical violence was involved.

"We talked. Or at least, *I* talked. He mainly asked questions. Why I was living alone. If I had ever had a husband. Where I learned about plants and animals. When I was going to harvest my crops. How I got them to look so healthy. I thought it'd be impolite to ask him too much myself, so I refrained from doing so. Besides, the few questions I did launch were met with mostly cryptic answers. 'Where do you come from?' I inquired. 'From a tower,' he replied. 'Where have you been taught magic?' I tried. 'In the same tower,' he answered. Of course, I did ask him why he had come to this land. This necromancer, he seemed so cultivated, so knowledgeable. Not because of his words, but because of something even less tangible. So I wondered why he was visiting Barnsby, of all places! That was the first time I saw something else in his expression. Something... *darker*. His face turned grim and his voice grave. 'I have come here because, right now, this is the right place to be.'

by Dirk Vandereyken

A BlackWyrm Book
Louisville, Kentucky

BAOUR: STRANDS OF DEATH

Copyright ©2009 by BlackWyrm

All rights reserved, including the right to reproduce this book, or portion thereof, in any form. Written permission must be secured from the publisher to use or reproduce any part of this book, except for brief quotations in critical reviews or articles.

The characters in this novel are fictitious. Any resemblance to actual persons living or dead is purely coincidental.

A BlackWyrm Book
BlackWyrm Publishing
10307 Chimney Ridge Ct, Louisville, KY 40299

Printed in the United States of America.

ISBN: 978-0-9820067-2-6
LCCN: 2008942315
Cover by Mark Vanco
Edited by Dave Mattingly and Jason Walters

First edition: April 2009

DEDICATED TO:

My parents,
for always believing in me
and letting me leave for conventions in the U.S. and the U.K.
when I was supposed to attend high school

Francesca Sorbie, for inspiring me

Sofie Hermans and Hanne Deputter, for the memories

Caroline Branders, for 'having issues' – she'll know what I mean

Jason Walters, for making me understand Republicans better
and being so kind and supportive

Tom Vanherck, for being the best Dynamic Duo Sidekick
I could wish for

Table of Contents

Foreword

There It sits, unmoving, in the middle of Its Web, oblivious to the scholarly debates about Its existence. Some claim It is only semi-sentient, others say the Spider is all-knowing and wise beyond the measure of any other intelligent being, while on certain worlds philosophers are branded as heretics, flogged, maimed, and decapitated just for insinuating that It isn't conscious at all, or, worse, that It does not exist.

Whatever the truth, even though Its body is gigantic, the Spider has not been misnamed, for it is just that: an arachnid. Its eight legs span entire continents and Its hairs rival the highest man-made towers, while Its faceted eyes are deemed to be the only visual organs capable of perceiving all of the Strands that It spins, whether they be connected to the tiniest particles or the largest objects.

Know the truth, for it is the truth on which all magic is based: every single particle in the multiverse, every object, and even the tiniest element within a thought pattern is connected to the Web. Most mortal eyes cannot see these colored connections, but they are there nonetheless; oscillating, fluctuating, but always present.

And so the Spider spins our reality and even our very existence, seemingly blissfully unaware of Its own actions. It just sits there, but to know Its motives or the reasons for Its existence is to start walking on a rarely-trodden path that can only lead to madness. Only the Seraphalim, worshipped as gods on many worlds, know Its true location. Only the Seraphalim can find It throughout the many layers of warped space, only they can ignore what most living beings experience as the passing of time long enough to find It again and again, and even they are unable to penetrate Its thoughts, if they exist at all. For they, too, are nothing more than bundles of Strands, wrapped into each other, connected by whim or design, ever-changing, but stable enough to form creatures and objects.

On this day, which is known as Judging Day on Aerkaron, but which in other places is a different day or even year or century entirely, the Spider stirs. It only does so rarely, but the events unfolding in the village of Barnsby seem to have caught Its attention, or at least to have provoked a reflex that defies interpretation.

On this day, in what later will be known as the Year of the Gauntlet, the Spider has moved and every universe in existence has moved with It, sending ripples through time and space, obliterating entire planes of existence within a single heartbeat, while in some galaxies only barely making a flower lose one of its leaves.

On this day something will change forever and the history of the universe will be rewritten.

Chapter One
THE CHARGE

"How… how do you plead?" Reald was very much conscious of the fact that he sounded insecure. It had been more than thirteen years since he had last felt like this. The part-time barrister still remembered his first few court cases, when he was young and inexperienced. Except for the local clergy, he was the only man in the village who had learned how to read and write, so it was only natural that he would take up the mantle of a lawyer during those few times that Barnsby had needed one. Most of his knowledge of the law was limited to the few specialized books he been able to acquire during his short travels, but over the last decade he had been very effective in settling disputes in subjects ranging from stolen livestock to the use of swearwords and besmearing the statue of a local saint. This case, however, was pushing his limits as a lawyer. Moreover, it was frightening the entire village. Humans are a curious lot, though, and so it was no surprise that most of the villagers had come to the makeshift court at the temple of the Seraphalim Gealius, whose domains were piety, family, and raising crops.

"Guilty."

It was a single word, but its impact was akin to that of the most potent magic weaving imaginable. There were ninety-three people sitting on the velvet cushions in the nave, but they gasped as if they were a single breathing entity. A gestalt, melted together because of a common fear.

Baour grinned as he looked at the crowd gathered before him. He was standing at the rear their altar, with the semi-circular marble apse behind him. Around the necromancer, crimson tapestries depicted the eight seasons, with embroideries showing Gealius offering presents to his followers on every single one of them. Happy scenes – but the contrast with the atmosphere inside of the temple proper had never been so big. The irony of it all had struck Baour since the proceedings had begun, almost half a sleep-cycle ago. There he was, standing in a place of worship, right where the priests were supposed to be, the cold metal of the altar touching his hands as he held it while slightly leaning towards his spectators. That was what they were, after all: spectators.

They must feel uncomfortable, Baour thought, *but still they are here, satisfying their curiosity and hoping that they will see with their own eyes that all will end well. Alas, it will not.*

"You look surprised," Baour said, locking his gaze with Reald's and then looking into the crowd. "Is this not what you wanted to hear?"

It took Reald, a middle-aged man with long wavy brown hair and a muscular build, a few moments to recover. "It is," he finally replied. "If it is the truth," he then added, almost as an obligatory afterthought. "You do realize that by pleading guilty to these charges, you forego the right to demand a lesser punishment?"

"A lesser punishment than what exactly?" Baour wanted to know. He sounded composed and it was his calmness more than anything else that was making the villagers feel uneasy. The necromancer defied the depictions of their best minstrels. Yes, his pearly white hair covered his lower back as well as it did his shoulders, but his face was youthful and he wore a constant healthy blush on his smooth skin. Yes, his penetrating grey eyes were the color of granite, but there was an apparent empathy there that necromancers weren't supposed to have. There was no evilness about Baour, no harshness, no viciousness, but that only made him appear more menacing. He was a death mage, after all, and no good could come out of such a vocation.

Reald frowned, shaking his head in disbelief. His hands were clammy and he had to fight his growing uneasiness, but he was also acutely aware of the prying eyes in his back as he stood before Baour, two steps down from the altar. The tall necromancer loomed over him and he felt smaller than he ever had before, even during his encounter with a garolda in Seador's Bay. If he were to fail now, though, he would incur the wrath of the entire village, small as it may be. "I have read the possible punishments to you when we first started this case, necromancer. Obviously being banned from this village is far less great a toll to pay than die while your eyes are being poked out with a hot metal rod."

Still the necromancer kept on smiling. He could almost hear people trying to swallow away their growing uneasiness. "You say that I can cheat death, that I can bend it to my will and make it dance before me like it was a puppet on a string. *My* string. So why should I not plead guilty to your charge? You think even the most painful death sentence holds no true risk to me, do you not?"

Silence. Baour took care not to enjoy the moment too much. These were living beings, after all, and they were scared out of their wits already. It was unfortunate, but it was also necessary. When he saw that Reald had regained his composure, he added, "Still. I know you see death as my willing companion, my mistress even, but I shall not embrace her."

A collective gasp, again.

"But... the only punishment to your guilty plea is death," Reald stammered.

"It is not."

"It... it is!" Reald had been sure about it, but now his mind started to drift to the ancient texts. The words started to appear to him again, the beautiful calligraphy secondary to their content. An execution. That was the only way, wasn't it?

"Again I say to you it is not," Baour repeated, this time raising his gentle voice to a powerful baritone level. "I plead guilty to conferring with your dead, but 'tis a transgression to Divine Law!" He pulled up his right arm, waving his hand towards the villagers, one of his fingers raised to the sky. "The Law of the Kings only concerns the living, not those who have departed from this existence, whether it be a beautiful or a tortured one. The realm of the dead *is* subject to Divine Law only, but..." Baour twisted his torso towards the Seraphalim's statue, pointing at the villagers' deity, "I do *not* recognize Gealius's divine authority!"

This time, some of the villagers' more fiery emotions got the better of them. "Heathen!" one of them shouted. "Blasphemer," two others screamed. "Demon brood!" another one exclaimed without thinking.

"I am no heathen, no blasphemer, and if I had been demon brood, I would have melted away your flesh as if it were burning wax covering wiry frames before these proceedings had even started," Baour stated, immediately thereafter lowering his voice to its usual honey-sweet level again. "I did not denounce this Seraphalim, nor did I deny or even question his existence. I only question his authority, as he is no more or less a living being than we are. As such, he has no divine, moral, nor spiritual prerogative over my actions, however repugnant they may be to you."

Silence again. The mage looked at one face in the crowd, then at another. Everyone seemed to be unified in his or her expressions, horrified but puzzled at the same time. As someone who could manipulate the Strands, Baour spoke with greater authority than any peasant ever could. He wore a mantle, but it was not just a physical one. It was a mantle of wisdom and of knowledge, one that granted senses far beyond those possessed by mere mortals. Still, the villagers' beliefs were ingrained deep into their collective psyche, passed on from generation to generation and Baour knew that it was only a matter of time before their faith would take control over their thoughts yet again. There was only one strategy to follow, only one way that might lead to eventual victory.

"So silent," Baour whispered. He took another pause, just to heighten the drama. "So silent!" he repeated, this time almost shouting into the crowd. The echo carried through the air for a while, adding strength and – yes – *meaning* to his words. He knew full well what he wanted to say next. No, he hadn't rehearsed beforehand, but Baour firmly believed that intuition is nothing more than the ability to think so quickly that thoughts which can't even be properly perceived form into coherent ideas with lightning speed, only to become obvious upon later reflection. He knew that the ability to communicate well is also the ability to improvise and still be structured and logical. "So where are they?" he asked defiantly. "Where are those who represent this Law that I will not abide by? Where are those that should speak up?" Before anyone could answer, he stressed, "*Where are your priests?*"

He pretended to scour those present, even though he had known where the clergymen were sitting since the procedures began. He could see people trying not to turn their heads towards Gealius's robed servants, but they were unable to control their eye movements well enough to hide their true intentions. The three priests saw it, too, and they rose, all at once, but each one of them just as reluctantly as the man next to him. One was old, one was middle-aged, and one was too young to be a priest in any of the major cities, even those abroad, where youngsters are revered and cuddled and mounted by grown men as if they are manifestations of the Seraphalim themselves.

"Here we are, necromancer," the cleric who was closest to his end days said. "We were not hiding as you implied. Reald has been appointed as the barrister for these proceedings, we have not, and so we abide by the King's Law." He pointed towards the hapless villager, who by now was nervously shifting his weight from his left foot to his right.

Baour could see the attendees' attention shift from the trio to Reald. He smiled cynically and put his hands together: once, twice, thrice.

"Well done, old man," Baour said, "but you know that your barrister is a scribe by trade." When he saw that Reald wanted to say something, he added, "A scribe who has settled many a dispute, no doubt, but not one who can speak for your Seraphalim himself."

The ancient priest nodded and Baour could almost hear his colleagues' sigh of relief. They were glad he was doing the talking, because they had no idea what to say. "It is true our Reald cannot speak for Gealius, but he *can* enforce Divine Law. Thus it has been written in the charter that made this country what it is today."

"You are right," Baour agreed willingly, "but how can he do that correctly if he does not know how to interpret it?" This time it was Reald who seemed to be relieved. He stopped shaking and turned towards the necromancer.

"There is no interpretation needed!" the elder said, offended. "The Divine Law is clear on dealings with the dead: you shall not commune with them in any way or form possible!"

"I wonder…" Baour replied, looking into the crowd again, "what, than, does 'communing' with the dead mean precisely?" He pointed at Merielda, who was known to be a healer. "Did this woman have to stand trial when she brought a child back from what you think is the netherworld?" He chose the undertaker next. "Or does Tealus have to be executed because he needs to touch a corpse before putting it to rest in your hill tombs, where it can be eaten by the birds?"

The priest laughed. "Preposterous!"

"Is it?"

"Of course it is!"

"Why?"

"Any intelligent soul here can understand why!"

Time to shut up again, Baour thought. *Let them reflect on those words for just a moment. Let me be their champion, because I need them to choose my side before I can save them.* Then, his voice went back to a whisper, but thanks to the acoustics it was still heard by everyone present. "I am glad you can read your flock's thoughts, old man."

The priest was no fool, though. "I cannot read their thoughts, black mage, and neither can you. But these people can think for themselves and they are not stupid. They know that the way you communicate with the dead is different from how we handle them." His two underlings nodded in agreement. Baour thought it was funny, because it made them look like they had no personality of their own.

"So you admit to handling the dead?"

To his left, a young woman started talking to her mother. In the middle of the temple, several friends exchanged viewpoints. To the right, a lively debate between two would-be philosophers started. Baour stroked his chin with his right hand, touching his elbow with his left, so that it would seem that any reply could only bounce off him.

"You offend us!" the priest shouted. The two others looked at each other for only a brief moment before nodding in agreement yet again.

"How, than, is what you do any less punishable by Divine Law than what I have done?" Baour asked, expressly sounding interested instead of condemning. It made him appear more sympathetic. "What do you do with the dead in this temple?" He was fixing the middle-aged priest to prompt an answer out of him, but the man just looked at his elder, his eyes as wide as his younger friend.

"We unclothe them. We bathe them. We sing prayers to them. We bid their spirits adieu. And we bring them to their final resting places."

"So you touch their bodies, you pretend as if they're alive and you try to commune with their souls before choosing where they will be eaten by poultry?"

"Do not mock us! By doing so, you mock all those present!"

Ah, another mistake.

"Is that so?" Baour asked, sincerely. He opened his arms wide as if he wanted to speak to everyone. "*Does* everyone here think these acts merit a different treatment entirely?"

"That... that is for the people to decide," Reald answered, almost reflexively. He gulped before continuing, "I am sure that no one here thinks Eldried has broken Divine Law."

Baour stepped in front of the altar and as he did so, most of those present held their breath. He laid one hand on Reald's shoulder, surprising the barrister, who froze almost immediately, terrified.

"Do not worry," the death-seer said, soothingly, as if he was teaching a boy the basics of art. "Do not worry!" he repeated to everyone. "I am not claiming that your priests have broken Divine Law. I only claim that what I have done is not fundamentally different than what they do almost every day." He shrugged. "And even if it is, I will not accept this Law of yours anyway."

"Why, then, even be here?" the one who was called Eldried wanted to know. "Why stand trial when you expect to resist judgment afterwards?"

Baour shrugged. "Because I expect to be exonerated. And because I want to help you."

"Help us in what way?" a woman wanted to know.

Their fear of me is bowing to their curiosity, slowly recognizing its true master.

"Later." He had always liked a well-staged show.

The old priest must have felt the tide changing, too. He was going to do what Baour had anticipated he would do – abandon reason and take up arms. "Lest you forget, black reaper, Gealius has given us power. This testifies to his existence and it shows us to obey Divine Law."

"'Tis true," Baour agreed happily, "your Seraphalim can manipulate the Strands like no worldly mage can. But you have used the correct words, elder: he has given you his power. *Some* of his power. But you are ignorant of how it works." Only now did Baour lift his hand from Reald's shoulder, which felt more relaxed than before. He walked up to the first few rows of people, but none of them rose, none of them looked scared, and none of them tried to avoid Baour's presence. Instead, a few villagers bowed forwards, their foreheads wrinkled. "I can see the connection between Gealius and yourself, priest. I can see how he controls the Strands around you when you ask him to... if he feels like it and deems you worthy. Why be scared of a gift I know far more intimately than you obviously do?" Before Eldried could answer, Baour changed the subject. "I am here, villagers of Barnsby! I want to leave this temple not only because I can do so at any time, but also because I want to leave as a free man, with enlightened countrymen in my wake! But before I do so, we have much to discuss. Sit, priests, and let this man continue the proceedings. We will have ample time to debate this issue later. Do not worry about my punishment yet, because I fully expect to go through those doors as a free man. While this court is in session, you can think, scheme, and try to figure out how to stop me and punish me if I am found guilty and still refuse to bow to Divine Law. In fact, I urge you to go forth and find allies, able men ready to halt me in my path and destroy me if you deem it necessary."

"We will sit." Eldried somehow sounded more serene now. The three clerics sat down in unison, just as they had stood up all at the same time.

Baour knew he could not be stopped. But he needed time to think himself. Those whom he had really come for were all present, except for one. He could see their Strands, corrupted, intertwined with black tentacles gripping at their selves, choking them like a snake would, connecting to the same Web everything connects to. His first attempt had failed and there was so little time left...

He smiled at Reald, gently. "Please continue, barrister."

Reald smiled back at the necromancer. "I will call the first witness."

"What is her name, my friend?"

No one seemed to notice Baour had called Reald a friend. Things were proceeding smoothly.

"Esmeralda," Reald replied. He scraped his throat. "The court calls the witch Esmeralda to the stand!"

Chapter Two
THE FIRST TESTIMONY
THE WITCH ESMERALDA SPEAKS

"I suppose some of you would like to hear me say that it was dark and cold outside, that the winds were howling and that the moons were full and screaming at the world underneath like they only do once or twice every year-cycle when I first met the man who calls himself Baour. Actually, I'm not so sure that's his real name, but I've never really cared about that. It's tough for a mother to hear her son call himself by a different name than the one she gave him at birth, but somehow I think this man before me has never had a mother. Right? But I'm digressing. I tend to do that, especially since my hair has turned grey and thin. Time has been kind to me, though, so I won't let any of you doubt what I'm about to say! I know some of you will, like you always have, but this time you shouldn't. No, no, not this time. Now hear me, Barnsby, and don't interrupt me! You can't, for once, because the Law says no one is allowed to interrupt a witness while she is still speaking, doesn't it?

"Anyway, it wasn't cold and the sun hadn't even sunk into the horizon yet. In fact, it was a beautiful day. The greens outside were vibrant, the browns stout and strong, the blues open and inviting, while the sounds were those of animal merry-making and courtship. I was baking in my cottage, a few miles outside of Barnsby. I've never been welcome in the village, but whenever one of you needs advice on more intimate matters, she comes knocking at my door. No, not at yours, old Eldried! So when I heard the first knock, and even the second one, I thought it was one of you, coming to me to discuss the absence of her husband in bed, or to ask me to concoct a brew which would make him more virile.

"By the third knock, I knew my visitor didn't hail from the village. Somehow, it sounded too forceful, too... *deliberate*. There was no insecurity there, no emotional urgency. For one moment, I thought the King's men were visiting me again, as they do every so often. They pretend to check up on me, making sure I don't violate any of the Laws, kingly or otherwise, but after a few questions they turn out to be as unsure of themselves as any of you, asking me to help them out with their problems. Some of them aren't very nice, though. They think the power to enforce the King's Law gives them the right to use and abuse, to levy taxes even nobles haven't heard of. In the end, it all balances out. One gives me coins, I give another one more than he should get.

"But there was no fourth knock. The King's men always keep knocking.

They're used to visiting people who pretend they're not home, just to avoid taxes or scrutiny. There was a stranger standing on my doorstep!

"So I did what I usually do when an uninvited guest shows up: I took my knives and hid them underneath my sleeves. I may be old, but I'm still swift and skilled at handling blades. One cut to sever tendons, another one to open up an artery.

"Of course I looked through the window first, but the angle was off. The only thing I could see was a light, red cloak, animated by a gentle breeze. It was an expensive piece of clothing, for sure, so I figured whomever it was, he wasn't planning on robbing me. Unless he would risk staining royal colors with blood, all for a purse with only enough coin in it to buy a handkerchief made of the same materials! I opened the door and there he was, a man like I had never seen. Tall and youthful, with delicate features and penetrating eyes, but with hair whiter than mine and with an aura that belies his apparent age. I only dabble in matters of the Web and I can't see the Strands the accused told me so much about after I got to know him, but my Sight is good enough to see some of the colors collections of Strands generate. I can tell you all, what I saw... what I *still* see... it... I'm not sure if I can describe it to you. I've always thought that actually perceiving a Seraphalim with the Sight would drive a mortal mad, and I've become even more certain of that since Baour first appeared at my doorstep. You can't see it, Eldried, and neither can you, Therionald and Ignetius, but this man, this *mage* standing trial... he is surrounded by colors, swirling colors, vibrant and lively and oh so painful to the Sight! A multitude of Strands have curled around him and he wears them like a mystic cloak. And I pray to Gealius that you are wrong, priests and blacksmith, you who are accusing this man and who have called for this trial, because his mastery of that which is unseen but far more real than what *can* be seen is such that none of us – *none* of us – can equal his power. Isn't it, necromancer? And even if we *are* wrong, I hope I've gotten to know you well enough, because I'm assuming you won't carry a grudge against us. I'm not so sure about you, priests, or you, smith Draudus!

"Ah, I can see my words pierce the hearts of some of you. And so they should! So they should! But my story hasn't finished yet. It has just begun.

"Where was I? Ah, yes, I had just opened the door. For a brief moment, I had to look away, as Baour's aura was overwhelming me. In that instant, he must have realized I have the Sight. It took me a few breaths to block it, reverting to my weary eyes and to the shadow most of us call reality. He didn't utter a single word, though. It felt like he was waiting for me to say something, and instinctively I dropped to one knee and bowed my head. 'Lord,' I stammered, but I'm not sure that I knew what to say after that. I didn't have to finish welcoming him, though. Instead, Baour gently lifted up my head with one of his delicate fingers.

"'I am not your lord'. That's what he said. Those were his first words to me. I may not recall every single piece of conversation literally, but I do recall exactly what he told me right afterwards, 'I am just a stranger traveling through these lands for the first time and I am in need of assistance. If anything, *you* are the lady, as I have seen crops growing outside of your cottage, healthy and strong. You have plowed a small patch of land and you have taken care of the plants around this building, nurturing them, caring for them like a mother cares for her children. I can see this. So do not bow for me, lady, let me bow for you!'

"With one hand, he pulled me up, while at the same time dropping to one knee just like I had done before. Then, he stood up again and he smiled at me. 'Forgive me, lady, for I haven't given you a name. I am Baour and I am honored to meet someone who respects nature as much as you do.' Or something to that effect. Most gracious, isn't it? Of course, that was before I saw him *kill* for the first time. But still...

"I must admit, he played on my vanity. I don't know for sure if he meant it, at least not anymore, but I think he did. Yes... yes, I do think he did. I was enchanted. 'My name is Esmeralda,' I told him, 'and to the people who live here, I am a witch.'

"He just smiled. It wasn't just a courteous smile, but a genuine one. A – dare I say it? – *boyish* one, even. 'I'm sure you are.'

"Baour looked over my shoulder and winked. 'I don't mean to be obtrusive, but as I have said, I have traveled far. May I call upon the King's Law and ask for shelter?'

"It occurred to me that for someone who claims to be a stranger, the necromancer had a good grasp of our customs. He knew it is forbidden to deny a traveler shelter shortly before evening falls if there is no inn nearby. Now that I come to think about it, he speaks our language fluently, as if it's his native tongue. Strange. I've never thought of that. Why didn't it cross my mind before? Ah, well, I guess it doesn't matter, does it?

"I let him in. I know some of you think I shouldn't have, but why not? I wasn't going to break the Law and this stranger had been kinder to me than any of you have in quite a while. He didn't need to, either. He knew I had to welcome him in anyway, as long as no physical violence was involved.

"We talked. Or at least, *I* talked. He mainly asked questions. Why I was living alone. If I had ever had a husband. Where I learned about plants and animals. When I was going to harvest my crops. How I got them to look so healthy. I thought it'd be impolite to ask him too much myself, so I refrained from doing so. Besides, the few questions I did launch were met with mostly cryptic answers. 'Where do you come from?' I inquired. 'From a tower,' he replied. 'Where have you been taught magic?' I tried. 'In the same tower,' he answered. Of course, I did ask him why he had come to this land. This necromancer, he seemed so cultivated, so knowledgeable. Not because of his words, but because of something even less tangible. So I wondered why he was visiting Barnsby, of all places! That was the first time I saw something else in his expression. Something... *darker*. His face turned grim and his voice grave. 'I have come here because, right now, this is the right place to be.' Or words to that effect, I can't remember exactly. In any case, it felt like he didn't want to say anything else about his reasons to come here, so I stopped asking.

"He didn't leave the next day. He was planning on visiting Barnsby, but he said he was afraid that you all would be wary of a mage. I told him that he was right. So he wanted to be prepared before showing up in the village. He asked me about all of you and about our customs. I thought he just didn't want to upset anyone, so I told him everything I know. Ha, that bothers some of you, doesn't it? No, I mean, I told him everything that is general knowledge. I didn't reveal any secrets, not about who is seeing a lover and not about who came to me to buy a love potion. He seemed eager to learn and I hadn't talked to any human being for that long since I first came to live here, so I guess I was a little drunk with excitement.

"Before I realized it, another day had passed, and then another. We often took strolls into the forest and I tried to teach him about herbs, but he seemed to already know everything. He never claimed to, though; but to tell you the truth I think he was just humoring me. It was fun to have someone around who was willing to listen to me, so I just kept going on about this weed or that plant, about that herb or that animal.

"I had earned enough coin since the last changing of the moons to avoid having to sell my wares on the marketplace for a while. I know you won't believe me, but I'd rather have earned less money, as a full purse usually means a lot of people have become ill lately. I know some of you are mad at me because the herbal concoctions I sold only alleviated the symptoms, but at least they did that. After a while I did need to travel to the village to sell some of my wares and I took Baour with me.

"After passing the first few farms, I actually had a great time visiting Barnsby, mostly because of the kids. Parents often tell me children are innocent and untainted, but they're not, you know. They can be just as harsh and petty as any adult, sometimes even more so. But they have something else going for them. Strangeness doesn't necessarily frighten them. In fact, it often fascinates them, especially if they're not amongst peers. That's why I like kids. They can see that I'm different, but they're not afraid of me, and when they saw Baour's nice clothes, they wanted to ask him questions, not drive him away. I know none of you can see the Strands, but I guess to most in Barnsby, Baour was found guilty by association as soon as you saw me walking next to him. I had warned him about that, of course, but he didn't seem to care.

"After helping me to set up my booth, the necromancer left. He told me he wanted to stroll through the village, small as it may be. I didn't see him again until sunset, but news travels fast and before I had sold my third ointment, Therionald and Ignetius had already found me. They wanted to know about Baour, asking all of the standard questions. I had nothing to hide – still haven't – but there wasn't much I could tell them. I get why priests want to know about new arrivals and I must admit that they were very friendly. You understand why people travel more than anyone here, Therionald, being a wandering priest and all. And you, Ignetius… you still have some of that childish inquisitiveness in you. Not like you, Eldried! I wish your fellow priest and initiate would always treat me like that, though. I think they were being kind because they needed information, but I don't hold that against them.

"Roaldus the tailor visited me as well. Apparently, Baour had asked him to make a new set of clothes for him and he wanted to know if the necromancer could pay for the fabrics he had ordered. In a strange way, I was happy to hear about this, 'cause the cloth had to be imported from Greensdale and that meant Baour was planning on at least staying until the moons had changed again – another twenty more sleep-cycles or so. I had grown quite fond of my companion, you know. I had never asked him for any money, though, so I didn't know what to tell Roaldus. He asked me if I could vouch for the mage and I said yes. Of course, that was before I knew what kind of magic he was practicing and what he was doing with it, so maybe I should've been less eager doing so. Even hindsight isn't always perfect, though.

"Baour finally came back while I was already breaking up my booth. Something was wrong. I could see it in his face. I had seen that expression only once before – when I had asked him why he'd come to the village. But there was something else in there too. He seemed pensive, worried, even. I asked him about it, but he just ignored the question and he didn't utter another word that evening.

"The next day, things were back to normal, sort of. My guest was talking again, but he was more brooding now. He started visiting the village more often, maybe once every three sleep-cycles or so. He told me he was checking up on Roaldus, even though the fabrics couldn't have arrived yet. I let him be because he was never gone for long and there were other things on my mind. While searching for herbs, I had found the ghostweed had been disappearing all over the forest. Eradicating ghostweed is one of the many things I do for all of you, without begging for your appreciation, but there wasn't much left to find anymore. I wouldn't know how to manipulate Strands to the degree needed to cultivate certain properties out of herbs or plants or anything else for that matter, but I do know that some mages can use certain Strands attached to ghostweed to help them weave dark magic and we were all taught that it disturbs the dead if left to grow out in the open. But now? Almost all of it seemed to be gone. Even the shadows of the great greeshtrees didn't seem to harbor the herb anymore. It disturbed me a little, but the thought that maybe the ghostweed had been dying everywhere was more comforting than anything else.

"It wasn't until I spoke with Ewella that I came to suspect Baour. Ewella has been living in the woods for many of our lifetimes, as most of you know. She's in charge of the part of the forest where I live, connected to the land like no other creature. The sprite visited me for the first time when I built my cottage, demanding that I'd be good to her land and I've always been so since. I like to look at her through the Sight. Her colors emanate out of her, becoming one with her surroundings. It's a beautiful thing to behold, especially since she doesn't visit often.

"I was gathering some plants when she whispered to me. Usually, her voice is like the wind, airy and sensual, and her words seem to float around for a while before disappearing. This time, though, she sounded heavy and chilling, as if the northern wind had hit, heralding the coming of Winter.

"'Esmeralda!' she whispered. I was surprised, but, uncharacteristically, she didn't wait until I had regained my composure. 'Esmeralda!' she repeated.

"'Ewella?' I asked.

"'It's me, Esmeralda,' the sprite answered in her own, beautiful language. 'I've been hiding here, in the treetop, trying to catch whoever has been stealing ghostweed without my consent.' She wasn't really using the word 'ghostweed,' as forest sprites have many words for every single herb, each one describing many different unique properties, differentiating between subspecies, but she was referring to the only kind of ghostweed that is able to grow here.

"'So it's true? The herb hasn't been dying?' I replied in her exotic tongue.

"'No, it hasn't,' Ewella replied. 'Someone has been taking it and I'm afraid that it's being used.'

"At first, I thought she was confirming that the stories about ghostweed are true, that it does disturb the dead, but Ewella assured me that wasn't what she meant. She seemed genuinely upset and we talked for a while, but she used many words I don't know yet. I was puzzled. After all, she had always encouraged me to root out the ghostweed; and if it wasn't going to anger the dead, did it really matter that someone else was taking it? Or so I thought. After a while, she got tired of trying to explain to me what she meant, so she stopped talking and we kissed for a while before she left.

"I never saw Ewella again. Not like she was then, with her white furry skin, oh so soft, and beautiful, glazy, purple eyes and long golden hair that flowed in the wind like it was alive.

"When Baour came back, I discussed the meeting with him. I still trusted him then and I thought he was being sincere when he told me he didn't have any use for ghostweed. He didn't seem too troubled about it, though. It was as if he had something else on his mind, but still the mage refused to tell me what. I'm a witch, not a tracker, and Baour claimed he didn't have any experience in looking for, or identifying, tracks, so the only thing we could do was try to be more vigilant. I started switching to the Sight more often than before, just to make sure no one had left any colors behind. That would make it easier to find out who was taking ghostweed. After a few wake-cycles of searching in vain, I asked Baour to look for Strands, since his Sight is so much more accurate than mine is. That's when he told me something that made me a little suspicious.

"'As you know, no human is capable of seeing every single Strand,' Baour explained to me, even though he knew I'm familiar with the Web. 'To see the Strand connected to every small thing, every single particle, would lead to insanity. So we specialize. We learn how to see certain Strands and filter out others, or we use the Sight to only visualize the Web on a larger scale, like you do. I have chosen to specialize.'

"We'd never discussed Baour's magic skills before. I knew he didn't like to talk about his past and I had been content to leave the subject well enough alone, but this time I wanted to know more. His refusal to answer even that question eventually started to make me angry. I felt betrayed. I shouted at him. He had been my guest for so long, I had told him so much, and I was so tired. Tired because I had been looking for a possible culprit and didn't have anything to show for it. Tired because I had felt Ewella's warm embrace eight sleep-cycles before and I was missing her love. Tired because Baour kept hiding underneath of a cloak of mystery even though I had been so kind to him.

"He never raised his voice.

"Even while I was shouting, the mage looked me in the eyes and asked me if he should leave. That calmed me down. 'Of course not,' I said. 'Of course you don't have to leave.' Now I wish I had took him up on his offer. I didn't and we went to sleep.

"I later realized that it probably was of no use to look for a ghostweed thief. After all, he had already gotten his hands on just about all of it, so why would he be back so soon? Ghostweed grows fast, however, so a few cycles later I started to look for possible miscreants again. I stumbled upon a few kids learning how to make love behind some bushes, a centaur visited me to heal a broken leg, and I had to turn Darius the lumberjack away again because he wanted to chop some young trees, but nothing unusual happened. Baour had started to take care of a flower field just outside of the cottage and I learned that he's a pretty bad cook. His soups are edible, but not much more than that.

"Then, everything changed. *Everything.* Please excuse me. I need a moment.

"I could feel it even while I was just waking up. There was something different about that morning. The light coming in through the windows was somehow duller than usual, the colors less vibrant, and I could feel a chill running through my spine. I looked to my right, where Baour usually slept, but he wasn't there anymore. That was the first time he'd gotten out of bed before me.

"I didn't even bother to put on decent clothes as I rushed outside. Out in the open, I could feel it even better. There was a strange aura permeating the place. Everything seemed darker than before. The birds were singing sad tunes instead of happy ones, a male rabbit was sitting in front of a female one without doing anything, and a squirrel almost tumbled out of a tree. Even the wind was different. It had less... *personality.* I'd never known the forest to be so infused with melancholy.

"I got back inside, put on a dress and took my blades with me before venturing deeper into the woods, without really knowing what I was looking for. Everything seemed to have changed ever so slightly. There was no pattern, no trace to follow.

"A noise. That's what I heard. A noise that didn't belong somehow. I already had one dagger in my hand when Baour walked out from between some bushes. He seemed calm, but solemn. We exchanged glances while I slipped the blade back underneath my sleeve.

"'There is death here,' Baour stated. I agreed. I knew he wasn't just talking about any death. Creatures and plants die every day in the forest, but this was something different. It impacted the Web more than the demise of any animal ever could. I told the mage that the ripples of whatever had happened were felt all over the place, but that I was unable to locate the source. He nodded. 'You don't need to,' he said. 'I can take you to the center of this.' That made me frown. He hadn't used much magic since he first came knocking at my door and I was still curious about his abilities, but how could he find what was causing such a general transformation?

"He did, though.

"Baour led as he walked through the trees, using the same ill-trodden paths I had gotten to know intimately but that most people know nothing about. He didn't run, but his pace was swift and it was clear that he knew exactly where he was going.

"It didn't take long before we got to a gathering of large trees, their leaves obscuring much of the light above. Baour cleared some dead wood with his feet, revealing a low pile of earth that had been freshly dug up. He dropped to his knees and started digging through the dirt while I only watched. I had time to think then and I was starting to realize what must have happened. It horrified me.

"I saw her hand come out from under the ground first. Baour pulled her up by her small, slim fingers, then grabbed her elbow, and finally wrapped his hands around her shoulders to drag her body out in the open. Her golden hair was stained now and it had lost its gloss. Her purple eyes were black, as is usual when forest sprites die. I started crying, but the necromancer didn't lose his composure for a single moment.

"But it wasn't the cadaver that made me throw up. Baour stroked some of the dirt off her lithe body and that's when we saw it. Ghostweed. The mage looked at me and this time I saw he was disgusted too. He wanted to say something, but I keeled over and started puking. Baour pulled me up after a while, clenching my face between his two hands.

"'The ghostweed hasn't compromised her spirit,' he said. 'Whoever did this, he knows nothing about how to use its Strands.'

"I asked him how he knew and he looked down, as if he was feeling guilty. I thought he felt that way because he hadn't told me about the necromantic magic he practices yet, but now I know he probably killed Ewella himself!

"We didn't even bother to look for tracks. Experience has taught me many things, but not how to be a ranger. Baour seemed more anxious now, though, and he was constantly looking around while we carried Ewella's body to a clearing. Many animals followed us as well. It was as if they felt that we were going to bury the sprite and they were grieving for her. Two stags appeared from out of nowhere, followed by rabbits, squirrels, badgers, and even a few gerrystul. All of them had sadness in their eyes and they all moved slowly, almost painfully.

"In the stories, rays of sunlight hit when a creature of nature is buried, but they didn't. Above us, grey clouds were packing together, but the rain never came. There wasn't even lightning or thunder to accompany our improvised ritual. Not even that. If not for the animals gathered around us, it would have felt so mundane, so utterly different from the special being she was. Of course, we didn't call for you, Eldried. You would have charged us coin to bury Ewella outside of the temple here, just because she isn't... *wasn't* one of us. What'd been the honor in that, huh?

"I was hardly able to do anything. I'm almost ashamed to admit it, but I was overcome by grief and I had dissociated from the happenings. It all felt like I was living in a painting. I found myself hoping that it was all a dream, but it wasn't.

"Baour made me snap out of it. After digging a hole deep enough for Ewella to be buried in, he turned his head towards me and he asked me if I wanted to have her back. Of course I wanted that! But how could he ask me such a thing? The sprite was dead. Her eyes had darkened. She was lost to this world.

"I told you before that I remember exactly how Baour introduced himself to me. I remember the words he spoke then as well, 'I can bring her back,' he promised. 'But she won't be the same.' He swallowed. The mage seemed so unsure. I think he hated himself for asking me, probably because he must have realized too late that he wouldn't be able to keep up his mystery-act anymore now.

"'How could you bring her back?' I stammered.

"My companion stood up, his robe fluttering in the breeze. 'I am a necromancer, Esmeralda,' he finally said. 'The Strands of Death are but strings on my instrument.'

"I gasped, clutching the cold earth, burying my fingers in the ground. I could feel it slip underneath my fingernails and the smell of my own vomit was starting to sicken me. Everything was spinning.

"I didn't know what to say. All kinds of thoughts were dancing in my head. It wasn't a beautiful dance though, nor was it a pleasant one. It was a chaotic mosaic of all kinds of different motions, some crashing into others.

"Before any of you judge me, what would you have answered if this man had offered to revive your own lover? Or your daughter? Yvonnia, who died of the illness just one changing of the moons ago? Yes, I am not ashamed to admit that I thought about it. Of course I did! She was my only real friend! Her... and the man who had just put me in the position to make such terrible a decision. I felt my head throb and the blood was coursing through my veins far faster than ever before, cascading from my heart to my extremities at such a pace that I thought I was going to find my death in that clearing, only a few leg length's away from my beloved Ewella.

"I'm not sure if I ever came to my senses. I'll explain what I did, but maybe it was just raw emotion taking control of me. Or maybe I just wanted someone to blame. I pushed myself up and faced Baour. Even though tears were obscuring my vision somewhat, I could see him well enough. I clenched my fists, suddenly aware of the textured, loose dirt in my palms and between my fingers.

"'No!' I shouted. 'No! You bastard! How could you? How could you ask me? You know her spirit is gone and I do, too! You wouldn't have been able to get that back, would you? Only her body – an empty shell, a constant reminder of what was once so beautiful, so pure!'

"I launched myself at him, but I never even thought of using my blades. I wasn't thinking straight, but I made the right decision nonetheless. I punched the necromancer, I tore at him, and I think I even tried to bite him. He never struggled, but took a few steps backwards. I tried to jab him again, and again, and he stepped to the side. My movements were too uncontrolled, reflecting the thoughts in my head, and I lost my balance.

"I fell down, right inside the hole, next to once-beautiful Ewella. Oh how cold she was and how devoid of life! I started sobbing and I didn't want to move anymore. I just wanted to be there forever. Baour said something to me – maybe it was just my name – and he kept trying to talk to me for a while before he gave up and let me be. It wasn't until the following morning that I was finally able to muster my strength, get out of the hole and finish burying Ewella. She smelled of death by then, and all her beauty was gone. As one would expect, Baour had left my cottage, taking all of his possessions, but none of mine, with him.

"That was about a single changing of the moons ago. I was stricken with grief and I didn't go to the village. I just wanted to be left alone.

Besides, I didn't think Baour was responsible for Ewella's death anyway, but my judgment was clouded. How could he have known where her body was? Offering to bring her back… it must have been a cruel, *cruel* act. Did you enjoy it, necromancer? Did you revel in watching me break down? Or… am I wrong? Please forgive me, but I hope I'm not. I hope it was you, so my nightmares about faceless murderers can finally end. Gealius forgive me, but I truly hope it was you.

"I didn't expect to be able to stroll into Barnsby, ask everyone I'd meet if he or she was the murderer and get a sincere answer, of course. But when the first visitors came to ask for my advice on matters of the heart and body, I informed about the goings-on in the village, trying to discover a motive – *any* motive – for killing Ewella. I never heard of one. I was told about Baour. How he had rented a room in your inn, Mildrieda. How his new set of clothes had finally arrived and how he had paid for them. How he was looked upon with fear by most of you. How you all were becoming increasingly suspicious of him. How more and more people were becoming ill after his arrival in the village. Still I spoke no evil of him. Not before the one time that I saw him again before appearing here at this trial.

"I had finally started to leave my cottage again. I need herbs to make my potions and my supply was running out. I still didn't find a lot of ghostweed to eradicate, but I did need to go deeper into the forest to find some rare plants.

"It was broad daylight. The day was pleasantly warm and the stuff I was looking for usually grows where the sun can get to it, so I took paths that weren't cut off from the sky by leaves or branches. That's why I noticed when something big passed above me. It made everything turn dark and its shadow slowly crept over the ground, like a snake sneaking up on its prey. I had wondered when the first gorogons would be back after Ewella's demise. Soon, it seemed. The position of forest watcher Ewella had taken upon herself hadn't been filled in yet and there was no one strong enough to stop gorogons from coming back to my section of the forest. The thing is… I still didn't expect to see any of them. We all know they like children and kids don't usually venture out of the village that far. When I finally made myself look up, I saw that the creature was slowly descending, though, so I quickened my pace and ran into its general direction. I can't run very fast anymore, but as I've said earlier I'm still in good health and I wanted to know what it was doing there.

"I heard why the gorogon had come before I could see why it had. A scream shattered the calm of the day. High-pitched like a girl's, but young enough to come from a boy. I knew an angry gorogon could kill me easily, but I hadn't cared about my life that much lately. Maybe I could calm it down. Curse you all for not teaching your children how to deal with one! They're just curious, gorogons are, but they absorb emotions and they can't handle being scared, so they react aggressively. By the way the kid was screaming his lungs out, I figured he would be dead before I got there.

"Then, before I got there, the screaming stopped. There was no time to sneak up on the scene, so I came crashing through the bushes, both of my blades in my hands, ready to strike and willing to give my life. More than willing, perhaps.

"The kid had started to make a small cottage out of dead wood. I guess it was supposed to be his secret hiding place, but it wasn't even half-finished yet. Much to my surprise, he was still alive. Just a few arm-lengths in front of him, the gorogon had wrapped its body around the tree. That's how they make sure you can't spot them from afar that well, even though they're so big. They don't have bones, you know, and their six paws are nimble, so they can climb easily up and down just about anything using those limbs and both of their prehensile tails. Scaly things, gorogons, but beautiful in color. I know some of you have already seen one, but they're all colored differently. The bright hues don't serve them as camouflage, though... they just attract children more easily. Despite their snake-like snouts, their big round eyes do that as well. There's nothing reptilian about those eyes, just something childlike and cuddly. Gorogons aren't very intelligent, either, but they mean well. Good intentions combined with natural killer instincts. It's a dangerous combination.

"The creature had its wings folded onto its body and it was showing its long split tongue, which usually means they feel at ease. Poison was dripping from its mouth to the ground; nurturing stuff to plants, but deadly to humans. Gorgons don't understand that, though, especially young ones like the tree-length specimen before me. They show their fondness by licking children, killing them in the process and usually killing themselves as well as soon as they're overcome by the emotions of a dying kid, and the bare tongue didn't bode well for the boy.

"Normally, the gorogon would have struck soon after the boy – *your* boy, Reaphrastus – had started screaming, but it was feeling comfortable. That was because the kid – Zeitas, I believe his name is, right? – was breathing slowly, his eyes fixed... on Baour's.

"The mage was standing on the other side, his gaze locked with Zeitas's. It was as if he was hypnotizing the boy, but I could see that he was looking at the gorogon as well, ever so subtly. He hadn't seen me, but I hadn't had time to process what was happening yet, and I shouted, 'Baour!'

"The necromancer lost his concentration. I... it was my fault. My fault entirely. Baour snapped his head towards me, surprised, losing contact with the boy in the process, and Zeitas started screaming again.

"It's tough to describe what happened next with any degree of accuracy. Everything happened so fast. The gorogon threw back its head. Its eyes widened, reflecting the boy's fear, and it threw part of its upper body backwards, swinging around the tree to lunge at the boy. I thought he would die for sure, but Baour jumped in between them, grabbing the gorogon's tongue with both hands. The necromancer screamed as the poison penetrated his skin, but he kept holding on while the beast wrapped its upper paws around his body. I yelled at the kid to run, but I didn't and neither did he. We just... stood there, watching as the gorogon buried its claws in Baour's shoulders. First blood spouted out of the mage, but I knew the creature hadn't hit a vein as the blood only started to drip out of the wounds after the initial hit, ruining the mage's new clothes. The gorogon pulled Baour up until the mage's face was right in front of its eyes... and Baour smiled.

"There he was, possibly mortally wounded, and he *smiled*, at the same time letting go of the tongue. His hands were turning black already, but the poison of a young gorogon isn't strong enough to kill an adult human being, at least not after touching skin for just a while. I had never seen anyone hold a gorogon's tongue in his bare hands, though. Even so, I thought Baour's puncture wounds looked a lot worse than his blackening lower arms did.

"Compared to normal reptiles gorogons can show an amazing array of emotions and... it looked happy. It moved its tongue like a dog waging its tail, ready to wrap it around Baour. That would've killed him, I suspect.

"I had finally come to my senses by that time and I stepped towards the kid, pushing him into the general direction of the village. 'Go!' I commanded, but still he didn't move. I was keeping an eye on Baour at the same time and what I saw next made me a lot more scared than the presence of even an adult gorogon would have.

"Even while the gorgon's tongue was slowly curling around his lower body, Baour was moving his hands, playing the Strands like one plays an instrument. It all looked so precise. One moment, he was weaving invisible Web-stuff together, another he was pulling at it.

"Gorgons feel the same emotions we do. That's why what happened next was so horrifying. It started with its tongue. Something happened to it. As if it was decaying at a tremendous rate, maybe hundreds of years in only an instant. The gorogon realized it, too. It's eyes, it's innocent eyes... it knew it was going to die somehow, and it was afraid of losing its grip on life.

"But it didn't just die.

"As its tongue crumbled, it sank its claws even deeper into Baour. The mage screamed and I could see that he was having trouble moving his arms now, but he kept weaving, pulling at certain Strands and hammering on others. His blood was dripping to the ground in huge amounts now, but just as the gorogon was preparing to sink in its third and fourth claw, the skin over its head started to wrinkle, turning into something like parchment first and then falling to the ground, leaving only dead muscle tissue and skull. It tried to scream, but it only managed to make a hoarse noise as the rest of its body was being unmade as well. As its paws disintegrated, it dropped Baour to the ground. The necromancer hit the forest floor hard, but even while on his back he continued gesturing. His movements were snappy and painful now, there was no elegance in them anymore, but they were effective. Before it could even try to attack again, the gorogon tumbled off the tree, transforming into ashes as soon as it hit the ground. Its remains were picked up by the wind and entered our noses and mouths. They tasted like dust and made us all cough.

"The most amazing thing was that Baour got up. He was weaving Strands again, but this time he was... sewing up his wounds somehow. I grabbed Zeitas's clothes, threw him around my waist, and started running to the village.

"I had seen what Baour could do. He's dangerous and I fear that he's a killer. That's my testimony."

Reaphrastus stood up, pointing at Baour, enraged. "He didn't help my son!" the bearded man with the sheepskin vest shouted. "Since Zeitas came back home, he's been ill! He couldn't even come to this trial!"

Esmeralda looked at Baour, bit her lip, and then looked at Zeitas's father. "Who says I was able to bring your son back alive?"

Chapter Three

THE CROSS-EXAMINATION OF THE WITCH ESMERALDA

A wave of commotion not much weaker than the concussion blast of a large fireball rushed through the crowd. It had a direction – from the middle of the group of villagers to the ones sitting at the periphery – with Reaphrastus at the epicenter. Some people stood up and stepped backwards towards the walls of the temple almost instinctively, inevitably stumbling into each other, with others following their lead without thinking too much about their own actions. All of them had turned their heads either to Esmeralda or to Zeitas's father: a simple woodcarver but a respected member of the community nonetheless. No one was looking at Baour anymore. The fact that he, if the witch's suspicions were true, might be responsible for the un-life of one amongst them almost seemed to be relegated to a fait divers. Right now, at this point in time, only the present was on their minds. The issue of what to do next would have to be dealt with later.

"Haven't we heard enough?" the rugged priest called Therionald finally asked the crowd. It was a rhetoric question. The cleric wasn't expecting an answer. To his left and right, people were nodding, so the surprise on his face when his elder halted him was apparent.

Eldried held his outstretched arm before the streetwise priest, who looked at him as a child who feels betrayed by his own mother might look at his parent.

"Quiet, Therionald. Sit."

Wh–why?" the middle-aged disciple of Gealius asked with a bewildered look on his face.

Baour grinned. He knew the answer. But he also knew not sharing it with the others would strengthen his own position, at least if things kept on going as he had envisioned beforehand.

As Baour had expected, the old cleric didn't answer. He only looked his younger colleague in the eyes, hoping he would comprehend, but he didn't seem to. Every heartbeat that this scene would last was to the necromancer's advantage, Baour knew. Not a single pair of eyes was diverted from the subtle power struggle that was unfolding in that sacred hall, but no one present doubted the outcome. Indeed, it was not a matter of who would gain the upper hand. The question was how long Therionald's disobedience would last.

The answer was: longer than anyone felt comfortable with.

Finally, Therionald sat down, but not before growling with frustration.

Reald was the first to realize something had to be done to avoid the proceedings falling to chaos. He scraped his throat, this time loudly so, and turned towards the villagers. "Wise Eldried is right. We cannot judge yet. The mage is allowed to show he is innocent first."

"I don't want to," Baour said. It sounded emotionless, but inside of his mind emotion was twisting around emotion, moving like a wild animal, but without a single feeling that could be expected in the given situation being present. For one brief moment, Therionald and the necromancer glanced at each other, each one knowing what the other was thinking.

The newly appointed barrister turned towards Baour, frowning. "That is a most surprising decision. Again, as the guardian of the King's Law, I am required to inform you that if you do not prove your innocence in this matter..."

"Yes, yes," Baour interrupted, slightly annoyed, "I will have to be executed. I just think that... what is that man doing?"

Almost everyone turned around, but it was too late. The great doors that led to and from the temple already slammed shut.

"This is a trial!" Reald yelled, exasperated. "No one is allowed to leave! Not at this time!"

Baour stepped forward. "Who was it?" he screamed at the people in front, but they only looked at him, petrified with fear. Given the choice between fighting and fleeing, they were too terrified to do either. "Who was it?" he asked again, this time sounding even angrier. "Curse your colors, Esmeralda!" It was a great insult to a fellow practitioner of magic.

"I only said what I think might be right," Esmeralda answered, unimpressed but with a hint of both sadness and doubt in her voice. "If you're going to kill these people or me, make it quick!" That terrified the hapless villagers even more. One wet his pants. Another started drooling.

Baour ran up the middle of the temple, heading toward the door. The crowd split before him as if struck by a giant, focused wave of water, a force of nature they could not hope to stop. A woman fainted.

"Stop!" Reald screamed. "No one's allowed to leave! Certainly not you!"

Baour didn't hear the newly appointed lawmaster, or at least pretended not to.

"STOP!" another voice reiterated. It came from the front, where no one was standing anymore, and it was louder than any human voice might be. It boomed and echoed. It ricocheted against the walls, filling the hall and assaulting the eardrums without permanently damaging them. Everyone turned to see who had spoken, even Baour.

Behind the altar, the statue of Gealius stood, cold to the touch and unmoving, but commanding and forceful. It was no more alive than the rock it was carved out of; but it didn't have to be, either. A golden glow with a subtle bronze edge now surrounded the sculpture. Maerae the midwife and Aulea the cook fell down to the ground eagerly, Aulea instinctively following Maerae's lead, their bodies convulsed with spasms as they forced themselves to fake religious seizures. It did leave some of the other villagers in awe, though, and no one seemed to be immune to the sudden display of godly power unfolding right behind the altar.

No one except for Baour, that is.

"Do you really think your prayers impress me?" His question was directed towards Eldried, but he didn't wait for an answer. Instead, his pupils diverted, filling up and blackening his irises before growing larger still. Those who saw it started to scream, terrified. In moments people were running in every possible direction except towards the wizard, but no one was able to get outside. At the exit, too many were torn between leaving illegally, thereby risking a fine or worse, or facing whatever magic the white-haired mage was weaving… and perhaps getting buried in anonymity outside of the temple graveyard. To save time, Baour only focused his Sight on the statue. There they were, golden Strands woven tightly around the statue, tightly connected to the Web and spun masterfully but hastily by a force much more powerful than he. Still, even the work of a Seraphalim was easy to undo if it were only an impromptu patch job instead of a work of mystical art. Baour was sure he would be able to see the Strands that had caused the air to vibrate and that had made Gealius's voice to appear as well, but he didn't have time to sift through all of the different kinds of strings and decided to focus on the ones that were making the statue radiate light instead.

When using the Sight, mages usually feel time flow differently. The arduous study required to learn how to manipulate the handiwork of the Spider has a thoroughly profound effect on the brain, enabling it to group small pieces of information into far larger chunks in less than a heartbeat, thereby avoiding a short-term memory overload. Baour knew this all too well, so he felt confident he could look around and find enough Strands of entropy before Gealius could be asked to perform another Weaving. The necromancer grabbed hold of a few strings with one hand and of even more with his other. He let them glide through his fingers to get a feel of their structure without actually touching anything. By focusing on them he could get a sense of their true nature, dangerous and destructive, yet strangely alluring.

Baour had never seen the dark energies as agents of destruction. To him, they were catalysts of transformation, the promise of change, the seeds of wonder and adventure. Yet they were eating away at his body as they ate away at every single thing, living or otherwise. Now he needed them. His skill with golden Strands was that of a dabbler, but his mastery of the darkish, purple, crackling nature of decay was unsurpassed in this part of the King's lands. He pulled at the strings and threw them over the statue like a veil, taking care to filter everything that was not black or yellow out of his Sight so that he would not accidentally hit the patterns out of which the statue itself was comprised.

The golden glow around the representation of Gealius disappeared.

Baour turned towards Eldried, who stopped whispering to the deity he served despite having both hands folded into each other in prayer.

"It seems your Seraphalim did not care much for your frivolous plea, did it, old man?" the necromancer asked rhetorically. Much of his question was lost in the commotion around him, but the priest's expression changed nonetheless. He had understood.

Both Maerae and Aulea forgot they were supposed to be having spasms. They starred uncomprehendingly at what was happening right before their eyes, as were many of their fellow townsfolk. By now others had finally gathered the courage to open the doors. Rays of sunlight cavorted through the temple hall. The colored light coming through the stained glass windows revealed cracks in the floor, but nobody really noticed. Instead, before anyone could leave the sacred site, two silhouettes appeared in the opening: a man-sized one and a smaller one.

It was Reaphrastus who recognized his own son first.

"Zeitas!"

His voice had a strange tonality, as if it were composed of dissonant sounds. There was happiness there, but it was also obvious that Reaphrastus was not too glad to see his son.

"I'm sorry, my brother, but I had to fetch my nephew to show everyone what vile deed has transpired here," the man next to Zeitas said solemnly, as if he had just done something heroic.

Basking in the sunlight, Zeitas made quite an impression, but not in any positive way. His shoulders were slumped downwards, his body devoid of any lust for life, his skin pale and sickly. However, his eyes concerned those present more than any of his other features did. They were sunken deep into their sockets, accentuated by a bluish rim and dull beyond what is natural for a boy of his age.

"It's obvious, isn't it? The boy has lost the capability of speech. He's moved beyond the realms of the living!"

Reaphrastus looked more like he was going to throw up or impale his son through the heart himself than like he was going to defend him, but he still seemed conflicted – or shocked – enough to refrain from saying anything for now. Ignetius balled his fist, though, and Therionald, who had accused Baour only moments earlier, was flanking him eagerly... at least, until Eldried slapped the upstart initiate in his face.

"I told you to Ignetius! I told you *both* to sit! So sit! And remain on your bench, lest you incur the wrath of Gealius himself!" The priests obeyed, but only reluctantly.

"Tell them, Eldried!" Baour shouted.

"There is not much to tell," Eldried replied.

"Yes, there is."

Everyone was paying attention to the interchange between the two men. Esmeralda got it first. She nodded quietly, a single tear rolling down her wrinkled cheek.

"The boy is not dead," Eldried finally said reluctantly. His acolytes almost jumped up, but he was quick to hold Ignetius down by his shoulder. Therionald took the hint and decided to remain seated as well.

"Tell them, priest." Baour managed to make it sound more like fatherly advice than a command. He needed these people to start trusting him, but he didn't want to force his hand. Not yet. *One first needs to build a foundation before laying the first stone*, he thought to himself. *First follow, then lead.*

"I was going to tell them. Everything just happened so... fast." Eldried said. His attempt to put everyone at ease was counteracted by him turning away his face and looking to the ground. He continued, "Great Gealius would not veil that which composes life from me. I don't know what happened to poor Zeitas, but I do know that he is still amongst the living."

"For now," Baour added, shocking the villagers again. It wasn't going to help him establish rapport with them, but he was trying to use every sense of dramatic timing he had to make even more of an impact later on.

"That doesn't mean you have not bewitched my son, death-dealer!" Reaphrastus shouted.

"Your anger is not directed at me, it is directed at yourself for wanting to finish off your own flesh and blood, woodcarver," Baour riposted.

"Damn you!" Reaphrastus pushed several people out of his way, but despite of his strength and anger was pulled back into the crowd long before he could reach the tall, charismatic mage.

The boy's condition has worsened, the necromancer thought. "Zeitas shouldn't have been brought in here." He sounded sad.

"Why not, mage?" said someone Baour didn't know – yet wanted to know.

"Isn't it obvious?" another one said. "He's got the illness!"

Before panic could spread again, the mage waved his hands dismissively. "No, that's not it. He just seems sick." He didn't want anyone to ponder on that train of thought too long, so he added, "Let's get back to *my* trial! Reald, I *am* allowed to cross-examine the witch, right?"

The barrister needed some time to collect his thoughts, but he answered fast enough. "Yes. Yes... of course."

It was no use to upset even more people anyway. The sickness had already been present.

Baour didn't give Esmeralda much time to regain her composure. He couldn't afford to.

The necromancer applauded while he was walking up to the front of the crowd once more. The sound echoed through the hall. Out of the corner of his eyes, he saw the puzzled looks on the faces of a few of the villagers. Maybe it was because so much was happening so fast. Or maybe it was because their faith didn't allow them to understand how a manifestation of Gealius could be dispelled so easily. Baour knew the answer, of course. It had nothing to do with the Seraphalim's might. Eldried had just acted too quickly; without being able to state why the statue should glow. And maybe – just maybe – his faith was wavering in the face of recent events.

He continued clapping his hands until he was standing in front of Esmeralda again.

"I have to applaud you, Esme," he said, coming to a standstill. "Your recounting of the events was very accurate and sincere. Indeed, it was so truthful that, honestly, I find myself utterly unable to attack you on any part of the story you told so well, whether it'd be a specific detail or a generalization." The necromancer glanced at the people he was slowly coming to see as his audience. "However..." He paused and bit his lip. "It seems to me that your testimony is more a plea *for* my character than an indictment against it, is it not?"

"No, it isn't, Baour. I just... I *just don't trust you anymore.*"

The mage stepped closer to Esmeralda so that she could smell his breath, sweet but with a tinge of iron and death in it as well. She turned away her face slightly while Baour bowed forward, gripping the bench between them with both hands.

He looked at her, his eyes dashing from left to right, from top to bottom and up again, taking in every beautiful crack in her wizened old face.

"What have I done to make you doubt me, Esmeralda? What?"

"There's the ghostweed. And sweet Ewella. The long trips away. And the gorogon you killed..."

"I killed it to save the boy!" He pointed at Zeitas, who was watching the spectacle, unmoving, unfazed, more like a wax statue than like a human being.

"*Does he seem saved to you?*"

The necromancer looked at the boy for a moment, the bowed his head, gritting his teeth. "No. No, he does not." He turned his attention towards Reaphrastus. "I am truly sorry. I tried." He wasn't talking about the attack he stopped, but that wasn't important yet.

"A confession?" Reald asked with a sense of eagerness in his voice. At this point the best he could hope for was to close the proceedings quickly and smoothly.

"It is not!" Baour hastened to say. "I will plead guilty to the things I did do, but in no way did I want to hurt the boy. I wanted to save him." He looked over his shoulder at Zeitas. "Death will come soon. It will envelop you and it will be warm and soothing. Do not believe what your family is saying. There is no coldness at the end of your journey, only comfort."

The boy nodded calmly, the first sign of self-awareness he had demonstrated since walking into the temple hall.

"That is no way to talk to a young boy!" Eldried protested.

"Then what would be a good way, priest? Tell him that life and death are not intertwined, that they do not belong to each other like eternal lovers? That he should fear the things he does not know about? That he should spend the rest of his young life in agony over what will happen soon?" He spit on the floor. "No, I will not do that."

"Do not desecrate our temple, murderer!" Ignetius shouted. Again Eldried motioned him to shut his mouth. Baour could see the words form on the elder's mouth. *He will get his dues, Ignetius.*

"I have offended no one except for yourself, Ignetius. My contempt is not directed at your Seraphalim. He knows death far more intimately than even I, as he lives in a place where so many Strands start to converge. Gealius does not care about a drop of spit on the floor of his temple."

"Who are you to tell us what our god thinks?"

Baour grinned. "I... am Baour."

He savored the silence that followed before directing his attention to Esmeralda again.

"You have not answered the question to my satisfaction, Esme. Why?"

"I did answer, Baour."

"My trips, me killing that poor gorogon... it is all circumstantial."

"But it's enough. You won't be able to prove your innocence."

"Is that what you are looking for? A reassurance? Something to give rest to your own mind?"

"It's what I'm looking for because I believe you may have done something wrong, mage!" She addressed the villagers, "You've always treated me badly, as if I wasn't one of your own. But I understand that. I get it. Ever since I can remember, I've tried to help you. I'm not going to quit now."

"How is this helping them, Esme? If I'm innocent..."

"If you're innocent, you'll be able to prove it."

Suddenly, it hit him. Esmeralda had been fooling him. He cursed himself for not seeing her manipulations for what they were. And he cursed her for laying out the path he would have to take now. He looked the witch in her eyes, asking for a way out. She saw it, but she only closed her eyelids for a moment and rolled her lips inside of her mouth.

"Damn it..." Baour whispered. He didn't want to let go. Not without trying. "Esmeralda," he started, pleading, losing all sense of formality, "please! *Please* tell these people that you know I only had their best interests in mind."

The witch strengthened her back, more to summon up courage than because she was feeling strong and righteous. "No! No! This man is a necromancer! I believe he has come to do us harm!"

"Tell them that you are just jealous, Esmeralda! Tell them that I didn't want to share your bed!"

"That would be a lie. Besides, you've already told everyone that my testimony was complete and truthful."

He had walked into a trap, and a clever one at that. She was handing the next course to take on a plate. *Complete.* It was a single word, but oh so important. *Complete.*

"It's true, we did sleep together. But I didn't want to touch you much, right?"

"Wrong!" She pointed at herself while talking to the villagers. "This man loves every single weathered line on my face!" She stepped to the middle of the stage and pulled up her sleeves. "He loves the old flesh that just hangs here, to no real purpose whatsoever!" Next she held he arms in front of her, showing the back of both hands. "He reveres the brown blotches on my hands and arms!" The witch stuck a foot out. "And he licked these veins, these ugly green and blue rivers of my life's blood, eagerly!" She grabbed her left breast. "And he sucked on these, even though they've lost the firmness of my youth!"

Esmeralda turned towards Baour again. He had understood the last hint as well, but he wasn't going to give up just yet and switched to more formal speak again.

"Than it was jealousness!"

"What would I have been jealous of, Baour?"

"Me leaving you alone after being so intimate. After all, by your own testimony I started spending a lot of time in the village soon after meeting you."

"You *know* that's not it."

The necromancer looked Esmeralda deep in the eyes once more, searching for a way out, almost *pleading* the witch to abort her current course of action. She sighed, but it was obvious now there was no other way. "Damn your colors, Esme," Baour whispered. "You don't have to do this."

The witch swallowed and looked over Baour's lowered shoulders, addressing the crowd. "He is a necromancer! He brings death!"

She was almost leaning against the mage now, showing him what he had to do. Baour tried to refrain from crying as he grabbed hold of her collar. With a single scream of agony and regret, he pulled the shirt open, tearing her clothes and stepping aside immediately. He made sure to keep his back turned towards the villagers in an attempt to hide his sorrow from them.

Screams. Commotion. The trial had devolved into chaos from the moment Zeitas's uncle had left the temple and it didn't seem like order would be restored any time soon, leaving Baour to wonder how long it would take for some of those present to either sink into insanity or be otherwise overcome by their emotions.

Esmeralda was now crying, but despite the shamed look on her face, she held open her arms wide, so that everyone could see what was going on.

There, grasping both of her breasts tightly was a small, shriveled creature. It was sucking one of the witch's nipples as it clung to Esmeralda's skin like parasite. Its hairs were now thin, leaving bald spots all over its body. White had turned to a sickly grey, gold to the color of rigid stone. Its eyes were black and lifeless, but open and functioning nonetheless.

"You said you never saw Ewella again. *Not like she was then.* You didn't mean her corpse, did you, Esme?" Baour finally asked.

Esmeralda shook her head. "No. No, I didn't."

"Why, Esme?"

"I… I just couldn't handle it." Baour realized his former lover wanted to say more, but she couldn't.

"I'll try to make this quick," he said, but he knew he couldn't really comfort her. "Is this why you turned against me, Esme?"

"Esmeralda is a healer!" someone shouted. "The necromancer must have brought the sprite back!"

"Did I, Esme?"

"No. No, you didn't. No, he didn't! He didn't. It… it was I."

"Maybe you should *complete* the story, Esme. Get it over with, so you can rest."

She nodded, wiping the tears from her cheeks with her sleeve. Without even trying to close her shirt, she resumed her recounting of the facts.

"As I said before, Baour didn't want to talk much about the magic he wields. But after Ewella died, I guess he took pity on me. While carrying her to the clearing where we were going to bury her body, I asked him questions about death and un-life, about the Strands of entropy the Spider weaves ever so diligently. He tried to console me by telling me about these dark strings and about how they work together with other colors. I tricked him. I don't think he knew I was planning on bringing Ewella back until we buried her. He… he *did* ask me if I wanted him to revive her, but only after it became clear I was going to try to do it alone. And his intonation… the *way* he asked me… he didn't want to do it, that much was clear. So I became angry. Angry because he asked me if I wanted him to use his magic on her while at the same time implying it would be a bad idea. Angry because he asked me without really intending to act. I thought he was being cruel, but I don't know anymore. Later, when he stopped the gorogon, he fueled my rage even more. It looked so… *easy*. How easy it must have been to you, Baour, to resurrect Ewella! But I watched. Oh, yes, I watched! I told you I didn't run, but it wasn't out of fear. Partly, I wanted to keep an eye on the boy. But partly... partly I wanted to see what the necromancer was doing. I wanted to see the blackness consume the beast and watch Baour's fingers manipulating creation.

"You had told me that the ghostweed hadn't compromised her spirit, mage. I had buried her body just underneath the soil, almost filling up the hole before I finally laid her to rest. But I couldn't bring myself to try. Not based on a tensed conversation about death and the Spider. After I saw you work your magic, however... I thought I could replicate some of your movements. So under a starlit night, with both moons bearing silent witness to what I was doing, I returned to the grave with a shovel. All around me, the creatures of the forest were trying to stop me. Insects screeched, a rabbit tried to bite my ankle and an owl almost clawed my face open. It succeeded in scratching me twice before I hit it with the shovel, thereby betraying everything I had ever believed in. There was only one thing on my mind. One thing! By now, I was bleeding. Red drops of sticky fluid fell to the earth underneath me, one after the other, but still I continued to unearth Ewella's corpse. After I had removed enough of it, I kneeled down and I used my hands to brush away the dirt. She was pale, but the worms hadn't gnawed at her. She wasn't decomposing. Maybe faeries never do, I don't know. All the while, I kept murmuring to myself, repeating what Baour had told me. Ghostweed has to be harvested in a certain way before it can prevent a spirit from leaving. That was what I clung unto.

"I brought Ewella to my cottage, where I shifted my Sight, trying to sift through the colors and grasping at them without truly being able to see specific Strands. I had trained on what I thought to be Baour's techniques, though. Without him knowing, I had become more adept at guessing where the Spider connects his fabric to things both living and un-living. I grasped at the Strands, mixing colors, pulling some of them away from Ewella and adding others. It didn't work at first, but I kept trying. I took some time to heal my wounds and sleep before I started again. Days. It took me days. The warning signs didn't matter. Not my cats, suddenly so loveless and aggressive, not the birds outside, that had stopped singing, were able to prevent me from continuing. And certainly not the thought of Baour, who had been so ambiguous about bringing back my lover. So one day... one day it worked.

"I don't know if I should say I got lucky, but it happened on a breezy afternoon. It just... all came together somehow. Like some other force was helping me. I strained to get everything right and the pressure on my eyes was tremendous. It was like my brain was going to explode or turn into goo and seep out of my ears, but I just kept going at it because I felt *something* was happening. And it was. Ewella... she started moving. Not like before, not with the grace and suppleness that is still burned into my memories, but moving nonetheless. She didn't say anything, though. Try as I might, since then I haven't been able to get a single word out of her. But she did recognize me. I know she did. When I held her, she clung on to me and when I pressed her against my chest, she sucked my breasts like she had done so many times before. Different, but the same. I cried tears of joy. I admit to that. But I know now I did something... wrong, didn't I?"

Esmeralda looked down at the hapless creature that was hanging on to her. "Didn't I?" She started sobbing again, but this time, no one reacted for a while. Despite the horror that had come over the Barnsby villagers, everyone present seemed to silently agree to let the witch deal with her emotions for now. After all, everyone also knew there could only be one ending to the sad story that was Esmeralda's. Baour let his right hand rest on her shoulder, but he, too, didn't speak.

As custom dictated, it was Reald who broke the silence. "How say you?" His question was directed to the three priests, all of which nodded slowly, deliberately.

"Divine Law has been violated!" Reald announced without any joy. "The verdict is death! These proceedings shall be interrupted until such time as the priests have carried out the sentence outside."

"Is this what you wanted?" Baour asked Esmeralda in a hushed voice.

"Yes. It is."

"Than I am happy for you. That which cannot be thought is yours, as it has been Ewella's."

"Will you accompany me to the door, Baour?"

"I will. You know I cannot go outside with you, but I'll take you as far as I can."

The witch smiled. "Thank you." In front of her, the villagers that had been sitting were standing up solemnly. Eldried and his colleagues made their way through the crowd and stopped at the corridor in the middle of the temple, waiting.

"Don't thank me, Esme. If I hadn't met you, you would never have been able to animate Ewella."

"Is that the only thing I managed to do, Baour? *Animate* her? I didn't bring her back?"

"You didn't. I can't bring a spirit back either, Esme. Not in its normal state. It's impossible. Even without ghostweed." He took her by the hand and they both started to walk over to the threesome that had taken up its mantle of judge as well as jury.

"You know," the witch smiled, "I still don't know if you're the one who killed Ewella. I hope you aren't."

"Maybe in some ways I am."

"What do you mean?"

"Don't ask. Your worries will be over soon, no need to create a new one."

"If you're responsible... then I hope you die as well."

"I know."

"It felt... good, though, Baour. Weaving that magic. Good and evil all at once."

"You never succeeded, Esme."

Esmeralda stopped, turning to face Baour. The necromancer saw the waiting priests coming over to them now, ready to take the witch away.

"What do you mean, Baour?"

"No one can animate the dead with only the small amount of knowledge you have, Esmeralda. It just isn't possible. Even experienced necromancers often never develop the necessary skills."

"Then how..."

Baour swallowed, than looked away as the witch realized what had happened. It was too late, though. Ignetius and Therionald were already wrapping their arms underneath hers. Suddenly, Esmeralda tried to resist, almost surprising both men, but they didn't lose their hold.

"Stop!" she screamed. "Stop! I want to amend my story! It wasn't me! It wasn't me!"

Esmeralda was dragged away, kicking and screaming, flailing about as the living corpse that clung to her was swayed from side to side. It was swinging wildly, a dead thing holding on to someone who would be just as dead – or even more so – soon. Baour turned around and walked back to the altar, shaking his head. *It didn't have to end this way*, he thought, *and yet it did.*

He ignored the horrible screams outside as he moved to the front again. "I call forth Roaldus, the tailor!"

Chapter Four

THE SECOND TESTIMONY
THE TAILOR ROALDUS ACCUSES

"As you all know, my family is well-traveled. We have to be. Tailors, all of us, and nowhere near enough animals or plants to make enough clothing for the entire village. One of the first things I learned when I was young had nothing to do with sewing, working leather or anything like that, but with how to tend a horse. Even though there are not many of them here in Barnsby, my father always took pride in having the best one in the village.

"Still... it seemed to me that none of you really cared where this necromancer came from. No one asked if I knew and I didn't think it was necessary to tell you. But, yes... I knew he was coming.

"I remember the first time I heard of Baour. It must have been a moon-cycle before he arrived at the village. I was at Greensdale to buy linen and wool, maybe even some silk if I got lucky and the merchants from Illexalluh had passed by. There's this trader I know, a ship captain called T'Halek. He's a strange old man, with skin as black as the night, while only his eyes betray his Sakhovan heritage. A half-breed, he claims to be of royal blood, but the monarchy of H'Lam has never recognized his claims to a title because he was born out of foreign loins. He's crossed the oceans many times and the smell of sea-salt follows him everywhere, always masking the far more unpleasant smells a man starts to carry with him when he spends too much time in crowded quarters with no land in sight.

"As far as sailors go, T'Halek is a calm person, prone to lose himself in introspection if you let him, so I was surprised to see he was agitated. His usually peaceful eyes were blazing and he didn't blink, as if he was afraid to close them, even for a moment. I picked up on it, but sea rats usually keep their worries to themselves, so I decided not to ask him about why he was so obviously agitated. However, decades spent on ever-moving waters have not done anything to change T'Halek's people sense. He must have seen that I had noticed his uneasiness and he started to talk about it himself.

"'I will not be staying in this harbor for long,' he said. 'I can take your order, but you will have to get your wares before the night sets in today.'

"I asked him why he was so anxious to leave. The sailor looked at me, as if trying to gauge if I would deem him crazy if he told me, then shifted his eyes to his left and then his right before finally answering me.

"'Bodies have been disappearing,' he whispered.

"'What do you mean, bodies have been disappearing?' I wanted to know.

"'The dead," he answered. 'Since we have docked, our dead have started to disappear.'

"At first, I didn't know what he was talking about. It seems like sheer folly to carry corpses with you on a ship. Even the strictest Seraphalim allow for the deceased to be dumped at sea in order to prevent the stench of rot from demoralizing or otherwise destabilizing the crew. Or so I've been told. But T'Halek explained to me that burial customs are far different in H'Lam. Even though he is banned from his own court, he tries to adhere to the old rites of his people, which mean the dead are not burned or buried, but... *preserved.* He never told me exactly how, but there's no magic involved. At all. In fact, the Sakhovan don't like the mystic arts too much.

"Anyway, apparently, according to T'Halek, despite a number of setbacks during his long journey across the sea, everything was going well until his ship – the R'Lallon, I believe – arrived in Greensdale. Only one day after docking they were visited by a man who called himself Baour. 'Tall and lithe but muscular, dark yet delicate, wise yet young, and wearing a black robe.' That's how the old sailor described his appearance. *Your* appearance, necromancer. Apparently, the mage had stopped by in order to ask T'Halek if he could... *buy* the corpses. I think the old man told me there were five in all. Two of them had fallen during a pirate attack, while another one was knocked on his head during a storm and never woke up. The remaining two had fallen prey to disease. How Baour knew about all of that, I don't know. Maybe he overheard a conversation between the crewmembers and a prostitute or a patron in one of the inns. Apparently, he wasn't planning to pay in coin, either, but T'Halek didn't tell me what recompense the necromancer had offered.

"Naturally, the captain declined. He is an honorable man and he would never have sold his dead friends to another, not even for a dozen bars of gold. The incident had alarmed him, though. He figured Baour was a mage, probably a necromancer, and he shares his race's suspicion towards all things arcane. The next wake-cycle, one of the corpses was found to be missing. No one had heard or seen anything and there were no signs of any burglary. Up until then, T'Halek hadn't told his crew about the wizard. He didn't think it was necessary and most of the sailors had wandered off into town anyway. After his first mate told him about the disappearance, he called those who served under him, and who were still aboard, together. T'Halek is a shrewd, intelligent person, and he knew a confrontation between his men and a mage could only result in even more fatalities, so he ordered everyone to stay put and not venture into the city on a wild quest for revenge. He did go to the watches' council chambers, though. The Greensdale watchmen are notorious for getting the job done and, even though I've seen a lot of money pass from the hands of eager traders to them, they usually can be trusted upon to act and try to solve crimes in some way or the other.

"As it turned out, they knew *exactly* who Baour was. He had already come under scrutiny after asking strange questions about recent deaths in the city during the past few wake-cycles, but he hadn't committed any offenses. Greensdale is a big city, especially in comparison to our town, but tall strangers with long white hair and black robes have a tendency to stand out. It's always amazing to me how well all of those citizens seem to know each other, even though there are more inns, shops and brothels within those stout stone walls than I can count on both hands. You would think a single man would have an easy time to get lost within the sheer number of visitors, but you would think wrong.

"After a sleep-cycle had passed, the guards stopped by the R'Lallon. I know most of you have never seen a ship with three masts before, and there's only one or two of them in the harbor at any time, but that's how big T'Halek's vessel is. Whenever he's not at the market, he can be found in his quarters, savoring the slowly moving waters like a baby likes his cradle. He was already waiting for the watchmen, eager to find out how justice had been served.

"Alas, the guards had talked to Baour, but he had denied any involvement in the matter. Of course, the watchmen – being the thorough kind of chaps they are – had rummaged through his room at the inn, but they had found nothing out of the ordinary. They had even retraced Baour's footsteps and talked to some of the other customers, only to find out that he was actually well liked at the inn. They told the guards that Baour is a great storyteller. Every night, he had entertained them with tales about heroes and dragons, wizards and monsters, swordplay and magic. I must say, when I finally met the accused, a full moon-cycle later, I found out that he is, indeed, an amazing conversationalist. He reminds me of the best of bards, sometimes. But I guess that's irrelevant, right? Even the most famous minstrels sometimes hide terrible secrets.

"T'Halek had no choice. After all, he couldn't even be sure that the mage was responsible for what had happened. He ordered his crew to continue their business as usual, but the atmosphere had changed. 'They became anxious,' he told me later on. 'They've weathered hurricanes and pirate attacks, illness and the occasional fistfight, and they had been living together fairly peacefully for more than half a year-cycle, but there was something different about what had happened.' I saw it for myself when I met the captain. His men had become more taciturn and brooding than usual. There was none of the merrymaking I usually found when I visited the ship to get my fabrics directly from its hull instead of haggling for what I needed at the marketplace. No one was singing, no one was playing *tracelines,* and no one was engaged in an animated conversation. They were all so uncharacteristically silent, focused on their chores and on the small waves slowly crashing against their ship and the docks.

"No wonder. Because by then, a second corpse had gone missing.

"Of course, T'Halek alerted the watchmen again, but they returned with no evidence whatsoever. In fact, they didn't even have leads. The captain told me there was talk about hiring a mage to find out what happened, but the only Greensdale seer he knew of had died during the past year-cycle and it was hard to sell the idea to his crew anyway. I guess he didn't really put in an earnest effort, either. It's hard to believe how the Sakhovan evolved the way they have without magic, but evolve they did. I'm always amazed at the contraptions their ship carries with it, but I've also learned not to ask too many questions about their technology, as they don't like to share their inventions to foreigners. It's what keeps things even when they encounter enemies who can weave magic.

"Even while I was bargaining for a good price, T'Halek was ordering his hands to prepare his ship to leave Greensdale. He was anxious to go, even though he made sure the remaining bodies were carried to a Sakhovan temple first. They still rest there, as far as I know. I've seen them. But I'll get to that later.

"After leaving Greensdale, T'Halek's story kept haunting me. There was something strangely eerie about it, as if I had touched upon one of the Great Mysteries, tasting it for ever so short a moment without smelling or seeing it, without actually being able to make any sense of it. It was a strange feeling, but while traveling back to Barnsby I decided the captain didn't single out the right suspect. It was obvious Baour couldn't have done it. The watchpeople would have found out if he had, right?

"At least that's what I thought then.

"Even though the worn faces of the R'Lallon crewmembers were etched into my memories, I almost forgot the name of Baour altogether. He didn't seem pivotal to the story somehow, so it took me a few heartbeats to realize who was standing before me when he first visited my shop.

"It had been a slow day. It usually *is* during market days, but I prefer keeping my clothes inside and you all find your way to my place when you need me anyway. I was patching up that old brown coat you brought in, Seelin – the one you're wearing right now – when the door opened. I wasn't expecting anyone to stop by at that hour of day, what with the market in full swing and all, and certainly not a tall man clad in one of the most expensive red cloaks I've ever seen. He largely fit the description T'Halek had given me, but he wasn't wearing a black robe. Instead, he almost looked like nobility, maybe even royalty. No man clad like that had stepped into my shop before. I knew he wasn't from around here, of course, and I was filled with all kinds of conflicting emotions and thoughts. What was a man like him doing in a shop like mine? Sure, I sell the best fabrics and clothing in town, you all know that. And I think I can make better cloaks and tunics than most of the tailors' guild members in Greensdale. But this village is small, you know, and it has no strategic, economic, or political importance whatsoever. I don't mean that as an insult, I like it that way. It's nice and quiet and still we can earn good money here. So why was someone who quite obviously is as affluent as Baour visiting us?

"Yes, I saw opportunity there. But I also found it strange. Maybe the man had stolen his clothes from a noble and had come to Barnsby to hide from the authorities. Or maybe he was on a secret mission that could spell no good for us at all. Those and many other thoughts went through my mind when the man standing over there entered.

"Of course, I didn't show any of it. I just greeted the stranger, bowing my head slightly. For all I knew, he might have been of royal blood. I did glance at his hands, but there was no signet ring there, no noble seal and no other indication of his status other than the clothes he was wearing.

"'You don't have to bow,' the man said. 'I am Baour and I am nothing more than a humble soul searching for some new clothes.'

Baour. I knew I had heard the name before, but the realization didn't sink in just yet.

"'I will help you out to the best of my ability, sir,' I said, 'but I'm afraid none of the materials I have here right now will accommodate a man with such clearly high standards such as yourself.'

"Then the mage said something I still don't really understand. 'That's what I was counting on.' Or maybe 'I know. I was counting on that.' No, wait. 'That was what I was expecting.' It must have been that. Either way, the meanings are similar.

"Baour told me that he had been wearing the same clothes for quite a while now and that they were in urgent need of being washed and repaired. I offered to do that for him, but he declined.

"'It would be better if you didn't touch anything I'm wearing right now,' he said.

"'I assure you that there's no place to run in a village like this,' I answered. 'There's not even anyone who would be able to spend enough coin on a cloak such as yours. I would need to travel to Greensdale and leave my shop behind, shattering my reputation and losing my customers.'

"The necromancer shook his head. 'I'm sure you're an honest man,' he said. 'But I'd prefer to wash these clothes myself. You can have them afterwards, so that you can repair these stitches.'

"I told him we wash anything brought in for free, but he insisted on doing it himself. What is it you said, necromancer? Let me think. It sounded strange… 'It's the only way.' That was it, right? 'It's the only way.' Yes, yes, I remember. Why was that, mage? Were you afraid I might notice that the stench of death soaked into the fabrics?

"Baour then started to explain what kind of clothes he wanted me to make for him. Red and blue trousers, a bliaud of the same colors, a red tabard, a green surcoat and a cloak trimmed with ermine with a pin of gold in the shape of a skull. His shoes were to be made of velvet, his buckle was to resemble another skull, and his hat had to be large and bright. He asked me to provide for breeches, a chemise, and a hose. He wanted me to use silk, velvet, and expensive furs as materials. He was very particular about the kinds of animals to be used, as well. Well, animals… he talked about reganths and thebelisks, ythallans and djervisjt. Monsters, all of them, fancied by hunters who like to claim they are protecting humanity as well as providing for food and comfort. I told him there was no way I would be able to find the furs of each one of those, but he just smiled and said two different kinds would be enough.

"I also warned this man that the cost would be prohibitive and that I would need to travel back and forth to Greensdale a few times in order to find all of the necessary materials. That didn't seem to be a problem, either, and he was willing to advance all of the coin I would need.

"It was only when he left that I remembered. Baour. A name shrouded in mystery, no? At the very least an unusual name, one that invokes dark passages and forgotten gods, great dungeons and the legendary mages of old. Or at least that's what *I* think. Maybe it's only because I know who this man is now. Maybe the associations only stem out of the stories we have all heard. I don't know.

"I had always remembered the conversation with T'Halek well, but now Baour's name was occupying my thoughts as well. Clearly, the man was no noble, but he seemed to have enough coin to rival with royalty and he certainly dressed like nobility to boot. I wasn't sure if he was to be trusted, so I closed the shop and ventured out into the village. You all had seen Baour pass by, but none of you seemed to know who he was.

"Reginae over there told me he had been seen nearby during the last few wake-cycles, and Merielda had seen him stroll through the woods with… you know. The witch. Do I have to pronounce her name at this trial, Reald? I prefer not to. It spells misfortune to speak of the dead before a full cycle has passed after their demise. Even if they were clearly in league with dark forces. *Especially* if they were in league with dark forces. Good, thank you.

"I knew the witch would be at the market and she always set up her booth at exactly the same place, didn't she? In the northeastern corner, next to Tora's building. I never liked the woman much – I guess I was right not to – and neither did most of you, but over the years I've seen many friends and acquaintances pass by her booth to buy some of her trinkets or powders. The entire tabletop in front of her was obscured by potions, elixirs, candles, and charms. It was very colorful and the incense smelled spicy yet sweet, but I was hardly impressed by any of it. I just wanted to know about Baour. Was he trustworthy? Did he indeed steal two corpses? Why did he offer to buy those bodies? I asked her all of those questions, but she refused to answer most of them. As if she was trying to protect the mage. The one thing she did want to tell me was that he would be able to pay me. 'He's good for it,' she said with that crackling voice of hers. She told me I could trust him. Ha! As it turns out, she didn't even trust him herself!

"She hadn't lied about the money, though. Only three sleep-cycles later, the necromancer visited me again. I don't know where he got it from, but he had a purse with him that contained more gold than I would need to buy the materials for every single article of clothing he had asked to sew together. There were a lot of coins in there, but they were minted in a wide variety of nations: Tormar and Ür'd, Byrmur and Thoufeldt, Arrkon and Illexalluh. All of those kingdoms, fiefs, and duchies use pure gold, though, so it would be easy to melt everything together. Except for maybe the coinage from Arrkon, but the exchange rate has been favorable since the old king Morr'Dir passed away and his armies withdrew from the neighboring lands.

"I know the witch told you that Baour said he visited every three wake-cycles or so, but he didn't. Yes, I saw him walk through the streets sometimes and he never neglected to greet me, but as you all know he didn't visit the village all too often. I've got no idea what you did while you were neither at the witch's place nor in Barnsby, necromancer, but it's quite obvious to me that you lied to the old hag, didn't you?

"During that moon-cycle, I did visit Greensdale twice instead of once. It was impossible to find all of the goods Baour had asked for after only one roundtrip, but I had enough contacts in the city to make only one other trip necessary.

"The first time I returned to Greensdale after Baour had stopped by, I took the opportunity to visit the Sakhovan temple. I've never really liked the Seraphalim those island dwellers worship, but he doesn't seem to be preoccupied with concepts like shame, guilt, sacred places, and the like. Or, for that matter, tidiness and cleanliness. The temple halls aren't particularly foul smelling, but there's always a faint stench of rot permeating the place. Its crudely shaped walls are made of yellowish brown sandstone, none of the pillars inside have the same shape, and the altar is a rough, vaguely circular affair set into the middle of the main hall. Sakhovan do like nature, though, so they let vines grow over the walls, moss over the doors, and mushrooms over the floors. They shape everything, and one can find interesting patterns and even drawings in their growths, but aside from that Sakhovan priests don't seem to worry too much about keeping anything clean.

"As weird as the upper halls might seem, the lower levels are a different kind of strange entirely. There's only a single stone staircase, winding down through dozens of levels, each of them pretty much identical in layout. It's an underground labyrinth lit only by two torches set at the entrance of every level. The priests who accompanied me told me they do that in order to keep the atmosphere solemn and respectful. Visitors take a torch and enter one of the different levels and they're supposed to return it to its former position when they exit, even if they want to visit a different level. That way, there's never more than two persons or groups visiting any single level, so that the dead are never disturbed too much.

"The smell of death and rot is far more present underneath the temple than inside of it, but it's also far less prevalent than one might expect. Even though there are dozens of dead Sakhovan bodies at every level, they don't reek as much. Captain T'Halek once told me it's because of the way they're preserved. He must have been right.

"I was brought to the lowest level of the temple. Sakhovan holy houses are always built on firm soil so they can dig ever deeper as the number of dead corpses accumulates. They believe that when they reach the center of the world, the Seraphalim will return for good, the fallen will rise from their niches and a new age without death will begin.

"Since there aren't that many Sakhovan in Greensdale at any one time, it was easy to find the dead sailormen. I'm pretty sure that I would still be able to find them, even without the priests being present. Go twelve levels down, take the eastern tunnel, find the last alcoves.

"Some of you might have been horrified, but the corpses weren't decomposing. At all. Sure, their eyes had sunken deeper into the sockets, their skin had caved in and they had lost half of their weight, but they were still recognizable as human beings. Their clothes were gone, though, but Sakhovan aren't ashamed of nakedness. I could see their battle scars, still clearly visible through their paled flesh. One's belly had been cut by a fearsome blade, another one had so many puncture wounds that he must have bled to death. The third corpse didn't show any wounds that would have been able to cause his demise.

"Each of the bodies was standing up, as if it was ready to walk out again, held upright by an ingenious contraption made entirely of rope. In front of them were plaques, but I can't read Sakhovan so I can't say what was on them. The clerics told me they commemorate the dead by listing their names, their occupations, their birth year, and the year as well as the cause of their death.

"I stepped through the tunnel to look at the remnants of the sailors. The priests knew exactly who they were. They keep extensive records, of course.

"And then, I saw there were two more alcoves. Puzzled, I stepped forwards. I counted the dead and asked the priests if they were sure they weren't mistaken.

"Five. There were five bodies there.

"Someone had brought in the two missing corpses.

"I asked the priests who was responsible, but they claimed not to know. Apparently, both sailormen were found on the steps leading up to the temple. Someone had left them there at nighttime, only a single sleep-cycle after the R'Lallon had left Greensdale. There was no way to get into touch with T'Halek, so I guess he still doesn't know that his men have gotten a decent burial. His ship hadn't returned yet when I visited the city again, either, but I should get back to the moment when I first saw those bodies...

"It was... it was horrible. Please excuse me for not sharing all of this with you before, but the sight of those dead sailormen has been haunting my dreams ever since I stumbled upon them.

"First of all, they looked sickly, in a different way than the other corpses did. It wasn't just the dried skin or the bones showing through, but the skin *color*. It wasn't just yellowish. There were darkish brown spots all over, as if they had contracted some sort of terrible illness. But that's not what was disquieting. The priests told me they had checked for contagious diseases. They had found nothing, but the bodies bore... I think they were *incision marks*. I'm not talking about the kind of wounds a slashing weapon leaves behind, but about deliberate incisions, as if someone had wanted to see what was *inside* of those people. They were everywhere. And... they had been stitched up. The Sakhovan don't do that. I don't know how they manage to preserve their dead as well as they do, but they believe in the sanctity and beauty of the entire body. That's why they don't want it to decompose. That's why they keep their dead in alcoves instead of burning or burying them. That's why they leave them naked. It was horrible, not because of the ugliness of it all, but because of the disturbed mind that must lead someone to do such a thing.

"During the entire trip back to Barnsby, those sailors didn't leave my thoughts. Not even for a heartbeat. I wasn't going to confront Baour about it, though. First of all, I didn't know if he had anything to do with it. Secondly, if he was responsible, I most certainly didn't want him to know that I had been to that temple. Who knows what you would have done to me, necromancer?

"About twenty sleep-cycles after he first entered my shop, Baour visited me again to check up on my work. I was a little nervous, but somehow the mage always seemed to make me feel more comfortable after talking to him for a while. He can speak like a poet when he wants to and it's difficult to remain suspicious of someone like that. We talked about the shape of the gold skulls he wanted to have made as adornments, about the exact color combinations he wanted to use, and nothing more, but the conversation was entertaining nonetheless. No offense, but none of you know so much about fine clothing as this man does, and I try to savor the rare occasions when I can talk to someone who's so knowledgeable about my field of work.

"He was wearing the same cloak I had seen him in when he first came by. His clothes were perfectly clean now, but I could see that some of the repairs he had made were rather poorly done. The pockets in particular needed more work, so I bent over and I reached into them with the top of my fingers in order to pull on them and show the mage that the stitching needed to be redone.

"That's when I saw it. I think I hid my shock fairly well, but... the stitching... It didn't look like a tailor's technique at all, but I had seen it before. On the bodies of those sailormen, yes! Yes, necromancer! And it's still there! Look at it!

"I found something else, as well. Baour stepped back as soon as I had touched his pocket. He said he was only a little surprised, but I think he was afraid that I would discover what he had been keeping inside. Some of it clung to my fingers, though. It's sticky. Everyone knows that. I keep it as well. It didn't make much sense to me until the witch's testimony, but here it is. See?

"It was no ordinary plant. It was ghostweed!

Chapter Five
THE CROSS-EXAMINATION OF THE TAILOR ROALDUS

Baour smiled as he locked eyes with Roaldus. It was a heartfelt, genuine smile, but one that made the tailor feel uncomfortable nonetheless – not because of the way the necromancer looked at him, but because he didn't avert his gaze for one moment. After a few heartbeats, the villager's neck hairs began to rise. A moment after that, a chill ran down his spine, and a little later he had to force himself not to turn his head away.

Roaldus wasn't the only one who felt it, though. Reald cleared his throat as loudly as possible. "Mayhap the..." He swallowed his words and corrected himself. "Mayhap Baour will care to start his line of questioning now?"

The death seer kept his gaze fixed on Roaldus.

"A-hum. Baour?" Reald tried again.

When he was confident that those present had other things to think about than the presence of ghostweed in his pockets, the man with hair as white as fresh snow broadened his smile and nodded, offering everyone some relief before he started to speak. He had already decided to switch to a more formal vocabulary one again; especially since Roaldus and he had become more than mere acquaintances and he wanted to leave that friendship behind.

"It was 'I expected nothing less.'"

"Excuse me?" Roaldus asked, puzzled.

"I expected nothing less." He swiveled around to face what he now perceived as a private audience that had come to see a performance the likes of which it had never seen before. "I ask of you, is that such a strange comment?" It was rhetorical. Baour waited for everyone to find the answer for him- or herself and turned his attention towards Roaldus again. "Would you say my tastes are expensive?"

The tailor had to laugh. He couldn't help himself, but he was only playing into the necromancer's hands. "Yes! Yes, mage, I'd definitely say that."

"So it is only natural that I would say something like 'I expected nothing less.' Or 'that was what I was expecting.' The exact phrasing does not matter all that much."

"Well... I don't know."

"If a wealthy man who likes fine clothes walks into a shop such as yours – as beautiful as it might be – in a village such as this – as nice as it might also be – would it be a stretch of the imagination to assume that this man would know he might have to wait for a while before expensive fabrics can be made available?"

"No. No, I guess not."

"So why did you find that statement to be so strange?"

"It wasn't the statement so much..."

"You dwelled on it during your statement. Everyone could see that. Such things might make an innocent man look guilty."

"I... apologize."

"You apologize?"

Roaldus felt trapped and maybe even a little angry. He narrowed his eyes and balled his fists before answering. "Yes, necromancer. I apologize. But that wasn't really what worried me." He sought his friends, then the other townspeople. "I mean, why would such a wealthy man stop by our village to order such expensive clothing to be made?"

"So what you really are saying is that you think this village is nothing more than a backward watering hole, a place where only the poor, the unskilled, or those with cheap or poor tastes stop by?"

Baour reveled in the murmur that started behind him. Esmeralda had already told him about the way the other inhabitants of Barnsby viewed Roaldus before he first visited the tailor. *"They think he sees himself as an upper-class citizen,"* the witch had said. *"It's like he puts himself above the others sometimes, probably because he's well-traveled while most people around here stick to Barnsby and its environs."* Then and there, he had decided on the line of questioning he would use at his inevitable upcoming trial.

The craftsman didn't hide his anger anymore. He lunged forward a little and warped his mouth to an ugly shape before spewing out his words. *He doesn't look charismatic anymore now,* Baour thought gleefully.

"I never said that! Of course Barnsby is a great place to live!"

"Then why not accept that an out-of-towner might come here to buy something?"

"Oh, come *on*! Obviously there's more choice in Greensdale!"

"You have a passion for the city that is Greensdale, do you not?"

Roaldus hesitated. "I... *have* to go there if I want to keep my business running."

Baour sought out Zerezsta in the crowd. She was following the proceedings with her chin cupped inside of her hands. "Maybe I should call your beautiful wife, Zerezsta, to the stand to ask if all of your visits to Greensdale are truly necessary? It seemed to me that there is a decent supply of fabrics in the back of your shop?"

"You know I don't carry a lot of expensive stuff, necromancer!"

"I am truly sorry, Roaldus. Perhaps I did not understand what you said before. I was under the impression that you were of the opinion that affluent, honorable customers would never visit Barnsby to buy expensive clothing in your shop. Perchance you wish to change your testimony?"

The tailor gritted his teeth. "You're twisting my words."

Baour nodded. He didn't want to look like a bully and he had already made his point anyway. "Maybe I am. I apologize. Let us not dwell on this subject any longer, but instead entertain a hypothetical possibility. You stated that the coins I handed to you were of many different currencies, is that so?"

Roaldus relaxed a little. "It is."

"I believe you named Ür'd, Tormar, Arrkon, Byrmur, and Thoufeldt?"

"And Illexalluh, yes."

"It seems to me you even forgot about the coinage from Erwould."

"True."

A nice opportunity to subtly remind people of what I've just said before, Baour thought. "It seems to me you are well-versed in the art of geography, my friend. Obviously, you are a man who has found other places to be of particular interest." The necromancer paused just long enough to hear Roaldus grind his teeth. "Would you say many of the nations you mentioned are far away?"

"Yes, of course."

"So it is reasonable to assume that I have traveled much?"

"Either that or you're a passionate collector."

"Which means it would also be reasonable to assume that I have slept inside of many a ship?"

"I guess." He looked at Reald. "How is this relevant?"

"I will come to that soon, my impatient friend," Baour soothed. "You also stated that you visited the – what was its name again, the R'Waun?"

"The R'Lallon," Roaldus answered, annoyed.

"You often visited the R'Lallon instead of going to the market place. Did you get to see the vessel from the inside?"

"Numerous times."

"Do you think traveling on such a boat is comfortable?"

Roaldus laughed. "No! It's not!"

"Which would mean that I am used to sleeping in places that are less than hospitable." He turned to his audience. "Perhaps I do not need cities to be majestic and cater to every single one of my admittedly luxurious tastes in order to appreciate them!" There was laughing, but not from Roaldus. He directed his next question to the tailor again. "Did I ever indicate to you that I did not appreciate Barnsby for what it is: a nice, cozy village, with charming inhabitants?" For a moment, he thought about the body of Esme hanging outside, but he didn't show it.

"You never spoke badly about this village."

"That is because sometimes I like to immerse myself in the simple life, which often is more pleasant and earnest than the life of a noble, bound by etiquette as the latter is. But let us entertain a second hypothetical line of thought for a while. Imagine that you are – maybe not a noble, but at least someone who is accustomed to life in high society. Now suppose you have been traveling and your next stop is the High City of Cadelberas. You do not want to attract too much attention – after all, you are not a native in these lands and the King's men usually do not pay much heed to a stranger. Robbers most often concentrate their attention on the larger roads and there is no hurry, so you decide to use the smaller paths leading from Greensdale to Cadelberas. Upon arriving, you will be greeted by royalty, so it is only natural that you want to present yourself in attire that is suited to such an occasion. However, while on the road, your clothing has sustained some damage. You hit a village like Barnsby, meet some people, decide you like the place, and order new trousers, a tabard, a surcoat, a cloak, a chemise, and more to be manufactured. Are you able to conjure up an image that suits this premise, dear Roaldus?"

"You're saying that you're here to visit the King's family in Cadelberas?"

"I said no such thing."

The tailor's eyes narrowed even more. They looked more like arrow slits than visual organs now, and if Roaldus could have killed from behind them, he probably would have tried to do so. His facial muscles contracted even more. "Are you toying with us, necromancer? You're at least *implying* to be here to visit the royal family. I'm sure it'd be easy to prove you're not lying. We could halt the procedure for a few weeks while a delegation rides up to the High City to investigate your claims." He smiled.

Baour shook his head. "Sadly, you are mistaken. First and foremost, there is the issue of plausible deniability. If the King has entrusted me with a mission of some kind, I am sure he would deny having done so to anyone who does not enjoy the privileges of a high noble. It would be bad policy – nay, it would even be dangerous – to do otherwise. Also, I would not be at liberty to divulge any details, as poor Mildrieda so tragically found out when her son, Arimarus, got hanged after the King's men found out that he had told everyone about our ruler's favorite meal. The poor man had only been invited to the palace once to receive a decoration for his heroism during the Battle of Kharûd-Lad, but unfortunately our ruler considers his eating habits to be a state secret." Baour paused for a moment so that everyone could hear Mildrieda's sobbing. *Always make it personal*, he said to himself. *Always.* The many wake-cycles he had spent wandering around the village, talking to the inhabitants as well as Esmeralda, were paying off. "Why, then, would I be allowed to tell you about any dealings I may have with His Highness?" Baour showed everyone the palms of his hands, and then lowered his voice once again. "Still, I am not saying that I have been summoned by the King, or that I wish to visit him and am allowed inside of his domain. I am just pointing out that there could be a million reasons to visit Barnsby, have new clothes made here, and stay here for a while."

"Granted, in that you may be right," Roaldus agreed. "But all of these other things..."

"We will come to those soon," Baour interrupted the tailor. This time, it was the necromancer who narrowed his eyes, but there was only implied curiosity to be seen there, not resentment or hate. It didn't make him look less beautiful or charming, only more astute. He lowered his voice even more, this time to a baritone whisper. "Why the sudden attacks, Roaldus? You said yourself that our conversations were interesting and involved. Why so eager to prove my guilt now?"

The question obviously caught the tailor off-guard. When he finally answered, he sounded smug, but it felt more like a too hastily built defense than like an inherent characteristic of his own. "I don't have to answer your questions, mage!"

"Yes, you do. This is a cross-examination. As soon as you decided to step up to this stand, I earned the right to ask you anything I want."

"We *did* have enjoyable conversations. About clothes and colors and Greensdale. But everything changed when I saw those corpses. Whoever... *borrowed* them did something unnatural to those sailors. As long as you weren't accused, I kept up appearances. Now, I don't have to anymore."

Baour raised his voice again. "I see that you are lying about your motives," he said, choosing to walk the thin line between talking and shouting. Before Roaldus could react, he continued, "But all of that matters not. Not right now. Please tell these people about your other misgivings, tailor. So far I have heard nothing that might indicate my guilt in any matter, past or present." His accusation would have to wait. After all, he knew exactly why Roaldus had lied about why he was pursuing him so aggressively, and who was responsible. He was only going to use the information when it really mattered, though.

"There's the stitches," Roaldus said. "Why would the stitches that I saw on those bodies look like the ones you used to repair your clothes?"

"You are a good observer, Roaldus. Maybe you would make an excellent *spy*." He stressed the last word, leaving people to wonder why he did so. "Or maybe a jester, they have to be very perceptive too," he added. He grinned when he heard laughter behind him. "Your line of reasoning is, most assuredly, valid. Let us go back to what you told us earlier. This captain – T'Halek – told you that I offered to buy his corpses?"

"He did."

"Did he stipulate how many I wanted to buy?"

"Wh–what?"

"Did he tell you if I had tried to buy all of them... or just some of them?"

"Does it matter?"

"It may."

"No. He didn't tell me."

"So possibly I only wanted to take two bodies with me?"

"Um... yes."

"Good. Now, did anyone claim to have seen the thief?"

"No."

"So T'Halek pointing at me as the prime suspect in the case of the missing dead sailors was purely based on me showing up at the R'Lallon and trying to make a deal with him?"

"Yes."

"Hmm. Let us call upon your imagination once again. This time, suppose you show up in The Black Stallion, Mildrieda's inn. During your last visit, you have gotten a taste for her special brew. You ask for a mug of it, but she declines, telling you she only has a small quantity left and she wants to keep that for a special occasion. She asks you to come back during the following moon-cycle, when more will be available."

Roaldus looked away, sighing. He knew where this was going.

"Now... The next wake-cycle, Mildrieda is playing host to an old friend of hers. She decides to get some of her brew out of the storage, only to find out that it has disappeared. Does this mean you are the culprit?"

The tailor didn't answer.

"Roaldus? Could you please answer my question?"

"What you described happened maybe a moon-cycle ago. I did ask for the divine drink you mentioned, and she did tell me to come back around this time. I believe you found it to be gone the next wake-cycle, Mildrieda?" The woman nodded. "I'm sure a lot of people asked about her brew, though, not just me."

Before the innkeeper could answer, Baour asked, "Still, how is what happened to Mildrieda any different from what happened to T'Halek?"

"I just asked for something every able-bodied man in this village likes. You asked for *bodies*!"

"Or so you claim."

"*What*?"

"It is of no significance. Whether the question itself is common or rare, the line of reasoning is exactly the same. If my offer means I have to be the body snatcher, you asking about Mildrieda's drink also means that you are the thief."

"What about the stitching, mage? There's no denying that!"

Baour shrugged. "If memory serves correctly, you only took a good look at five of the thousands of corpses underneath that temple, correct?"

"That's right."

"How are you to know that most of the other corpses are not stitched in the exactly same way?"

Roaldus was flabbergasted. He felt his shoulders lower, even though he didn't want to show any sign of weakness.

"Would you say that the way I stitch my clothes indicates only a passing knowledge of sewing?"

"It probably does."

"Do you think the Sakhovan priests are tailors?"

"I'm sure some of them are capable craftsmen."

"Some of them... or *all* of them?"

"Some of them," Roaldus repeated in a way that made clear to Baour he was almost ready to give up.

"Could you please repeat that answer so that the good people in the back may here it?"

"Some of them!" the tailor said again, but this time his voice ricocheted of the walls.

"So it would not be unreasonable to think that the kind of stitching you are talking about is fairly common?"

The tailor didn't answer.

Baour formed a sentence with his mouth, without actually speaking. He was pretty sure Roaldus could not read lips, but he was also certain it would make the merchant feel even more uncomfortable. *"I know who paid you."* Without making a single sound, he repeated the words, *"I know who paid you."* Roaldus caught it and swallowed. Baour knew that, even though the tailor probably didn't know what he had just accused him of, the possibilities that were now raging through Roaldus's mind were even more unsettling than if he *had* understood.

The necromancer made a gesture to indicate that what Roaldus had said up until then was insignificant. "It seems to me there is no way to connect me to the disappearance of those dead sailors. And, even if you could..." he paused, "that would be irrelevant to the charges brought before me anyway."

"You forgot about the ghostweed," Roaldus tried, but the tone of his voice was lacking conviction.

"Ah, true. Tell me again, how much ghostweed did you find in my pocket?"

The tailor brought both of his hands together to indicate a small sphere.

"Would that be all of the ghostweed one could find in the forest?"

Roaldus laughed weakly. "Of course not."

"I do not understand. Why is finding ghostweed in my pockets important, then?"

"Because Es..." Roaldus stopped, terrified. "The witch. She told us all of the ghostweed had disappeared, and..."

"Exactly!" Baour exclaimed, as if Roaldus was helping him with his defense instead of putting substance into what he was charged with. "Such a small amount of ghostweed, while you fear that I stole the entire supply nature had given us!"

The tailor sought out a man in the hall. Baour smiled as he turned his head to see whom Roaldus was looking at, even though he already knew. He just wanted everyone else to notice as well.

In the crowd, Ignetius nodded quietly, quickly, maybe hoping that no one had seen what had just transpired. He obviously meant to secretly support Roaldus, but Baour was sure at least some of those present were aware of the priest's reaction.

"Why would anyone carry ghostweed with him?" Roaldus tried. It felt like his last stand and Baour was ready to strike. His smile broadened now, but he made sure only Roaldus could see his satisfaction.

"Because, as you have pointed out so many times during this trial, I am a necromancer. We do use ghostweed from time to time, but what would I gain by taking so much of it?" He directed the next part to the villagers. "Apparently someone *did* want the ghostweed. One of you. I am sure we will be able to find out who was really responsible before these proceedings are through." It was a challenge, a straight attack to weaken the defenses before he would come in for the kill later on. He swiveled back towards Roaldus, this time almost as if he was dancing. He cursed himself even while doing so. *Keep your emotions in check, Baour. The hardest part is yet to come and you need these people to like you before you are done! Do not show your appetite for destruction just yet!*

"Can I be excused?" Roaldus asked Reald.

"I think you can," the barrister answered.

Baour let Roaldus step down before he halted him. They were better positioned now: the tailor standing on the floor, Baour on the platform, towering above the hunter who had become his prey. Maybe the necromancer could have won right there, but he needed the villagers to keep guessing, to stay alert.

"One more thing, Roaldus," Baour said, stopping the tailor in his tracks. The man froze without turning. Baour could see him shiver. *He thinks I am going to question him about the aggressiveness with which he was pursuing me. He must fear that I know the name of the one who bought him.* "Those bodies... let us suppose I *was* responsible for their disappearance. Under what laws would I have to be prosecuted for such a transgression?"

"I... don't know," Roaldus answered, genuinely sounding as if he hadn't thought of that before.

"Reald?"

"Um... As far as the abduction goes, since that happened at the harbor, it would fall under the King's Law. But the bodies were returned to the temple, making it subject to Divine Law."

"Divine Law I do not recognize. But please refresh our collective memories, Reald. Would that be Gealius's Divine Law?"

"No," Reald said decidedly. "It would be the laws of the Sakhovan faith."

"And do we know what those laws are?"

"Huh... No. We don't."

"Ah." Baour paused. Even though Roaldus still had his back turned towards him, he could see the man was relieved. He let the tailor take another two steps before he halted him again.

"Roaldus?"

The tailor stopped moving.

"You told us about five bodies. I believe you said that one had been cut through his belly, the other one had puncture wounds, the third one did not have any visible wounds, and two of them bore brown spots and yellowish skin. That would be consistent with what the captain had told you, right?"

Roaldus swiveled around, puzzled. He nodded. "True."

Baour's facial expression turned serious and grim. In other circumstances, one might even have said 'stately.' He searched through the crowd quickly before finally resting his eyes on the woodcarver.

"Reaphrastus, would you be so kind as to lift up your son's chemise?"

The man still seemed afraid of his own blood, but he approached nonetheless, motivated by curiosity as well as the sense of urgency Baour had managed to convey. *He seems alarmed, as they all should be,* Baour thought.

Zeitas looked more like a statue than like a child now. He was almost motionless, but he didn't show any fear while his father lifted his chemise in a single motion.

Baour waited until he had seen what he knew was there, then turned away and closed his eyes, as if he wanted to give the villagers some time to take in what they had just been shown. For that moment, he was captive to his own sadness.

The youth's pale body was slowly turning yellow. Large brown spots had appeared around his nipples and on his belly and new blotches were already vaguely showing themselves elsewhere. People started to scream.

Baour looked up at Reald and whispered, "May I call Zeitas's brother, Matthayas, to the stand?"

Chapter Six

THE THIRD TESTIMONY
THE APPRENTICE MATTHAYAS UNVEILS

"Well, I don't have as much to say as Esme... What? I don't care. Esmeralda. That was her name. Esmeralda, Esmeralda, Esmeralda! You should all just shut up and sit down. I haven't been struck by a firestorm yet, right? Don't feel any worse than a few seconds ago, either. It's all just superstition. Lord Baour taught us that. Yes, Zeitas and I have known him for a while now, and at least he's been treating Zeitas like a normal kid. None of you have. No, dad, you haven't either. In fact, you've just been hoping he would die on the spot, haven't you? Can't hit me now, can you? Can't hurt me while I'm standing here! None of you can. So I can tell all of you – including you, Eldried and Therionald and Ignetius – that I think this trial is a charade. I've gotten to know Lord Baour pretty well during these last few moon-cycles and he's got more integrity than any of you. That makes you angry, doesn't it? Ha! My bags are packed and, if Lord Baour hadn't told me everyone has to stay in the village, I would have left before this damned thing even started.

"I guess I was kind of looking forward to this trial anyway. I'm eager to leave, but I knew the truth was going to come out before this altar. Which truth? That most of you are hypocrites, trying to keep up appearances while pretending to mind your own business. But as soon as a wealthy stranger comes to town, everyone seems to want to destroy him. Even though I'm sure Lord Baour could've killed all of you if it had suited him. Still, no one here dares to ask him why he hasn't. Why is this man standing trial? He's risking everything, but you're all so afraid of the answer that the subject hasn't been brought up at all during these proceedings, even though the fear in your faces is apparent to anyone who cares to look.

"Don't call my testimony a sign of weakness or youth after all of this is finished. I may only be sixteen, but I'm just as much of an adult as any of you and maybe my age brings with it advantages. Like honesty and bravery. No need for me to be a minstrel to my own life, however. Not while all of you have witnessed how my father acted when the subject of my poor brother was brought up. You wanted to look the other way; well, that's your choice. I'm sure you will be punished for it in the end.

"But I was called up here to talk about Lord Baour and talk I will. As I said, I... *we* know him, better than any of you, except maybe Esmeralda. I'm pretty sure Zeitas and I almost spent as much time with him as the witch did, though.

"I think we must have met Baour just a few sleep-cycles after he first came to the village with Esmeralda. If any of you are going to stand up once more to stop me from saying her name, I'm going to repeat it a dozen times! I'll shout it and I'll chant it, may you all be damned! Thanks. Much obliged. Anyway, Zeitas and I were playing by the river. My brother was throwing rocks in the water to watch the ripples while I was watching Aulea's daughter bathe. Ah, don't act as if I've insulted anyone's dignity! Our women wear clothes when they bathe – why do you do that, anyway? – and any healthy young man who claims not to watch while they stroke their wet breasts and sometimes even caress places only men are supposed to touch is a liar! Come to think of it... Eaerae, will you accompany me to Greensdale? Your mother seems so bored that she prefers to feign seizures instead of working hard and your father is at home, trying to fight a hangover. Seems to me there's not much here for you, but in a great city... there our futures lie! Hush. You don't have to speak now. Aulea's already turning pale and I'm sure she'll need your assistance when next she plays the Feigning Saint Thersela!

"So, where was I? Ah, yes! We were playing by the river. I was the first to notice the sound behind us, as if someone was moving through the brushes. I mean, a lot of people come to the Lorenlon, but why would they choose to go through the undergrowth instead of just taking the well-trodden paths leading up there? There are lots of them. It sounded too large to be a small animal, but it didn't frighten me either. Barnsby is a pretty safe place and I never really got into trouble before. Sure, there's dangers lurking in those woods, but surely even the forest isn't more dangerous than life in the city is, right? I never understood why any of you like living here. It's so cozy, so... *uneventful.* So when Lord Baour finally showed himself, I was actually glad. Glad that I saw something else than the same familiar faces over and over again. Glad that this stranger wore clothes that clearly didn't belong to a commoner. Glad that he seemed like someone who had stories to tell other than what animal he had sculpted out of wood.

"Lord Baour must have noticed that he had surprised me, though. He bowed.

"'Forgive me, young sir,' he said, 'I didn't mean to startle you.' His smile was disarming. It wasn't just that he seemed so kind, or even warm and friendly. There's just... something about him. You told us you liked talking to him, Roaldus. Well, if you looked into his eyes... the man standing here has a quality none of you have. Maybe Eldried, but his mind is bound by religious restrictions and ancient ethics that have no place in this modern world. Not anymore. But when I look at Lord Baour's face, I see wisdom and knowledge. Knowledge about the outside world, about science and magic, about the natural order of things, and about the Spider. He's attended the academia. I think no one else present in this temple has, except for Therionald.

"Some of you will think I'm impressionable, that Lord Baour made me drunk with promises of greatness and power – while in fact you *all* know that my words are the truth. He scares you and you feel threatened by him, so you want him gone. And yet you fail to realize... I may be wrong here, but I think Lord Baour *will only leave if and when it suits him.*

"So, here I am, looking at this stranger, wondering why he didn't just use the path and avoid his clothes being stained. I think he actually tore that beautiful red cloak he was wearing while doing so, but I may be wrong. Maybe he damaged it long before that.

"Almost reflexively, I called out to Zeitas while I stuck out my hand, waiting for him to grab it. He didn't need much motivation. My dear brother was already rushing to my side, his attention captivated by the appearance of this stranger.

"'You didn't startle me,' I finally said. It was a lie, but I think it didn't fool Lord Baour. However, instead of saying anything, he just smiled.

"He humored me. 'Good. I am Baour and I came from far to visit this village.' I don't care about the other testimonies. I know that's what he told us. *He came to Barnsby to visit us*. I didn't ask about the reason, though. I was much more interested in other matters.

"'I am Matthayas, and this is my little brother, Zeitas.'

"Zeitas has always been a shy kid. He didn't really say anything, but he nodded, soaking up the rich red colors of Lord Baour's cloak with both eyes while he was holding my hand.

"Lord Baour kneeled down and stroked Zeitas's face.

"'So young, so seemingly untouched by entropy,' he murmured. I could hear his words, but I didn't understand what he meant. Not yet. It was a powerful experience: a stranger of his obvious stature kneeling down for my brother, both of them losing themselves into each other for what must have been at least a dozen heartbeats. Lord Baour's eyes widened and I could almost hear him gasp for air. Then, he closed his eyes and looked down.

"'Is something wrong, Sir?' Zeitas inquired, his shyness overcome by his curiosity.

"The white-haired man shook his head. 'No, nothing's wrong.' He got up and he pointed to the river.

"'Is that the Lorenlon?'

"I nodded. 'It is. Goes all the way up to the Sundarun realms.'

"Eaerae and her friends had stopped bathing now. They had noticed Lord Baour and were just standing there. He waved at them and yelled, 'Sorry for the intrusion! I am but a stranger in these lands!'

"As the girls started to wade to the river bank to get dressed, Lord Baour turned his attention to us again. He was frowning.

"'Forgive me for asking, but does everyone in this village bathe in this river?'

"Zeitas started laughing. Even he knew it was a preposterous thought, boys and men – or even women – bathing in the same river as our girls. Young women are still pure and blessed with Gealius's energy, while those born with a lance pierce the innocent to make them part of the world of work and war, of child-bearing and care-giving, of housekeeping and responsibilities. Or at least that's what Eldried teaches us all. Amused, we explained everything to Lord Baour. He listened to us as if our beliefs and customs were of the utmost significance. It felt good. It felt like – even though I realize what we had to say couldn't have been of much real interest to him – we were two of the most important people alive.

"'How many girls are there in this village?' Lord Baour wanted to know. Zeitas started laughing again. He really likes Dahlia, so I teased him with that and then turned my attention towards the stranger again.

"'There's not many of them, I'm afraid,' I answered. 'Nobles don't usually visit this village to find concubines. You may not find what you're looking for.'

"'Rest assured, I *will* find what I am looking for,' Lord Baour said. He was deadly serious about it. He put one hand on my shoulder and looked me in the eyes. 'How many girls?' he repeated.

"Zeitas answered, 'There's Dahlia!'

"I laughed. 'Yes, and there's Dahlia, right! And Dahlia, and Dahlia, and Dahlia!'

"My brother ran around Lord Baour and me a few times before I took hold of his hand again.

"I continued the conversation. 'So you know about Dahlia. There's twelve others, I think, but only half of them already have breasts. They're the only ones who have reached the wedding age.'

"'I do not care about weddings, let alone the feasts that accompany them, or the life sentence they entail,' Lord Baour claimed.

"'He wants to pierce them!' Zeitas joked. I told him to shut up for a while and when he didn't, I just squeezed his hand a little tighter. It's our signal. When I do that, he knows I'm serious. Lord Baour didn't seem to be offended, though.

"'No, I do not want to pierce them.' He winked at me. 'But I would be very grateful if you told me all about them.'

"We spent the whole wake-cycle talking about girls. *Our* girls. Lord Baour wanted to know what their names were and where they lived. We told him how Tressa once fell into the well, how Yvonnia wandered off into the woods and got lost for a while, and how Eaerae and I first kissed. It may seem strange to you that we spoke about such things when we didn't even know Lord Baour yet; but I like someone who's direct and asks the questions he wants to ask instead of covering them up with flowers and perfume, or of masking them with tall tales and misdirection. If Lord Baour hasn't been like that to everyone here, I'm sure it's because he knows most of you would react badly and think of him as nosy and lacking etiquette. Well, I don't care about etiquette and Lord Baour seemed to understand that.

"There's also... there's also this *quality* about him. I felt like I could confide in him, like I could tell him anything. Like he would keep my secrets and tell me about his own.

"After a while, Lord Baour looked up. We were sitting on the grass and Zeitas had fallen asleep, but our new friend seemed to see something in the skies.

"'I have to excuse myself.' he apologized. 'It's time for me to go. There's someone waiting for me. She'll wonder where I am.'

"I smiled. 'So you already have someone to be with.'

Lord Baour nodded.

"'Who is it?' Zeitas wanted to know. He had woken up, or maybe he hadn't really been sleeping at all.

"It doesn't matter,' Baour said. 'What does matter is that your parents may have started to worry about where you are. It *is* getting late and I would like to see my companion and kiss her before she journeys to the

Dreaming Lands.'

"I shrugged and told him that our parents don't really care about us anyway, even though they pretend to. They wouldn't come looking for us. Not unless we were gone for more than a wake-cycle. They need our hands and muscles to help them at their jobs. Don't you, mum and dad?

"Lord Baour seemed to care, though. He told us about his parents – or, actually, about how he didn't have any. About how he was found after... but I've promised not to tell. We both did. It would be our shared secret. The first of many.

"Before our new friend left, we agreed on meeting each other again. On the riverbanks, but somewhere the girls wouldn't notice us. Can I tell them, Lord Baour? Can I tell them now? Good.

"A few wake-cycles later, we met up with Lord Baour again. We weren't really sure he would come, but Zeitas and I had been telling each other stories about what it might be like to have someone like him as a friend. We didn't know he was a mage yet, but people were talking and we'd also heard he was staying at Esmeralda's place, so it seemed logical that he was, indeed, a mage. Between the two of us, we had imagined great works of magic, dragon riders, royal feasts, and mage battles, but we didn't think we would actually ever be involved in any of those events. History doesn't seem to have many inhabitants of Barnsby in it. I know there's Reginauld the Rockslinger, but that was ages ago and the fact that his name is still being mentioned every few wake-cycles is rather sad. You all seem so proud of him having been a villager here, but he left when he was seventeen and he never returned! Am I the only one who understands how pathetic that is? I guess I am.

"I don't know if we really expected Lord Baour to show up, but just to be sure we had made it to the river early. Much to our surprise, our new friend was already sitting there, watching the girls with a single piece of straw in his mouth. It almost seemed playful if not for the expression on his face. He was obviously concentrating. I don't think he was actually enjoying himself, or even taking time to admire the beauty in the water. It took his a few moments to notice us, but when he did, he greeted us cordially.

"My little brother was still full of life then and he tugged at this man's clothes. 'Are you a mage, Sir?' he wanted to know.

"I wasn't expecting Lord Baour to answer the question, but instead he smiled. 'Yes, I am.'

"'Please excuse my brother,' I said, but my heart was racing just as much as his was. A wizard in our village! I almost hadn't wanted to believe it and now that I knew, it was so different, so... exciting.

"Baour waved his hand. 'Do not worry about it, Matthayas. Your brother asked me a legitimate question.'

It was the last piece of the puzzle. Lord Baour had told us about his childhood, but he had omitted some details and everything seemed to make more sense now. My initial apprehension was gone as well. Our friend had made clear that our questions would not be deemed foolish, or – worse – irritate him. I know Esmeralda could weave magic, but she was pretty much a recluse and I had never needed to visit her cabin, so I was very much interested in seeing magic be performed.

"'Please, Lord Baour, could you weave a spell for us?'

"'Well, there *is* something I must do,' Baour replied. Then, it was as if he had an idea. He pointed at us with his index finger and asked, 'Would you both like to help me while I am weaving my magic?' Of course, he didn't really have to ask us. We jumped at the opportunity, eager to experience something wondrous and new. Lord Baour suggested playing a game and we immediately agreed. He wanted us to go a little further down the bank, where no one would come, and dig out a small water basin with our hands. 'Be careful not to fall into the river,' he said, but we often played at the riverside, creating miniature walled cities out of sticks and rocks and digging out small canals out of the Lorenlon to get some much-needed water to the inhabitants. Our canals were usually just as long as my arms and only as wide as my sandals are, but this time we wanted to impress Lord Baour and we eagerly started to shovel the dirt away with our hands. We stained our clothes and the earth crept under our nails, but it felt like we were doing important work, even though we didn't even know what Lord Baour had in mind. We pretended that it must be something important, though.

"While we were digging, Baour was entertaining us with some of his tales, but long before we were satisfied with the results, he stopped us. 'That's enough,' he said. Maybe he lost patience, because what happened next made clear to me that he really didn't need Zeitas and I to do anything. I think he just wanted to involve us in the process.

"The mage knelt down and started to concentrate. His eyes glazed over and he just seemed to be in another place, but this time he was pulling and tugging at invisible strings, almost as if he were making a work of art. Before we knew what was happening, the small canal we had begun to make started to deepen. In and out of itself, or so it seemed. It was as if an invisible force was eating at the dirt and expanding our ditches. Zeitas and I gasped, watching it happen without uttering a single word. When the mage was done, our canal and its two branches were each just as long as a grown man, and deep enough to sink an entire finger in them. The river water started to flow into our canals without being absorbed by the dirt too fast, filling them completely.

"'This is how some countries get water to their cities,' Lord Baour explained.

"'We know,' I said, 'but how do you keep it from being absorbed back into the ground after a while?'

"'A very good question, sir Matthayas!' the mage replied. 'First of all, the canals have to be level and their bottoms need to be flat. Or at least it's preferably that they are. But – more importantly – you will need to puddle them.'

"I didn't know what that term meant, but Lord Baour explained to me that he wanted to line the cut with a watertight material. Actually, he asked us if we knew where to find some clay. I told him about the Layn Hills just outside of the village. He patted me on the back, saying, 'Excellent! If you want to, this will be your first assignment as an engineer. When you and your brother are finished lining these canals with clay, I will show you more magic.' He closed the entrance of the main canal with some dirt and covered everything with some branches and leaves.

"It may seem like a small, insignificant thing, but that's because none of you have witnessed what Zeitas and I have seen. Maybe using magic to make small ditches doesn't impress anyone here, at least not if I only tell you about it, but to see something being shaped without using proper tools... it's *different*. It's *wondrous*. And it's why everyone keeps coming to this temple, isn't it? If we're all really honest, we pray to Gealius because we've *seen* Eldried summon light and heal the sick, not because we all like the Seraphalim so much. Do you think that's blasphemy, old priest? I don't think so. It's just the truth. If you couldn't work your miracles, maybe some people wouldn't even believe Gealius exists. Some would start to doubt the invisible forces that shape our world. Religion would stop being fact and become belief. Can anyone imagine something more frightening? Having to *believe* the Seraphalim and lives past this one exist, instead of *knowing* they do? There would be a lot less heroes, for sure. The world would become a darker place. People would be more likely to only look after themselves, without realizing they'll indirectly hurt themselves in doing so, because we're largely defined by society. So I don't really care about your rules and regulations, priests. I only care about the fact that I *know* there is more to this life than what we usually see. If you want to call that blasphemy, that's fine by me. I'll be gone soon anyway.

"So. As I said, we've all seen Eldried's magic, but Lord Baour... his magic is different. It just feels so much more potent, so much more... *direct*. When our priest illuminates the temple, I feel the existence of Gealius and that comforts me, but it's like I've bought a loaf of bread at the market. Bread is a miracle to me, but the merchant isn't responsible for it. He bought it from a baker. When Lord Baour wields his powers, you can feel the energy inside of him, pulsating, radiating. Like a living creature. In a lot of ways, he *is* the magic, while Eldried isn't. This mage has *bought* the power, our priest has *borrowed* it. You know what I mean?

"Yes, I've thought about it long and hard. None of you ever gave me enough credit, though. You all wanted me to just be the next woodcarver and you were content to let me play with Zeitas and learn how to work wood in between. But I think about things, and when Lord Baour called me an engineer, that made me feel... *special*, I guess. Before he came, maybe I *would* have stuck to the woodcarver trade, even though I've always wanted to be an adventurer. An archer, maybe, someone whose skill with the bow later becomes the stuff of legend. Or maybe an academic who spreads his knowledge around the world. Since I met Lord Baour, I've learned that people can accomplish amazing things if they really put their minds to it. And they can stand up against the ones who keep them from becoming what they can be. Even if those people are your parents.

"During the next four wake-cycles, Zeitas and I brought some clay to the river bank. We started to line the canals, but it was so much more fun than you would expect. There was a sense of purpose behind it all and my brother and I shared a common goal. We wanted to see more feats of magic!

"Lord Baour appeared just when he had told us he would. He looked at our handiwork and he assured us we had done a good job. 'Now show us magic!' Zeitas yelled. The mage pointed to a berry bush.

"'Get me some berries,' he said. 'I'll need at least several handfuls.'

"We plucked away until the berries were falling out of our hands and gave them to Lord Baour. He removed the dirt from the canal entrance and asked us to squeeze them above the ditch, just where the water from the river started to flow in. The reddish, syrupy juices trickled into the water, staining it, while our friend's eyes started to focus on something invisible yet again. His hands were in constant motion, and it was as if he was pulling something out of the canals.

"I guess maybe he was.

"After a while, the red water started to clear up again. It was hard to see at first, but soon it looked like we had never added the berry juice. Lord Baour seemed content.

"'What did you do?' I asked him while Zeitas was sifting through the water with his fingers, wondering where the color went.

"'I am a mage who specializes in entropy,' Lord Baour started to explain. 'It's most often used for... other purposes, but if the Sight is developed well enough and he keeps an open mind about it, a mage can manipulate the forces of entropy in any matter.'

"'What is entropy?' I wanted to know.

"'I suppose you could say it's got to due with decline, degeneration, and – eventually – death,' Lord Baour answered. 'But it is also loss of information, randomness, and the amount of energy that isn't available to work in a certain process.'

"In fact, I had to ask Lord Baour to explain several times. He was more specific about it, but I couldn't grasp everything he was trying to teach me. I see most of you don't understand my words, either. Let's just say necromancers usually study a specific aspect of entropy, but Lord Baour's Sight is very well developed and he has learned to touch that force in all kinds of different ways.

"Zeitas was getting tired of playing with the ditches and stood up. 'What are we gonna do now?' he wanted to know.

"Lord Baour didn't answer. He just looked at the river, then at our canal and its veins, then at the river again. I finally understood.

"'You're going to clean up the river!' I exclaimed.

"Our friend nodded. Zeitas understood as well and he started to jump up and down, but the mage lifted one of his hands. My brother doesn't always listen to others well, but he could see Lord Baour was being serious and he stopped.

"'What is it?' I asked, alarmed.

"'It would be very difficult to purify the river entirely. Even for me. So many Strands connected to it... so many different ones. It will take a lot of effort and energy to draw even one kind of tiny Strand out of the water if I want to get all of it. But the time has not come yet, and hopefully it will never come.' He looked at me. 'I have walked through Barnsby several times now. I cannot continue to analyze everyone, not even a dozen people. Sometimes they are in one place, sometimes in another, and the villagers will start to wonder why I am looking around so much. I will not be able to come to this river every time the girls bathe, either. The borders have to remain closed, except for some. Yes... for now, some may leave...' He pronounced the last words as if he was talking more to himself than to us. Then, he seemed to remember that we were still there. He looked Zeitas in the eyes, than me.

"'Will you help me?' He didn't sound like he was begging, but still... there was an urgency in his voice he had kept from us up until then.

"Zeitas clapped his hands and screamed 'Yes! Yes! Yes!' I wasn't so quick to answer. Not because I didn't want to help Lord Baour, but because I really had no idea what he was talking about. I asked him what he wanted me to do exactly.

"'I just want you to watch the girls,' he said.

"I laughed. 'I do that anyway! Well, I watch Eaerae...'

"'I want you to watch *all* of the girls,' Lord Baour specified.

"'Why?' I asked.

"'You see colors, don't you?' he inquired. 'Around people? And objects? You see colors.'

"I was stunned. Yes, I see vague colors around everything. It's like a very thin, colored fog that surrounds anything I see and I've been seeing it since I was nine or so. I've never told anyone, though. Always figured it was some kind of affliction. Bad eyesight. To a kid who would like to be an adventurer – even if he grows up thinking he will just be a woodcarver – that's pretty scary. Tough to be a great bowman if you can't see clearly, right?

"I needed some time to collect myself, but then I finally affirmed Lord Baour's suspicion. I was stuttering and I felt pearls of sweat start to form on my forehead, but the mage calmed me down by stroking my leg, my buttocks.

"'You're a beautiful boy, Matthayas,' he said, 'but you haven't been using your Gift.'

"'I have a gift?' I was shocked. Overwhelmed, even.

"Lord Baour nodded. 'I know you've been blocking it, but look at your brother. What do you see?'

"I concentrated on Zeitas. He laughed, because I don't usually look at him like that.

"'I can't see much,' I apologized. 'Just the same vague haze I see always.'

"'Good,' the mage said. 'Now try to tell me what colors you see.'

"It was hard to say, but Lord Baour kept pushing me. Still no success. I felt bad and the stress was getting to me, so the mage told me to stop. 'It would be unusual for you to already succeed in what I am asking you. We have some time left. You two just meet me here after another three sleep-cycles have passed and we will continue.'

"So we did. We kept on seeing Lord Baour every three cycles. Every time, we met at the same place at the embedment, and every time Lord Baour asked me if I could distinguish the colors surrounding my brother.

"Don't try so hard," Lord Baour used to say. "You're just straining your eyes. Don't do that. Relax the muscles in your face. Look beyond everything; but in doing so, *see* everything. Your Gift isn't well developed, so forget about the Strands. Just look at what you already know. Look at the colors!"

"Three meetings after Baour first let me use the Sight consciously, I started to distinguish the different colors around my brother. First the greens of emeralds, of leaves and of grass. Then the reds of blood and of berries. Finally different shades of grey. They were shimmering, fluctuating. And then, on the morning that we met Lord Baour for the seventh time, two sleep-cycles before the forest lost many of its colors, I saw it: small, thin coils of blackness swirling about my brother, as if he were bound by an evil serpent.

"I was pretty shaken up. Lord Baour must have seen it, because he grabbed my arm, pulling me against his warm body.

"'Now you know,' he said.

"Tears started rolling from my cheek. I looked at Zeitas and tried to smile while I wiped my face with my sleeve. My brother looked at me, questioningly, but I didn't know what to tell him, so I just kept on smiling.

"'It's too late for him,' Lord Baour said simply. 'But you *have* to tell me if any of the girls start to show the same colors. You have to tell me before it spreads to the Sundarun realms!'

"I sifted his white hair through my hands and kissed him. His tongue was warm and wet in my mouth and it moved gently, soothingly. Then, he stopped kissing me for just a moment. Zeitas was looking at us, amused.

"'And maybe,' Lord Baour said, as if he was only completing his previous sentence, 'we will have to kill.'

Chapter Seven
THE CROSS-EXAMINATION OF THE APPRENTICE MATTHAYAS

An icy chill crawled its way into the temple hall just before Matthayas finished his testimony. Outside the air was stirring, and a powerful wind came knocking on the door, as if to accentuate the weight of what the young man had said last. Eldried might have prayed to Gealius to warm up his holy house and make everybody inside feel more comfortable, but he felt that the villagers of Barnsby *wanted* to feel cold. It seemed to suit their inner thoughts, their misgivings, and their emotions like their patchwork clothing suited their humble backgrounds.

Most of Matthayas' audience had listened to him with a sense of aloofness that barely hid the disdain with which they viewed the would-be adventurer. His first words had hit hard, since they were directed at themselves, but there was little reaction to the rest of his testimony until his closing sentence.

We will have to kill.

Baour knew it really didn't matter anymore what else Matthayas had said. These people would only truly remember his last remarks. It was as if a ship had been wrecked in a storm. Most of the wood was drifting on the water and would eventually wash ashore, but the treasure hunters were only really interested in the heavy, intricately designed gold-filled chests that had sunk to the bottom of the ocean. For the first time during the proceedings, he was unsure of the eventual outcome. He grinned as he thought about how important Matthayas's testimony was. Even though his protégée had mentioned several facts that might eventually be of use in his defense, a new dilemma had unveiled before the necromancer's very eyes. It was too soon. Too soon to connect the dots, too soon to tell everyone what he was doing in Barnsby. The woodcarver's son had said too much, too quickly. It had thrown Baour off balance. He had to rethink his pacing, change his timing.

For once, the snow-haired mage was at a loss for words. Yes, he had nodded when the witness had asked him if he could say more, but he hadn't thought his young apprentice would go into that much detail. He hadn't told Matthayas about his most important – and darkest – secret, though. That would be the last ace up his sleeve.

"Your questions?" Reald urged Baour anxiously. The cold was getting to him too.

He needed more time.

"I believe Matthayas hasn't finished yet," Baour said.

"I have asked the question," Reald riposted. "He is now forbidden to talk unless a question is directed to him."

Baour nodded. "Very well. Matthayas, did I ever imply that maybe we would have to kill a *person*?"

Matthayas frowned. *For someone who's so bright, he acts astonishingly stupidly sometimes,* Baour thought.

"What do you mean, Lord Baour?"

The necromancer sighed. "I mean: Could it be possible that I meant we might have to kill a monster or an animal instead of a human being?"

His witness pondered the necromancer's words for a moment. *Now he's starting to think!* It might have been useful if the young man didn't think of Baour as being infallible. Maybe he would have been a little more cautious, but it was too late now. Eventually, he shrugged. "I guess so."

"You *guess* so?" Baour was unable to hide the surprise in his voice.

"I guess I just figured you meant that we would have to kill one of the girls."

The necromancer slapped his forehead with the palm of his hand. He could almost feel the smugness of the three priests behind him burning into his back. He sighed.

"Did I ever actually tell you we might have to kill a girl?"

"Not in so many words, no." Matthayas smiled. *He's being too sure of himself. Too sure of me.*

"Could it be possible that you misunderstood the meaning of what I was trying to tell you?"

Matthayas looked at his tutor questioningly. Baour widened his eyes, finally getting a reaction. Just not exactly the one he was rooting for. His witness's mouth fell open for just an instant. "Ah!" he exclaimed as if he had just had a revelation. "Yes, yes, of course! Of course I may have misunderstood!" He winked at the necromancer, who was painfully aware of the fact that everyone in the temple hall had noticed that small gesture. Matthayas went on, "I'm sure you would have stopped anything that might have entered the waters while tainted!"

Baour stared at the young man for a few moments, flabbergasted. For one brief moment, he looked over his shoulders, searching out Eldried. The priest didn't seem like he was praying – and Baour's Sight wasn't revealing anything that might have turned the otherwise-intelligent Matthayas into an idiot. He cleared his throat before going on, buying himself some valuable thinking time. He'd have to play more cards out of his hand than he had anticipated.

"You are talking about taint. I know this is difficult, but you said that I asked you to look at your brother's colors. On the fifth day, you saw coils of blackness surrounding Zeitas. What do you see now?"

Matthayas swallowed. A single tear appeared in the corner of his left eye, clinging to its well desperately before it finally had to let go. He shook his head. "I... I haven't looked at him for a while."

Baour tried to sound as soothingly as possible. "Can you tell us why not?"

"It's... It's gotten bigger."

"What has?"

"The blackness," Matthayas answered. His voice was cracked, his carefree demeanor shattered, all in just a few heartbeats.

Baour gently took hold of his chin and lifted up his head. He looked the young man straight in the eyes. "Can you do it for me?" he whispered.

Matthayas wet his lips as he thought over the question – it was something he often did when he felt nervous. Then, he grabbed Baour by the shoulder, trembling, and pushed the necromancer aside. His grip was weak, but the necromancer let Matthayas guide him, giving him a clear line of sight to his brother. Slowly, his pupils dilated, spreading out over his irises. It almost made him look less human. His heartbeat and his respiration started to slow. He was now aware of every heartbeat, his life's pump beating in his chest at a steady rhythm, almost like drums. Matthayas's cheeks took on a reddish blush as he focused on his brother, who was standing behind one of the benches, his upper body barely showing. It made some of the villagers feel uneasy but no one dared to move.

He had to focus. There were so many people in the temple hall, so many colors. Baour had taught him how to filter out the visual noise. Failure meant insanity. He imagined a tunnel, a narrow passageway leading up to his brother. Nothing – no one – existed except for Zeitas.

"Do you see it?" Baour asked.

"N... Yes! Yes, I see it."

"Can you tell these people what you see?"

"The coils. The... black coils. They've become more like thick, organic tentacles. There's so many of them, surrounding him... *clinging* to him!"

"Stop it!"

Ignetius was standing up now. He looked at Baour and Matthayas fiercely, defiantly.

"Stop this charade!" he added. "How are we to know this is for real?"

Baour looked at Ignetius, truly surprised. He turned his head to Matthayas, whose pupils almost covered both of his eyeballs now, and then back to Ignetius and to Matthayas again, finally settling for the priest. "Surely priest Ignetius cannot be serious?"

"I *am* serious!"

"Have you ever encountered someone or something – boy, man, girl, woman, animal or other creature – able to pretend being endowed with the Sight?" He almost couldn't believe that Ignetius wasn't just acting, but then it hit him. Baour had to fight his facial muscles from pulling his mouth into a smile.

Next to Ignetius, Eldried had buried his head inside of his hands. The young priest didn't know what to say. Baour turned to his elder. "You, Eldried! You recognize the Sight, do you not?"

The old man looked up. "I do," he said, reluctantly.

I've got you now! Baour thought, amused. *I've got you both!* It would have to wait, though. He wasn't finished with Matthayas. Not yet. He directed his next question to Matthayas again.

"Would you say these black tendrils indicate that your brother's condition has deteriorated?"

The young villager bit his lips. "Yes," he replied, fixing Zeitas with his eyes as if he wanted to apologize.

"All those present today have heard about how I asked you to watch the girls of the village. Can you please offer them your thoughts on this question?"

"I never took it to be a question," Matthayas said matter-of-factly. It almost didn't surprise Baour. Almost.

"Would you care to elaborate on that Matthayas?"

"It felt more like an... assignment."

"Indeed it would have been – if you would have been part of any organization under my control."

The young woodcarver-to-be nodded. "I understand. But, no, I'm not a member of any organization, secret or otherwise."

"Did you carry out this assignment you are referring to?"

"Yes, to the best of my ability. Roaldus talked about how he saw you wonder around the village. Well, if that's an offense, I am guilty as well. I started to keep an eye open for the girls. After I saw the black coils around Zeitas for the first time, I decided to help, but you told me to be discreet about it. To not get caught while I was using the Sight. Also, it's still difficult for me. It requires a lot of concentration, a lot of energy. At least for me. I tried to pick my moments. It's easier to look at people if they're alone, so I waited until I saw one of the girls walking around alone, or until they came to the river to bathe. There's a lot of space there, which allows me to focus on only one or two of them at a time."

"Did you ever see the black coils around any of them?"

"Yes."

"Who was it?"

"Laurelei, Yvonnia's daughter. Yvonnia's sister. She died one changing of the moons ago. It's easy to remember. It was only one sleep-cycle after the forest went to sleep. We had just met up – the first time after I'd seen the darkness surrounding my brother. You had seemed more... *anxious* than otherwise, but I guess that's because I'd kept talking about Zeitas's affliction. I wanted to know if you could take it away, just like you had removed the berry juice from our miniature canals."

"What did I answer?"

"That you had tried. Many times. I didn't understand, because only four people had died since you came to Barnsby, and as far as I know you never visited any of the villagers who were bed-ridden. You had failed, though. I was shocked. Didn't believe it could be so difficult at first. But it is, isn't it?"

"Yes, Matthayas, it is. Do you still remember why?"

"Because water isn't the same thing as a living creature. It's... *simpler*. In the river, it's easier to distinguish the black Strands from the rest of the Web. But if entropy wraps itself around a living being, if it's able to mesh with it... if it does, you might kill the one you're trying to save. You told me that it usually doesn't matter all that much if a mage accidentally messes up a few Strands while he's trying to purify water. But if you make a mistake while you're working on a creature, if you trip a Strand that should be left in place, or if Strands that don't belong together get intertwined... bad things will probably happen."

"But there is something else as well."

"Yes."

"You can tell now, Matthayas."

"The illness. It isn't... *natural.*"

Everywhere, people started talking. No one was trying to whisper anymore. The sounds of dozens of voices echoed in the hall, ricocheting off the walls, the floor, and the roof, tumbling back inside, and jumping up again. Matthayas was glad that he had only used his Sight for a moment, because the Strands of chaotically moving noise would have been too much too take in without focusing on something else. He could only see colors, which made it a little less likely he could get overwhelmed, but it was also more difficult to sift through separate color schemes and patterns.

Matthayas tried to grab the attention of the people sitting on the benches. He didn't like most of them, but he didn't want to see them all dead, either. "It isn't," he reiterated. Then, while fixing Eldried, "That's why you can't treat it. That's why Esmeralda couldn't, either."

"That's why so many people have been dying," Aulea, who was sitting only a short distance from Matthayas, said. He knew her voice and he could hear her words despite the tumult in the hall. "Yes," he answered, but he wasn't sure if Eaerae's mother could hear him as well.

"Please remain calm!" Eldried begged the crowd. Therionald and Ignetius were trying to contain the commotion as well, gesturing everyone to keep sitting and be quiet.

Baour waited until most of the villagers had regained their composure. Only Maerae was still crying, her hands raised up into the sky, shouting, "Gealius has punished them! It is his reckoning! It is his reckoning!" and words to that effect. Aulea remained still this time. She looked positively terrified, but she certainly didn't want to be compared to the Feigning Saint Thersela again and her desire to keep up appearances had gotten the best of her.

After everything had quieted down, Baour addressed his pupil again, "Can you tell what happened on the day Laurelei died?"

"I was never able to check up on her. She'd been taken ill only a few cycles after you first came to Barnsby and she hadn't ventured outside even once, at least not that I know of. That morning, people were already talking about the fact that she might not make it through the cycle. The illness... When it finally gets you, it shows itself. The brown blots turn black and... I'd rather not talk about the details. By now, everyone knows what happens. I had told you about it. It was on my mind. I'd just seen the blackness around Zeitas and then Laurelei reaches death's door..." Matthayas wiped away a tear with his sleeves. "It was a tough day."

"What did I do after I heard the news?"

"You told us that the time was right to stay in the village. I later heard that you'd just rented a room in The Black Stallion, even before the sun had come up that day. It was as if..." *Don't say it, boy!*

"It was as if you smelled Laurelei's death even while she was still struggling, trying to hold on."

"I did not," Baour lied. "If you remember correctly, I had just had an argument with Esmeralda. I had left her alone with Ewella's dead body. There was no other place for me to stay." It was a partial truth only, but it would have to suffice.

"Of course, Lord Baour." Matthayas didn't sound convinced. "Anyway, when they brought her body outside, most of you had gathered in the street. The weather had just started to change, as if it felt that the forest was sick, too. It became more fickle. The sun is supposed to cast its warmth on us for a while still; but oftentimes he just decides to leave us alone, in the coldness of our own hearts and bodies. At least the moons still keep the darkness away at night. That day, I just thought the sun had decided to keep his rays to himself, so that we couldn't find comfort under its guardianship while someone who had died much too soon was being brought to the Burial Mounds of Gealius out in the Layn Hills. Only those who die in good health are buried outside of this temple, aren't they, priests? Usually, we carry the bodies of our fallen to their final resting places, but this time..." The young man paused. "I guess I understand why you had a rope tied to her ankles, Eldried. I get why you asked other sick people to do it. But was it really necessary to have the retallons drag her over the ground for such a long journey? No animal has succumbed to the illness yet. You must know. You must know it's not natural! You must realize it only preys on *us*!"

Eldried didn't answer. The priest just sat there, outwardly emotionless. Also, Matthayas could see he had only succeeded in angering Ignetius – a feat that was, admittedly, not that hard to accomplish – while Therionald was nodding, but the would-be adventurer had no idea what that might mean. He continued his story.

"So I followed. While Lorelei's family and friends were trailing the retallons Eldried was leading to the Layns, I joined them. I was grieving, but I had an agenda as well. Out of the village, without so many of you around me, it was easier to shift my Sight without anyone noticing. And I saw it. The same blackness that was consuming my brother had covered Laurelei like a cocoon. I didn't even have to feign feeling bad to turn back. It's... hard to see what will happen to someone you love."

Baour waited a moment before his next question. The young man was in pain. And he hadn't even told half of the truth yet.

"What happened next?"

Matthayas looked the necromancer in the eyes. "Are you sure?"

The mage nodded and tried to pull off a faint smile. "You have told them so much already, you might as well continue the story. You are telling it well."

Baour stepped aside so that Matthayas might address the villagers more directly. The young man took a deep breath.

"Very well. I went back to the village. Lord Baour was waiting for me in the inn. We knew there would be a lot of people, so I could talk to him briefly without anyone thinking twice about it. Most of you were inside, except for the sick and the ones who were still traveling to the Mounds. I told Lord Baour about the black colors. 'It is as I had suspected,' he said, but I couldn't understand why he hadn't checked for himself. 'It was a hard night, Matthayas,' Lord Baour told me, 'I had to expend a lot of energy and my eyes needed to rest.' So I asked him what to do now."

"What did I say?"

"You asked me to bring you to the burial site before it would be too late."

"Before what would be too late, Matthayas?"

"Before you couldn't commune anymore."

"Who did I want to commune with?"

"Laurelei."

For the second time in a short amount of time, people started to talk amongst each other, but the conversations got cut short by Ignetius, "I told you! This is proof! The necromancer is guilty!"

Just as Reald wanted to speak, Matthayas raised his hand. "No! Wait! I haven't finished yet!" He looked at the barrister. "Please let me finish."

"If the man named Baour wants you to."

"Go ahead, Matthayas," the wizard said softly. "What did we do?"

"After the sun had set, I slipped out of my window. I didn't take Zeitas with me. He was sleeping and you had asked me not to. Our room is next to a deddallis tree and it's easy to grab hold of one of the branches, get a foothold on another branch, and then lower yourself down. I do it often when I want to visit Eaerae – sorry again, Aulea. I don't think my parents would stop me, but they've never listened to me when I tried to share my thoughts with them anyway, so why would I tell them about going out at night? As long as I'm present during the wake-cycle to help them with their work, they don't care. I met up with Baour just outside of Barnsby. It would have been exciting if not for the circumstances. My mind was constantly shifting between Zeitas, Laurelei, and the sickness and – even Lord Baour's kiss didn't bring comfort this time. We didn't say much to each other while walking up to the Mounds.

"Sometimes, when I talk to other people, they tell me how they think the light of our moons bathes everything in an eerie coat of blues and yellows. It's as if Uraniel and Emallae reflect the light of our sun, but not without the rays passing through the world of ghosts and spirits before they hit the ground. I guess that's why they say that the veil to the ethereal plane is thinner during a sleep-cycle, but Lord Baour has already told me that's not exactly true. That night, though… that night, I saw it for the first time, as if I was looking at the world around me with different eyes. Maybe in a way I truly was. There was something… *disturbing* about it all. I told Lord Baour, but he just smiled and he said I should see the other end of this world while the sun shines its beams on this side. 'It's far darker there,' he assured me. I want to visit that place. Sometime in the future I will."

Baour saw that Reald was shifting his feet. He was getting anxious and with him a lot of the villagers. "I bid you, Matthayas, can you tell everyone what happened upon arriving at the Mounds?"

"By the time we arrived about a third of the entire sleep-cycle had passed. Everyone knows what the Mounds look like. Like Death they are neutral: not great, not small, not green, not barren, not cozy, not uninviting. These days, however, the path leading through the burial site is well maintained. Our priests have to bury someone there about once every changing of the moons, so they make sure it's easy to get to. Lord Baour said he can't track well, but I know where people who have just died are buried; it didn't take us long to find Laurelei. We were expecting to need quite a lot of time to unearth her body. People who died because of an illness are buried deeper, aren't they? Of course, we knew the earth would still be soft…"

Matthayas looked away, lost in his own thoughts. Baour took hold of his arm. "Continue." The young man agreed.

"We knew the earth would be soft, yes, but we weren't expecting Laurelei to be just underneath. She was buried no deeper than my forearm is long. No deeper."

"That's a lie!" Ignetius shouted.

"No, it isn't, Ignetius. I'm not saying that *you* didn't bury her deep underneath the surface."

"Then what are you saying?" Eldried asked, curious, this time.

"I'm saying that someone dug her up before we got there."

Baour had already readied himself to ask something else before the commotion could start. "Why do you think that, Matthayas?"

"Because of the ghostweed. Someone had sprinkled ghostweed all over the body."

"What did I do?"

"You started cursing. I must say… I never knew someone could fire off so many profanities so fast."

"Why was I cursing?"

"Because you wanted to ask her about the illness. But the ghostweed… it keeps her spirit locked. You can't talk to her that way."

"Not even if the ghostweed is removed?"

"Not even. That's what you told me."

"I told you something else as well."

"That the properties of ghostweed can only be unlocked by someone who can shift his Sight. That this time, someone had used the Strands connected to the plant. Not to anger Laurelei's spirit, but to refrain it from talking."

"So I never actually communed with the dead?"

"You didn't."

Baour looked at the clerics, then at Reald. "Those are the charges, correct? That I talked to the dead?"

"Yes."

"Matthayas, did we ever even touch the body?"

"No. We were careful not to do that."

"Good. But that is not all, is it?"

"You mean the Lorenlon?"

"Yes. Tell them about the river."

"We got back to Barnsby before the sun set. I was able to get some sleep and when my parents woke up I pretended to still be too upset to start the wake-cycle early. They didn't understand of course, even though in a way I *was* still feeling bad and I *could* use my sleep, but they let me do what I wanted. It was a slow day anyway and I promised to get some more work afterwards. During the next twelve wake-cycles or so, I got to see Lord Baour more than before he started living in the inn. Roaldus finished his new clothes and he started wearing them as if he's royalty. Beautiful royalty. Everybody knows what happened then. I had to help out in the shop during the entire wake-cycle and Zeitas was off playing by himself. If I had known… how could you?"

Matthayas balled his fists and squeezed his fingers tightly together until the blood started to leave them, his fingernails buried in the soft flesh of his palms. "How could you?" he repeated in a softer tone, knowing his parents wouldn't answer anyway. He tried to relax his hands before going on. "At least he already had the illness. But if Lord Baour hadn't stopped that gorogon... well, I guess now you all know why he was in the neighborhood. He told me later that Zeitas hadn't been playing at the riverbank and he went out in the woods to look for him. Didn't think he would find him in the middle of that kind of situation, though. But that's all irrelevant now, isn't it? After the attack, I almost forgot about checking out the girls. Luckily, Lord Baour sensed my lack of perceptiveness. He didn't need me as much as before he rented a room in the village, but he wanted me to stay sharp as well, so every time we saw each other, he urged me to keep my eyes wide open. I was starting to learn how to shift my Sight without my eyes going all strange on me, but trying to see colors in that way is a lot more difficult. It takes even more concentration and sometimes it's easy to lose focus on what you're doing. Must be even tougher if you have to concentrate on single Strands, but my teacher seems to be able to do it well enough.

"Six or seven cycles later, I was strolling down Darius's street when Gearlinde caught my eye. She was returning home, but she was all wet. Her hair was still clinging to her head and her shoulders, her nipples, were visible through her shirt. It was obvious that she had gone bathing. Alone. The girls here don't usually do that. You almost always go to the river on the same days. Forgive me for saying so, Gearlinde, but... but seeing you like that... it made my stomach turn upside down. I hadn't looked at you... *really* looked at you since the last time I saw you all at the Lorenlon, but that was just before Zeitas got in trouble. So I decided to shift my Sight."

Gearlinde veered up, a horrified look on her face. She sought her mother's hand, but the woman hesitated to take hold of her and she pulled away from it. She was forming the words on her lips, but there was no sound. *Say it isn't so, Matthayas! Say it isn't so!*

Matthayas hesitated, shaking his head as if his thoughts might go away, but they didn't. "You're afflicted. I'm sorry. It's there. The black tendrils have gotten a hold of you."

Everywhere around the poor girl, people were leaving their benches, looking at Gearlinde apologetically while they nervously shuffled towards the walls.

"Please don't do that," Matthayas begged, but his words fell on deaf ears. It just made him remember how much he hated this place, these people. He continued, "I panicked, but Lord Baour had asked me not to tell anyone about our friendship yet, so I just ran to the river to wait for him. There was still some time to go and every heartbeat seemed to last an entire cycle. I sensed every single breeze, sometimes caressing my skin, sometimes playing frivolously with my hair. I saw the wings of birds moving while they were flying through the air. Up and down, up and down. I watched the silhouettes of fish carousing with each other in the waters. And there was noise everywhere. It was different than before Ewella had died, but in many ways the same nonetheless. The forest is still alive, but it's become so much sadder, even though some of the colors are returning.

The colors everyone sees, I mean. Finally, Lord Baour stepped out of the bushes. He looked at me and he knew. Must have read it on my face. 'In the water?' he asked. 'Was she in the water?' I nodded. My teacher cursed – second time I heard him do that – and he took me by the hand. Not like he usually does. There was a sense of urgency I hadn't felt before, even though I had sensed his uneasiness had been growing during the last moon-cycle.

"We ran. Ran as fast as we could. I didn't even try to talk, because Lord Baour was watching the water. I knew what he was doing. He wasn't looking at the river per se, but at what was inside of it. I had to guide him through the undergrowth. We stung and cut ourselves and my teacher stumbled a few times. I had to pull him up and make sure he didn't fall into the Lorenlon. I don't know how long we ran, but we were out of breath and far beyond our usual meeting place when Lord Baour finally stopped.

"In some way, I knew what he was going to do, but I couldn't really believe it. It was so... *unreal*. It seemed so impossible. But when he said we were lucky that the darkness moves slower than the water does, I realized he was going to try anyway. He started to move his arms in wide gestures, as if he was conducting a Tormarian imperial orchestra. His fingers were in constant motion as well, intricately slipping in between Strands and pulling them together or tearing them apart. His eyes were solid black. There was nothing left of the subtlety with which I saw him use the Sight before. He didn't hear me anymore, nor was he aware of my presence. I decided to shift my Sight as well, but I was overcome by the colors almost instantly. I hadn't decided on what I wanted to focus on and every single color of the spectrum was whirling around me, crashing into my mind through my visual organs. It was as if a pick had been smashed into both of my eyes, making its way through my head and puncturing my brain. I could feel blood running out of my nose and other fluids slowly seeping out of my ears, but I wanted to *see*! I tried to concentrate on Lord Baour and the river. Around my teacher, shards and sheets and flowing ribbons of yellow and brown and green and red were flying away from him, while he was drawing what looked like an inkblot as large as a man out of the Lorenlon. The specter kept growing, but it was also struggling, clinging to the water. It left a trail of darkness, but the top part was already slowly starting to fade away. Actually, I felt like I was fading away myself. I hadn't even noticed that I had fallen to my knees; my arms wide open as if I was inviting something or someone to come to me. But I wasn't. Or maybe I was, I don't know. I was struggling to focus, but my other senses were in overdrive, overloading me with sensations. My heart was bouncing in my throat, my blood felt like it was flowing outside of my body instead of inside of it and I had to expend all of my energy to keep a grip on my thoughts instead of letting them float away like leaves on the wind. And still Lord Baour was standing there, a commanding, terrifying presence. A man alone against the elements of nature: defying the Spider and ignoring the Seraphalim. But so was the blackness. It was made of nature and yet it wasn't. Someone has spun it, but not the Spider. And so it started to relinquish its grip on what is normal, on what is untainted by man.

"The rest of it happened so fast I can hardly describe it. I remember that I was lying on the ground, Lord Baour looming over me on one knee. He was bleeding through his nose as well and the blackness in his eyes was only slowly shrinking back to its original size. His sweat dripped down to my lips, a welcome reminder that I was still alive, and I could hear his breath, loud and fast. 'It is over,' he said, 'for now. I think I got most of it and that should suffice. No one down the river will become sick, but if we want to save the other villagers, we will have to find more clues, uncover more evidence."

"Was my desire to move faster substantiated?" Baour asked before he looked sideways, down and sideways again. His tongue was outside of his mouth, partly curled up, while he was thinking. He took a deep breath as Matthayas finally said it.

"Yes."

"Why, Matthayas?"

"Because it's here. I can see it everywhere, in almost everyone. The entire village has been afflicted."

Chapter Eight
THE TESTIMONY OF THE INNKEEPER MILDRIEDA

"I know you all want me to tell my story, but seems to me we should talk about how to handle this disease. Maybe the boy's right, you know? But you, necromancer... I just hope you know the cure. Doesn't matter to me if we find you guilty or not. If you're innocent, then I hope you will tell us how to get rid of this affliction 'cause we gave you a fair trial. If you're guilty, then I hope you'll have the decency to tell us how to handle this illness before you die. Might get you to the core of the Web, if you believe in that kind of thing.

"So anyway, I'm probably the reason why this man is standing here today, so I'll try to get to the point as quickly as possible. You all know I don't like to beat around the bush and we could use some food and a good night's sleep. But I also know I've got to tell you about the 'circumstances.' You know, the circumstances surrounding everything and all. The others have told you about how they got to know the mage, but I'll sort of skip that. After all, if anything happens in this village, I'm usually the second to know, so I knew the old woman had a visitor the cycle Merielda had seen them stroll through the woods, which – based on everything I've heard so far – must've been only one sleep-cycle after he had arrived at her cottage.

"Course, I was curious. Was curious why he would want to stay in that lousy cottage while I have perfectly good rooms available. Rooms that aren't used very often, I might add. They're in good repair. Maybe we should consider attracting more visitors. You would think more people traveling from Greensdale to Cadelberas would stop by, but they don't. Never have, and never will. Not until the King gives us some good roads.

"Got to admit, though. I'm scared outta my guts. Have been ever since the necromancer stopped by to rent a room. I checked the records, 'twas thirty-one sleep-cycles ago. Never was scared of Baour, though. He's a quite pleasant fellow and on top of that he attracted a lot of business. Many of you seem to have developed a taste for my brew over the last moon-cycle. It was you who scared me, my friends. A lot.

"It started with gossip, long before the necromancer came in to ask for a place to stay. The kids never seemed to mind the stranger, but you adults! Aulea visited just about every other wake-cycle to share most recent news with me. She's been doing so for a long time, but she's far more venomous now, talking about how she knew the witch and Baour were performing dark rites together in that cottage. Sure, she's never been to the woman's cottage, but there she was, raving on and on about how she saw them holding hands, rubbing against each other. She was very graphic as well. That's how you get the other customers to listen. Don't just say, 'I know they're lovers.' Nah, say, 'I know late at night they embrace each other in her creaky bed, chanting in tongues long since forgotten by the new races, and melting into each other. Their flesh waxes and wanes: a thick, unholy syrup that oozes with evil and deviancy. And as they become one, the dark Seraphalim take heed and they look down from upon the Web, granting them boons, tugging at the Strands to the tune of their sacrilegious love-making to make their presence known. On those nights, birds howl and wolves sing, squirrels take to the air and fish walk over to the cottage, dying in front of the door, a macabre nightly sacrifice to unspeakable powers we cannot fathom. And in the midst of those cloudless nights, Uraniel and Emallae cry as they are forced to see how the fate of the world is determined in the bed of two mortals, unable to warn us, their position in the sky their only way to tell us of the inescapable fate Baour and the witch are leading us to.'

"Chilling, isn't it? And most of you fell for it. At least you were right about some things, Aulea; but if all of it is true, it will be coincidental.

"Many times I asked you how you could know, cook, but you never really answered. 'Everyone can see,' you said. 'Everyone can see,' many of you said. It was like a mantra, a way to disguise your ignorance; and perhaps, a means to hide your fears. I've seen it happen before. I am the only one of you to ever lay eyes on the King, only moments before he gave the order to execute my son. There was no evil there, only fear. No bad intentions, only ignorance. Maybe those things are one and the same. I don't know. But the seed had been planted, right there in my tavern, and it kept growing.

"Soon the Black Stallion became less boisterous. There was still merry-making, but animated conversations were a thing of the past. You all started to whisper, thinking your poison would only infect whomever you were talking to. It spread, though. You didn't see, but I did. From behind my counter, I observed the distrust on your faces. Walking between the tables, I heard the hatred in your words. Serving your drinks, I saw your angst. And still whenever Baour came into the village, you were kind to him. 'Ignore him if you can,' I heard some of you say, 'but humor him if he speaks to you, lest he transforms you into something nonhuman altogether!' But, strangely, whenever the mage visited my inn to have a drink, you all flocked together to listen to him speak. He never told us much about himself, but he did regale us with his tales of faraway lands and strange kingdoms. During those times, you seemed to forget your misgivings. I don't think you were pretending then, but I do know that, once he was gone, his stories frightened you even more. Here was a man who had experienced so much more than any of us; an odd fellow with more knowledge in his fingertips than we have in our entire bodies. That's a scary thing, isn't it?

"Baour never stayed for long, though. He only ordered one or two drinks, then left. And, what's more, after he did so you all remembered his stories. I remembered how he'd only talked during half of the time he was staying in my tavern. During the other half, he *observed*. As you all tried to avert his gaze and make it seem like you weren't interested and didn't care, waiting for Baour to speak, he always took in every detail of the room, every expression on your faces. Watching. Thinking. I guess now we know he was using the Sight, but I can tell you for certain he wasn't only watching our young women. Then he left and you started spewing your venom again.

"Course, some of you didn't listen to the gossip. Roaldus seemed to care more about how much money Baour would make him. Eldried never even knew about what was being said in the inn. You've never visited the Black Stallion, have you? Not even when you return from your voyages to Greensdale, weary and thirsty. You go to this temple to pray and you only drink the water from the well in front, after adding some of your alcohol, of course. Your acolytes, though... Ah! You didn't know? Ignetius is quite the drinker and Therionald sometimes brings his own brews and shares them with my customers. Pays me handsomely for the opportunity, as well. Taught me some of his skills, too. Has a formula for every nation he's been to, but tells me my signature drinks are second to none.

"But there were others, as well. Not everyone listens and believes. Some have to *see*. *I'm* like that. Probably wouldn't be standing here if I weren't. And then there are the children, of course. The witch was right: they never talked about how Baour might be a creature of inherent evil, no, no! They came here to sip their drinks and, while their parents were whispering so that they wouldn't hear things they couldn't possibly understand yet, they spun their tales about the stranger as well. How beautiful those stories were! You were right, Matthayas, Baour never was an evil mage to your brother, and neither was he to any of his peers. Instead, he was their hero, a white-haired royal gladiator, or maybe an archmage, or maybe even a Seraphalim. He was the one who conquered the darkness and slew the beasts, their savior from the dreary village life, their hope for a more eventful life than that of their mothers and fathers, and the subject of their youthful imagination. And, yet, just like the old hag said, those who would have cared to listen would not have found innocence in their words. Their childish tales were strong with wish fulfillment, budding sexuality, anger they would otherwise direct at their parents or each other, and a need to gain power over a world they don't have a hold on yet. But never did they target Baour. He became the toy of their imaginations, the subject of their drawings, a man so clearly different from anyone else here that he sparked their creativity like no thing of nature ever has.

"And then came the first real warning signs. Those of you who work in the woods started to tell others about how the colors had dulled. It probably took you a little longer to catch on than the witch, but catch on you did. The sense of loss wasn't nearly as big as the woman's, but the dulling of the plants did heighten your sense of fear. Even though there was no panic yet, fruit lost some of its taste and the game shot in the forest made for tougher meat than before. The children noticed as well, but most only got more excited. They started imagining how strange, magical things would start to happen, hiding their own increasing sense of insecurity in doing so. Some of you talked about how the changes in the forest must be connected to the disease that had already killed a few of our fellow villagers. Others theorized Baour was to blame. Many thought Baour, the illness, and the strange occurrences in the forest were all connected somehow. Maybe today we'll finally find out.

"Only one sleep-cycle after everyone had started talking about the dulling, I opened the inn only to see him standing there. Him! Baour! The common room was still empty, I wasn't expecting any customers, but there he was, standing in the doorway, the first light of the wake-cycle throwing his shadow into my direction. I wasn't afraid, though, as the man just put one foot on my floor and bowed, introducing himself in a gracious manner. Course, he didn't need to do that. He had been to my tavern before, spinning his tales.

"'The cycle has just begun,' I said, 'and I have never taken you for a drinking man.' I tried to look casual, wiping a plate dry as if I hardly noticed him. Then, I looked up for just a moment. 'You've left the witch.' It wasn't a question so much as it was a statement. Taking care of my great-grandfather's inn for seventeen year-cycles, watching the wood it is made from slowly ripening and growing old... you learn stuff. Get to know how people think, why they do things. And even though this man is a necromancer, he's a man nevertheless. I may have vowed to remain faithful to my husband before he left Barnsby to come to grips with our son's fate, but I haven't forgotten what you are like.

"Usually, the next reaction says everything. Do they smile? Do they remain silent? Do they elaborate on their misfortune? Baour didn't do any of those. He nodded, but he had a serious look on his face, as if something bad had happened. 'You are right,' he answered, 'I have left.'

"Now, even though some of you may pretend otherwise, men usually don't leave their wives or lovers out of their own volition. They're kicked out. Sometimes, they cheat and keep lying about it. That gets 'em every time. Us women... most of us have a sense for that kind of thing. Problem is, a lot of us are a little *too* confident. I've seen intuition sniff out the bad ones, but I've seen it point a finger at the good ones, as well. I usually know the truth. If men cheat, I know of it sooner than their wives or male bed friends do. If they don't, I know about it too. With Baour... there was something different in his eyes. Something more... *sinister*. It just didn't mesh.

"I've listened to you during this trial, necromancer, and you can't fool me. There's something you're hiding. Something *dark*. But I'm not convinced that you're evil. You seem like you wanna do the right thing. I'm just not sure that what you think is right even resembles what we think is.

"I offered the mage a drink. He looked like he could use it. Gave him some of my brew, but he just kept sitting there, looking at it. Didn't even touch the jug.

"'You wanna talk about it?' I asked.

"'Yes,' Baour replied. I was a little surprised, but then he changed the subject completely. Wanted to know if I only use the rooms in the back to brew my drinks, or if I also make them at home.

"'I meant, do you wanna talk about what happened with...' Uh... I used the witch's name. Sorry, Matthayas, but I really don't think it's a good idea to go against conventions like that. A superstition? Maybe so, but I'm fifty-four now and that's too old to start taking chances on that sort of thing.

"Again, the necromancer said yes. And again, he repeated his question about how I prepare my specialty drinks. I figured he was confused. Never thought the old woman could make a man feel upset like that. Except maybe if she stopped giving him those love potions that made his wife still want to make love to him. I'm afraid you men didn't think about *that* before you executed her outside, did you? A lot of things are going to change here soon… if we live long enough to see the cycle, that is.

"At first, I thought Baour wanted to know about my brewing methods. As if I was going to share my secrets with him! Most of you brew your own drinks, but none of them even come close to my ale and mead. I don't think there's a single man in this village who hasn't asked me how I do it, though. Where do I get my hops? How much water and malt do I use? Do I smuggle in a dash of honey in my ales? Do I mix them with my mead? How do I get my brews to be so sweet, or so delightfully bitter, without ever overdoing it? Those are secrets of the trade, my friends, and if I were to divulge them, I would be out of business sooner than Reginauld the Rockslinger ran out of Barnsby! If nothing else, Matthayas was right about *that* one.

"So I started telling Baour what I usually tell you: I only use the best hops, my mother told me about the perfect doses, and so on and so on. But I could see he wasn't at all interested in what I was saying, so I ended my little monologue.

"'You really only want to know *where* I make the stuff?' I asked him.

"'Yes, I do,' Baour replied, almost apologetically. 'I just wondered where all of these great beverages hail from. I have traveled far and seen many cities, but nowhere have I tasted anything that made me feel so intimately familiar with the Spider and its Web,' he lied.

"I smiled. 'You're far too kind, white poet. But if you really like my brews so much, why haven't you even tasted what I just put in front of you?'

"The mage shrugged. 'For just a moment my desire to taste your ale again made me forget about the reasons that brought me here,' he explained, 'but I have many things on my mind and my body doesn't feel like being nourished right now.' He gently shoved the jug back to me. 'I will gladly pay, for it is a shame that a drink this divine is going to be wasted on the stones outside.'

"I laughed and saluted him as I grabbed the jug and put it to my mouth. "Fear not," I assured the necromancer, "it will not go to waste!"

"'Wait!' he shouted, as if I had said something terrible. 'I've changed my mind. If you still let me, I will drink!' I looked at him, confused. He had always sounded very composed and rational. His stories were prosaic marvels, but he seemed so out of it this time. He was feeling bad – that much was obvious – so I tried to show he hadn't offended me and laughed.

"'I'll pour in another one, then,' I said. 'We'll share a drink together and toast on what you've learned from the sad experience you've just gone through, whatever it may be.'

"'Very well,' Baour said, but it didn't really sound like he meant it. He was gritting his teeth and there was no sign of gratefulness. Then he changed his mind again. 'This is undoubtedly the best ale in the known world, but I haven't had the pleasure to taste your mead yet. I would be most grateful if you let me pay for this drink as well as for two mugs of mead so you can join me in the celebration of your craft.'

"Coin is coin and I've learned never to refuse a customer, so I agreed. I went to the storage room, but something was nagging at me. Instead of going straight to the cellar, I got a hunch and shuffled over to the door as quietly as possible. I hadn't fully closed it, so it was easy to take a peek at my customer. That was the first time that I saw him weave magic.

"The necromancer was still sitting down, but he was bowing over my counter, holding his hands over the jug, moving his fingers in intricate patterns while he concentrated on my ale. My ale! As if it was missing an ingredient or something!

"No, I can't really trust a man who messes with a perfectly good beverage! Maybe foreigners have different tastes, but even though people from abroad don't often visit Barnsby I've met my fair share of travelers and I've been to two of the great cities... and every single man, human or humanoid, who's ever tasted my ale likes it! Every single one! Taste buds are the same everywhere, no? Anyway, you definitely are a strange fellow, wizard.

"I opened the trapdoor, took some mead I had bottled out of the cellar and got back to the common room. Baour was still sitting on the same stool, sipping at the ale he had ensorcelled. He finished his beverage while I was pouring in the mead. Apparently, even mages' lips start to hang looser after they've had a drink. He seemed more relaxed now, and was willing to talk. I didn't even have to repeat my original question.

"He said he had left – I'm just going to say 'the witch', but he used her actual name, of course. 'We are not in agreement regarding several important issues,' he said, 'so I decided it would be best to move out. I assume you have a room available?' I hesitated. Of course all of my rooms were available, but I knew what you all were saying about him and I wasn't sure if I could afford to have a guest like that stay in my inn, you know?

"'It's bad timing,' I assured him. 'People will start to wonder. Only yesterday, the forest grew dull and less vibrant with life. They might think it's all your fault.'

"Baour didn't really seem to care. 'I will take responsibility for every one of my own actions when the time comes,' he promised, 'but I will not plead guilty to a deed that was committed by another.' It was a strange way to phrase things, so I got curious.

"'So there's actually someone who caused all of that?' I wanted to know.

"'Nature sometimes is capricious,' Baour mused. 'It is fickle and chaotic, yet structured and orderly. As long as the Strands are not disturbed, one thing will always lead to another.'

"'If the Strands aren't disturbed,' I repeated. The necromancer nodded, so I went on. 'Seems to me the Web is manipulated often enough.' It's something that annoys the hell outta me. Magic has its own merits, but sometimes nature should be left well enough alone.

"The mage stopped drinking his mead. He put the jug back on the counter and looked me straight in the eyes. 'Manipulating the Web *is* a natural thing, Mildrieda. It is how things are ordered. Scholars may debate whether the Spider does or does not weave its threads with any conscious purpose in mind – or even if it has a mind at all – but those who have the Sight know there is an order to things. A metaphysical and physical structure that must have been designed, not something that was created by fluke or accident.' He squinted his eyes. 'Do you believe this Seraphalim of yours truly guards this village?'

"'I do,' I answered. Now I don't know if I'm recounting all of this accurately, I'm sure Baour used a different phrasing and he sounded more eloquent as well… it's accurate enough? I'll continue, then.

"So, the next thing he says is something like, 'If you believe Gealius watches you, then he can only do so by interpreting the Strands that move around him, correct?'

"'I'm not very knowledgeable about that kind of thing,' I admitted, but the necromancer was adamant on not letting go of the subject.

"'If we cannot see him, than either he must be here, invisible, or he is sitting on the Web, but in the latter case he will not be able to see us with his own eyes… which means he must be using the Strands themselves to be able to perceive us.' He had almost lost me, but it sounded fascinating. 'Now, being present here as an invisible entity would mean that he is only aware of his present surroundings – in which case your assumption would be wrong since he would not be able to watch over an entire village – or that he is still acutely aware of the oscillation of the threads around him, which must mean that he does use the Strands continuously, or that the teachings of your priests are incorrect. Logic dictates no other possibility is even remotely plausible, at least not if one takes into account how the Web is structured.'

"'I think I understand that line of reasoning,' I said, hesitantly, 'but *seeing* or *feeling* isn't *manipulating*.'

"The necromancer smiled for the first time since he had set foot in my inn a little earlier that wake-cycle. 'Every interaction is manipulation. Let's say this room is stuffed with customers of yours and I enter. If I don't do anything except walk up to the bar and order a drink, will no one think of me, feel different, have an emotion connected to my presence, or react in any other way?'

"'I don't know,' I said. The mage was confusing me.

"'That is correct,' Baour agreed, even though I had just admitted to being ignorant. 'There is a possibility that not a single soul will notice me, but there is a bigger chance that the thoughts – the stream of consciousness – of at least one person will be changed by my mere presence alone. Have I, then, not manipulated the situation without even interacting with your customers?'

"'Ah, these matters are well beyond my capacity to truly comprehend!' I said. 'I am but a lowly innkeeper.' I wanted out of the conversation, but still the mage wouldn't have it.

"He knocked on my counter once, twice. 'Nonsense! Your ability to comprehend is not determined by your profession. As long as things are explained step by step, your capacity to acquire knowledge may even be greater than mine.'

"I started blushing. This man may burn this night, but he sure knows how to make someone feel good about herself. He noticed that I didn't know how to react and winked at me. 'Besides," he added, 'no one crafts better ale and mead than you do.'

"I was almost won over by his compliments until I remembered that he had weaved magic over his ale, but I humored him nonetheless. I think he noticed, though, because for just a moment I saw him frown. I wanted to change the subject to something more light-hearted, but he obviously wanted to make a point first.

"'I can assure you Gealius exists,' he said, 'but I fear the Seraphalim usually have better things to do than meddle with our lives.'

"'Some would call that blasphemy,' I warned. The conversation was heading in a direction that started to concern me.

"'Why would it be?' He didn't wait for a response and started to elaborate on his reasoning. 'If the Seraphalim intervene on a daily basis, why would anyone need priests? Why go to a cleric and ask Gealius's divine favor through him, if one can talk to the Seraphalim directly and be heard?'

"'Because the priests have a better connection with him,' I retorted. 'Because they know us. They know who's worthy and who's not.'

"'Ah!' The necromancer sounded almost as if I had proved his own argument, or at least supported it. He leaned over towards me in an almost conspiratorial manner. 'So the Seraphalim are not all-knowing or all-powerful. They *need* to use their priests as vessels. It's only logical that they wouldn't divide all of their attention over everything and everyone there is – is it not? Why would different Seraphalim reign over different communities or different spheres of influence, anyway?'

"'Maybe they need priests because we commoners aren't strong enough to channel their energy,' I tried.

"'Surely an all-powerful being must be able to channel its energy in such a way that it will not hurt anyone?' Baour riposted. 'If it cannot, by definition it is not almighty.'

"I didn't know what to say. I just asked him where he was going with the conversation, but the necromancer only shrugged. 'It seems to me most people lay too much of their lives in the hands of powerful beings who usually do not listen to their pleas anyway. Think about it! How much more would we be if we did not depend on them so much? Think about the wondrous things we could accomplish if we were not deterred by the supposed rules and commandments priests tell us to adhere to!'

"I was getting annoyed, maybe even a little angry. 'I know you come from afar,' I said, 'but please don't mock our customs or our beliefs.'

"'I honor your beliefs and I do not mock your customs,' Baour assured me. 'I am only saying there are so many more avenues to explore to those who do not see a tunnel, but an open field.' He saw that the conversation made me feel uneasy. 'Please forgive me for my exuberance. I was letting myself get carried away by my enthusiasm and will refrain from doing so again, especially with customers by my side. The room?'

"While I was thinking it over and trying to recollect my thoughts, the mage put his purse on the table. I heard coins ringing as they clashed against each other. 'I am a man who appreciates his privacy and I believe there is no one staying here at this moment. Please allow me to rent your entire second floor. I will pay double of what you normally ask.'

"I would have been stupid not to accept. That kind of money… even if Baour's presence had scared away most of my customers, I would still have made a profit.

"Just after I had showed Baour to his… *uh*… floor, the first customers started to trickle in. Most everybody was still talking about how the forest had become less vibrant only one sleep-cycle ago, and Baour's name was mentioned several times, but when he finally came down the stairs, it seemed like business as usual. The children were excited, but you adults ignored him until he started entertaining you with his yarns and strange logic. It convinced me I had made the right decision. In fact, even more people started flocking to my inn than before Baour came to our village. I guess it's not surprising. The last important thing that happened around here... the last things that really grabbed our attention was the exploits of my son. How proud we all were, how well he managed to do for himself and... how sad I was when he died. But during the last moon-cycles, we've had strange illnesses, a wealthy but mysterious stranger, the dulling of the forest... it's all been a bit much. We've become a sorry bunch of scared citizens, trying to find relief in the very things that frighten us. Except for the children. Even though they sense our panic, they're able to redirect and control their fears a lot easier.

"'I wasn't expecting so many customers that wake-cycle and soon I ran out of my signature drinks. I still had other ales to offer, but when Roaldus specifically asked for some of my brew, I had to disappoint him. I didn't have much left and because of the dulling, I figured it would take me another moon-cycle to make more. The plants outside still looked edible, but I didn't want to take any chances and I will never serve any signature mead or ales without being sure they're of the very highest quality. Besides, I was expecting a visitor during the next wake-cycle and I wanted to share some of my personal stash with him.

"It was a long night, but I managed to get enough sleep before getting up and opening the Black Stallion again. That morning, I went into the cellar to grab a bottle of my ale, but... it had disappeared. Actually, *all* of my signature drinks were gone. As if they had vanished into thin air. Only the stuff I'd bought from merchants was left. I didn't feel frightened, just angry. Got a big knife out of the storage above the cellar and started looking for any clues. I swear, if I had found who'd done it, I would have killed him right then and there. Checked the door, but it was still locked. None of the windows open from the outside, no glass had been shattered and there was no evidence of anyone breaking in. It was only after I searched everywhere that I remembered to look for my money.

"The strangest thing is, whoever it was, he didn't take my coin. I've started leaving my purse somewhere else now, but up until then I always stashed it underneath the mead bottles. That way, I always remembered where I left my money. But even though the bottles had been stolen and the purse was now exposed, it was still laying there, right where I left it. No thief can miss such a thing. Course, I figured whoever robbed me had probably taken the coins and left the purse itself, so I emptied it on the floor. My life's savings were still there. I started counting and then I realized the strangest thing.

"Someone had actually added some coins. Not small copper ones, I might add, but actual gold currency from Illexalluh. It was easy to distinguish from the rest. Most of you pay with local coinage, but Illexalluh mints its precious metal in a larger, circular form with a hole in the middle. They're really difficult to counterfeit. Only a couple would have been enough to pay for the alcohol that had been stolen, but I counted six. Wasn't sure what to make of it, though. I *was* feeling more relaxed by then, so I started looking for other, less-obvious clues. Couldn't find any. I'm not a tracker, but the dust on the floor didn't seem to be disturbed more than usual, the candles in the cellar looked and felt like they hadn't been lit since I had gone to sleep and even the trapdoor lock hadn't been pried open. So I was left with a shadowy thief who could move as silent as a cat, open locks without damaging them or leaving any other sign of tampering, and who had the power to see in the darkness.

"Or whoever did it was a mage staying in my inn.

"I slid my knife under my kirtle and ran upstairs. Hadn't checked up on Baour yet, so I didn't know which room he had picked to sleep in. I pushed open the door to the largest one without announcing myself in any way, saw that he wasn't there, tried another one and then heard a low-pitched groaning in a third room. I rushed inside, only to find the mage lying on the floor. The first thought that crossed my mind was that I was wrong and that Baour had probably been hurt, but then I realized he was still covered by a blanket. His bathtub hadn't been filled yet and he was moving slowly, jerkily, as if I had just disturbed him in his sleep.

"Either this man is a very good actor, or I really woke him up that morning. I've seen many men rise from their beds after dreaming about their latest sexual escapades, and they all look pretty similar. Tired eyes, red spots on their skin indicating their last sleeping position, a hoarse voice... even if they open their eyes just because they want to make love, the signs are there, and the mage conformed to every single one of them, or at least so I found out as soon as he started speaking.

"'Please excuse me,' Baour said, 'but it seems I was still sleeping. Can I assist you in any way?' He wasn't trying to cover his body with the blanket, so I could see he was still wearing his undergarments. A few drops of sweat dripped down from his bare chest and there was a faint smell of sleep, as well.

"'Well, I guess I'm the one who owes you an apology here, barging in the way I did,' I replied, 'but it seems someone has stolen my signature drinks.'

The necromancer reacted just like someone who's tasted my brews should. He wasn't just surprised, but horrified as well.

"'Not the mead!' It sounded like a reflexive reaction.

"I nodded, content to hear the horror in his voice, then thought it over for a moment and realized he had forgotten something, so I added, 'And the ales! My ales have gone as well!'

"'Of course. The ales,' he said, but I'm sure that he was only humoring me this time. His voice was flat and without much emotion. I found myself wanting to delve deeper into the subject – why did he seem to dislike my ales? – but I stopped myself, twisting my tongue twice before I said anything. I pointed to where he was sitting.

"'You haven't been sleeping on the floor, have you?'

"The necromancer shrugged. 'It brings me comfort.' Weird, isn't it? I heard the Sundarun like to sleep on hard surfaces, but a human in his right mind?

"'It usually works the other way around', I pointed out. 'Most people like to spend their sleeping-cycles in a nice, warm, cozy bed.'

"I must say, I think he understood perfectly well, yet he also tried to explain why he felt differently. 'It reminds me of where we all come from, and of where we are all going go. It makes me feel closer to nature and it confronts me with my humanity. It helps me not to grow indulgent or lazy, to remain vigilant even while I am sleeping, and to appreciate those things that we take for granted.'

"This time, it was me who shrugged. Didn't really understand what the mage meant, still don't, and if I did, I'm pretty sure I would still find it to be a little too much out there for my tastes. But he did change the subject soon enough, 'Your alcohol. Should we not go looking for it?'

"I folded my arms, straightened my back and tapped my feet on the floor. Didn't even have to summon the courage to do so, either. As I said: I was angry. Maybe not as angry as I would have been if the thief had also taken my money, but the thought of someone – anyone – entering and maybe even leaving my inn without being noticed made me mad as hell. Even if Baour had been a Seraphalim himself, I still wouldn't have cared. 'You're the only one who's staying here,' I said.

"The wizard looked at me. He waited before saying anything, as if he wanted me to rethink what I had just said. I wasn't going to, of course, so I pouted my lips and started to drum on my arms with my fingers in order to show that I wasn't going to allow myself to be messed with that morning.

"Baour got up. He didn't wipe his eyes clean with his hands and he didn't yawn even once. Even without his expensive clothes, even with his perspiration showing through his undergarments, even with the still-tired look on his face, his demeanor was... regal, somehow. For a moment, I thought I saw a hint of aggression on his face, but that emotion flashed by almost instantly and changed into comprehension and acceptance. Or at least that's what I believe.

"The necromancer bowed just a little bit, holding his right hand level to the floor, palm upwards and in front of his chest, in a gesture that seemed to match my interpretation.

"'I suppose it need not be said that I am neither thief nor liar.' He sounded calm and in control. More than I would be if someone had just accused me of a crime I hadn't committed. 'Neither would I benefit from stealing your brew.'

"'You did like my mead a whole lot,' I tried.

"'So does every single villager in town,' Baour fired back at me. He was right, of course. 'Not liking your concoctions, madam, would be a worse crime than stealing them!'

"'That's a true statement,' I admitted. 'Still, you're the only one inside and I can't see how anyone could get in, steal my stash, and get out again without leaving some sort of trace.'

"'Are you sure he or she did not leave anything?' the necromancer wanted to know. It didn't sound like just a question, though. He was *implying* something. It almost made me feel guilty for possibly being too impatient and rushing in, disturbing my guest – who had paid royally to stay here – and accusing him without any tangible shred of evidence. So when I said that I was sure, it didn't sound as convincing as I would have liked.

"'You said there was no sign of a break-in?' Baour asked. The mage clearly wasn't satisfied with the weak affirmative response that followed out of my mouth. With a renewed sense of focus, he stepped out into the corridor and started looking around. I didn't see anything, but the wizard started to climb the stairs hurriedly. He made me think of an animal that had just smelled its prey. I followed him to the upper level, where he stopped, motioning me to be silent. My guest took a few deep breaths, then asked me, 'Do you feel it?'

"I didn't feel anything until he clarified himself. 'The draft. Do you feel the draft?'

"Now that I knew what to concentrate on, I *did* sense it – it was colder upstairs than on Baour's floor. The necromancer looked around, and then pointed to a door. 'There.' I pushed it open and was greeted by a waft of air. Someone had opened one of the windows. I cursed.

"There's enough handholds outside to climb down fairly easily, so I guess almost anyone who's agile enough could have done it. Still, I wasn't prepared to give up Baour as my prime suspect. After all, the open window didn't explain how anyone could have gotten in from the outside, and the necromancer could have easily set everything up. When I told him about my misgivings, he actually agreed. He even lauded my sense of logic, even though it doesn't take a smart woman to pick out the necromancer as the most likely suspect, but the mage convinced me to let him stay in my inn nonetheless. He told me that the perpetrator would be revealed as soon as the missing bottles were discovered and that I should probably ask my customers and neighbors if they saw anyone climbing up or down the walls before deciding on Baour's guilt. It made sense. I mean, there's no one here who has the kind of money the necromancer has, and whoever was responsible left money to compensate for the loss. Never really believed in gentlemen thieves, but apparently they do exist, huh?

"That wake-cycle, I did decide one thing. I would keep a close eye on Baour and his activities. As smart and eloquent as he might be, he was still a stranger, maybe even a bearer of ill tidings. And he was staying at *my* place. Who better suited to reveal this man for what he was than me? There were other things to do as well, though. I had a visitor coming over and I had to make arrangements to accommodate him. And running the Black Stallion doesn't give a woman much free time. The mage would have to wait.

"Baour left soon after the incident, but I didn't follow him. He came back late that sleep-cycle, looking more tired than usual, and went to bed early, but the next day-cycles were pretty uneventful, at least compared to what had happened just before. You all kept coming to the inn, the forest slowly got most of its colors back and Baour got his new clothes.

"He did go out a lot, leaving for long stretches at a time. And me… I just kept waiting for an opportunity to follow him. It took six or seven cycles of patience, but one morning Baour left while I was still cleaning the main room. I decided to open the inn a little later and snuck out.

"I had prepared, of course. It's easy to slip in small questions while conversing with my guests. Even while talking about the weather, I asked some of you about Baour. Even while listening to your stories, I made sure to piece together a pattern to his habits. Even while serving you drinks, I was careful to listen to anything related to the mage. The stories about him were still being told, but I knew most of them to be grossly exaggerated and based on assumptions no one could prove to be true, so I didn't really care about those. As the wake-cycle passed and Barnsby quieted down somewhat, the tall tales seemed to lose their punch. There were no major upsets to speak of anymore and you all started to repeat the same stories over and over instead of finding new things to blame Baour for. It became easier to get the facts straight. I now knew Baour spent a lot of time wandering around town. Some of you felt like he was spying on you, but most of you didn't, as he always seemed to be courteous and to greet everyone he met. By name, I might add. I also heard he visited the forest quite a lot, though, and Tressa had seen him near the river banks more than once, so it was easy to anticipate and remain unseen while I shadowed him.

"I'm not exactly a trained spy and maybe most men would've noticed me, but Baour didn't. Not just because I had a general idea of where he might go to, but also because the mage seemed so ignorant of his surroundings as he strolled through the village. Yes, he watched everything and everyone carefully, but subtly, yet I think he was so focused that he lost track of what was present in his periphery. It was like watching a play so good that you lose track of everything else. I know we only get to see one of those once or twice every year-cycle, if we're so lucky to have a stage troupe visit our village, but I'm sure most of you can relate to that, right? Watching the necromancer for only a moment, you would hardly notice his over-concentration, but as I kept following him, it became more and more obvious to me.

"After buying bread, he started heading to the forest. Took one of the pathways through the deddallis trees. That scared me a little. There would be no one to run to, no one to help me if the necromancer caught me. I'm just an innkeeper, not a fighter, and I'm slowly growing old. No match for a magic-user. Still, curiosity got the better of me and I stayed on his trail. Made some distance between us, though. I figured it would be easier to follow someone moving through the woods than try to shadow a man walking through down streets. People leave tracks, right? Some of our men can find those easily. Alas, I apparently can't. Baour was already out of sight when I got to the path and I'm not much of a ranger. I went after him anyway, though.

'The forest doesn't hold much mystery to us, at least not in the immediate vicinity of Barnsby. We all know it pretty well and even though we may not wander off the known paths very often – our hunters will, but most of us won't – it's always familiar. Things had changed since the dulling, but after you got used to that, the woods – in some ways – became a *less* scary place. Before, a frightened mind could hear threats in the sound of the insects around it, a pet animal moving through the bushes could be misconstrued for a voracious monster, and the filtered sunlight could be perceived as shining on plants and animals with a purpose all its own. But now, there was far less noise and movement than before, without the forest quieting down altogether. There was, in a very real sense, less to be fearful of.

"And still… I was afraid. Must've been five or six since walking through the forest frightened me that much. It didn't have anything to do with the trees or the birds themselves, though, but with the man I was trailing. I couldn't find him. What if he was ready for me? Was he waiting for the perfect time to spring an ambush? Would I even notice? I started to remember all of the stories you all told about Baour. About the possible extent of his magic. Maybe he would weave an invisible web I couldn't get out of, or cast a spell to transform me into an insect. Or turn me inside out: a perverse, twisted epitaph with which he would first quell his deranged sexual desires before sinking his hands into my intestines and tearing them apart one by one. I realize that I was only succeeding in working myself up, but there was nothing I could do about it. My heart was throbbing in my throat as if it wanted to burst out of my chest; but, still, I didn't want to turn back. There is… *attraction* in mystery, *emotion* in danger, imagined or real, and more than all of those silly tales about Baour, I remembered my son. My dear son, the hero, a champion to the King before the very man whom he had served so valiantly ordered his execution. His death was too much for my poor husband, who left Barnsby soon afterwards because the inn only reminded him of happiness past. Dying of old age… it's what we do here in Barnsby, you know? If disease doesn't get us – and it seems it might leave none of us standing this time – most of us are content to lay down in our beds and quietly say our last goodbyes before finally wandering off to meet our Seraphalim. And I have to admit that I, too, would choose such a death. But right then, right there… somehow being cut into a thousand bloody pieces by Strands made tangible and sharp as knives seemed like a fitting way to honor my son and salute him one last time, with a final act of bravery.

"I gave up, though. I had been following the path for long enough and there was an inn to open, so eventually I turned back. With the village as my next destination, my fear started to abate… and then I heard a noise. It was faint and very much in the distance, but it sounded like a scream and it stopped me in my tracks. I tried to concentrate. Wasn't sure where it had come from. In fact, I even questioned if I had really heard something at all, but there it was again. A scream. I almost panicked, but instead of running back to Barnsby as fast as I could, I forced myself to stay put and take a deep breath. And another. And another. I balled my fists and started to talk to myself… *You can do it, Mildrieda. You can do it!* I repeated it over and over until I had sort of convinced myself it was true. No time to find help in the village, I was still too far from the edge of the forest. So I lifted up my skirt and started to make my way off the path and through the undergrowth. Slowly.

"The noises got louder and I knew what was happening even before I saw it with my own eyes. I felt my fear flow out of my body like a calm, continuous stream of water. It left through my fingers and my toes until it was gone altogether. Only had to push aside a few plants to get a good look at Baour. There he was, kneeling to the ground, straddling a naked Matthayas. They were so involved in their lovemaking that the chances of their noticing me were extremely slim at best. It was rough, but loving at the same time. Endearing, in many ways, these two men exploring each other. I watched them for a while, admiring their virility, their masculinity, the raw power both exuded, a perfect companion to their obvious affection for each other. But then... something happened. They changed position. Baour got out of Matthayas and the young man turned around to kiss the mage while they were both caressing each other's backs. That's when I saw Matthayas's eyes. Those weren't the emerald green eyes I've known for so long but inhuman eyes, pitch-black with only a hint of white in their corners. I understood immediately. The boy has the Gift. I didn't have to wait for his testimony to know.

"I left as quickly as possible. Didn't want to stay there any longer. Facing one mage sent chills up and down my spine. Facing two men with the Sight... No, I definitely didn't want to take that chance. Didn't want to share this with anyone else, either. Don't look at me like that, Reaphrastus. I respect you and I'm happy to have you as a customer, but you've always been tough on your son and it would be bad business to share other people's secrets, anyway. You all know I can be trusted not to divulge the things you tell me after having some ale or after the sun has gone to sleep and the Black Stallion is only lit by candles and the moons outside. I'm only telling you this because I have to. Can't lie in front of this altar, lest the fabric of which I'm made be damned. But I will never – ever – betray anyone without direct intervention by Gealius or his priests.

"Of course, seeing Baour and Matthayas like that... I didn't know what to think of it. On the one hand, the mage had shown his humanity in that single act of the flesh. On the other, maybe it meant that I shouldn't trust either of them.

"I tried not to think about what I had seen too much, but since then, every time Baour walks past me, every time he talks to me, I feel more awkward than before. I've hid it well, I think, but I've grown more wary of him. Rightly so as it turns out.

"I didn't follow the necromancer anymore, though; just tried to stay clear of him. We still had our conversations, but he must have sensed that I didn't want to spend too much time with him anymore and he often cut them short himself.

"Yes, I did stop following him. 'Til two sleep-cycles ago, that is. You see my bed is one floor down from where Baour is staying. I used to be a deep sleeper, but I got more cautious after the break-in or theft or whatever it was and since I'd seen Baour and Matthayas together, I had also moved my bed to be closer to the door. Just to make sure I wouldn't miss something important. Almost did, though. I was already sleeping for quite a while when I heard movement upstairs. At first, I was still too drowsy to realize it was a door opening and closing again. Had to tell myself I wasn't dreaming anymore. After pulling away from the sweet embrace of sleep, I started to hear footsteps. Someone was coming down. It could only be Baour. I grabbed a shirt and pulled it over me as I slinked out of the room. Don't think I had ever managed to be as stealthy as during that sleep-cycle, 'cause Baour continued on to the front door without the slightest hesitation. Uraniel and Emallae lit the common room just enough to see what he did next. The door was locked, as it always is at nighttime, but the wizard – who was fully dressed – just pulled out a fine piece of steel wire and fiddled with the lock for only scant heartbeats before it clicked open. He slipped outside, so I didn't waste time and did the same. Didn't have my keys with me, but who would know the inn had been left unguarded, so I felt it was fairly safe to leave.

"It was easier to feel secure under the blue and green light of the moons. There were shadows everywhere and Baour was using their cover, too. He ran from shadow to shadow, each time first looking around to make sure no one was there. I knew he was up to nothing good. It all looked *too* suspicious, *too* secretive. It was scary, but exhilarating, as well, and the need to know, to quench my thirst for the truth, was far greater than my fear was.

"After a while, the necromancer stopped on the corner of Vigilius's house. Vigilius had been showing signs of the disease for quite a while and he hadn't left his house a single time during the past cycles. A strong man, the blacksmith, but without wife and children – or at least not that we know of – and he had resigned himself to dying alone year-cycles ago, well before he got sick. Never one to talk much, he became even more taciturn after the first symptoms started showing and he had even demanded that Eldried and his acolytes not bother him during his fight with the illness. I guess he wanted to leave this life the same way he had lived it: sternly, and in solitude.

"It was obvious that this was the necromancer's destination. He seemed to relax, as if there was no need to hide anymore. But that's all he did. I mean, he really didn't do anything else. In fact he sat down. Just like that. On the ground. Shouldn't have been surprised – this is a man who likes to sleep on the bare floor, after all. Still... why would he do that? Why would he go through such great lengths not to be seen and then just sit down? It was as if he was waiting for something. I could just distinguish the look on his face: solemn, calm, almost respectful, but of what I don't know. It wasn't that cold outside, but I only had a shirt on and I didn't dare to move lest Baour might see me, so I tried to stay put and remain silent. Time seemed to crawl by slowly and I felt like I was freezing. Don't know how much longer I could have stood there, just behind Derek's house, using the walls as cover and sticking out part of my head once in a while to check up on what Baour was doing. Never seen anyone hold the same position for such a long time. Not even my son, back in the day when he was still guarding the gates of Cadelberas, before he got promoted. It must take year-cycles of training to be able to do that and not flinch a single muscle, you know.

"Just before I couldn't stand the cold anymore, Baour lifted up his head. He looked at the house as if he could see right through its walls. Maybe he could, I don't know. I, for one, had chosen my angle well. I was just outside of his field of vision. In any case, he got up and sneaked up to the door. He got that metal thread out again and got Vigilius's lock to open almost just as easily as he had mine, even though I know the smith had fashioned it himself. It had been too cold and too long a wait to feel scared, but that moment alone was enough to make the blood race through my veins again. My throat felt dry and even though it was chilly I noticed that my shirt was clinging to my armpits, held together by the perspiration of fear. Didn't want to turn back anymore, though. I had come this far and I wanted to know what was happening. So I monkey-ran up to Vigilius's door.

I was sure the necromancer hadn't locked it from the inside, but I wasn't prepared for what I heard.

"Voices. That's what I heard. Voices.

"Now, if I had just heard Baour and Vigilius talking to each other, that would have been one thing, but that wasn't what it was, at least not in any traditional sense. Yes, I could clearly distinguish the necromancer's voice, but Vigilius... he sounded so... *different.* It was still Vigilius, no doubt about it, but his voice seemed to be devoid of... *life*, I guess. There was a hollowness to it, and the blacksmith spoke in a register far lower than I've ever heard a man use. The weirdest thing about it... the *most unsettling* thing about it was the echo. It was as if three or four versions of Vigilius were talking all together, but with an almost unnoticeable delay between each of them. It chilled my bones far faster and deeper than the relative cold had done, like my flesh had been stripped away and someone was scraping my remains with large, pointy chunks of ice. As if my very skeleton was being polished by a frost so pure and intense that it more resembled an absolutely perfect *idea* of frost than the actual state itself. It froze me up, it left me petrified, a helpless shell filled with fear. But I still could hear what they were saying – and these words I remember well!

"'You woke me up!' Vigilius said. He sounded angry. 'You woke me up!' he repeated. 'How sweet a slumber this was!'

"'I know,' Baour reacted, calm as always, and with far greater empathy than Vigilius had ever known from us. 'The sleep of death is seldom welcomed, yet when it is there, it is embraced like an old friend.'

"'I had been waiting for it.'

"'This, too, I know,' the mage replied, 'yet it was necessary to wake you before the path back to this world got blocked by ghostweed.'

"'I don't know what you're talking about,' Vigilius's ghost said, gruffly. 'Leave me be!'

"The answer wasn't what the once-blacksmith was hoping for. 'I cannot. There is much to discuss first. I need to—' and then, he stopped talking, as if he had just noticed something.

"It wasn't Baour, but Vigilius who took up the conversation again. 'I sense a presence.'

"'I, too. Damn it! It's too soon!'

"They were talking about me, of course. You know how sometimes you freeze up because of fear? Well, as I said, I was already petrified, but the realization that Baour had heard me actually pulled me out of it. It took a few moments, but I started to run. Straight to this temple.

"That's where I told our priests about how Baour had woken Vigilius from the dead.

Chapter Nine
THE CROSS-EXAMINATION OF THE INNKEEPER MILDRIEDA

The atmosphere inside of the temple hall had completely changed. Before hearing they might all carry the disease, the villagers had been, in a sense, *enjoying* themselves; for many of the same reasons people flock to gladiatorial combats or other places where a disaster has occurred. The villagers of Barnsby were, perhaps, more susceptible to exciting events than the average city dweller would be, precisely because any of those didn't happen very often. They would never have admitted to it, of course, but Baour's trial was the best entertainment they had come across in a long time. Listening to the eloquent necromancer and the witnesses, trying to make sense of it all and connecting the dots, it had almost felt like a game to some. Even seeing Esmeralda carried away hadn't changed their enthusiasm. Far from it.

Just about everyone had heard Baour spin his tales, or had at least heard about it through a family member or friend, but to most the stories had been treated like faerie tales, not actual anecdotes. To many, the necromancer had refueled something they had deemed lost: a sense of wonder and imagination. Still, Baour's words had been like an inferior wine to them: yes, it tasted great, but the flavor soon disappeared because in truth no one had really believed in Baour's stories. Surely his depiction of Thoufeldt had been exaggerated, at best, while the supposed existence of a college for wizardry must have been wishful thinking. Telling people that everybody and everything consists of a nigh infinite amount of small particles the eye is unable to perceive was probably just a way to impress, and Baour couldn't really have gathered all of those different coins during his travels. After all, nobody ever travels that much, or that far.

The trial was a way to discover the truth, not only about Baour's guilt or innocence, but about his stories as well. Many wanted to believe they reflected reality, but just as many were scared by what that would imply. They needed to know the mage wasn't truly as powerful as they thought and that he could be brought to justice. Perversely, most wanted to see someone they secretly thought was greater than them fall, just to ease their fears. There were so many things to be frightened of: the unknown, magic, illness and, eventually, death. Not a single adult villager knew how to handle all of those conflicting emotions. They were interested and captivated and attracted and frightened and angry all at once. And it had to stop. The trial wouldn't be entertaining anymore if it didn't lead to a satisfactory conclusion.

So after everyone heard that they might die, they started to realize Baour's execution might not be a good closure after all. Even those who had wanted to believe the mage before were now hoping that he was a liar, scaring them with tales of death and disease only to further his own twisted purposes.

The human mind is a strange thing. If something threatens to shut it down or to make it feel too much discomfort, it tries to rationalize, hypothesize, delude, or deny its way out of the pain. Sometimes it's the only way to keep standing. Even though more than ever the villagers wanted to see Baour dead, it was becoming more and more difficult to deny he might be unto something. People *had* been dying, after all, and Baour wasn't on trial because of their *deaths*, but because of his involvement with the *dead*. The only thing left to do was hope that, if the necromancer were indeed a living bringer of disease, this trial would eventually force him to undo the damage he had caused. Or that he was actually a good man who was going to cure them all. The former hypothesis was a lot easier to believe in, somehow. The priests hadn't been able to cure anyone, so how would a necromancer be able to do such a thing anyway?

Baour knew the proceedings would soon come to a conclusion. Whether that would lead to a bloodbath or to redemption, he couldn't predict yet; but so far almost everything was going according to plan. The next two cross-examinations would be crucial. He folded his arms as he looked at Mildrieda. His expression was now more that of a jester than of a man who was accused of a deed punishable by death.

"Did I ever in any way imply that I hated your ales?"

Mildrieda turned away her face and pouted her lips. "You most certainly acted that way!"

Baour smiled. "You told everyone that you saw me... *ensorcell* my beverage. Did I drink the ale afterwards?"

"Yes, you did! After first altering its taste! As if it *needed* to be altered!"

"I fear that, to everyone present, your supposition says more about the pride you rightfully feel in your brewing techniques – admittedly unparalleled in the known world – than about my taste buds. Do you feel certain that I wove Strands just to change a flavor?"

Mildrieda still refrained from looking her questioner in the eyes. "I can't think of any other reason."

"I can," Baour retorted. "In fact, I *know* there was another reason. It seems clear that you are judging me based on unproven – nay, *unprovable* – assumptions. I first decline to drink of your ale, and you assume I do not like it, even though I have sung its praises before. Then, you see me weave magic above my mug, and you assume that I am altering its taste somehow."

Mildrieda turned towards the necromancer. She was angry and her demeanor obviously in now way reflected how dangerous her interrogator might be. "Then tell me the reason why you did it, necromancer! Tell us all!"

"I will," Baour promised, "but you will have to tell everyone the truth as well."

"I have told the truth!" the innkeeper protested. Her face was red now.

It made Baour think of the forest berries a friend of his liked so much.

"The entire truth, Mildrieda."

"I *have* told the entire truth!" the woman insisted.

"Fair enough. Maybe you do not even realize what I mean, but it will become clear soon enough." He purposefully looked askance. It fitted in well with his performance. After a brief pause to make sure everyone was making up his or her own mind about what he had just said, he continued. "It did not occur to me until the following wake-cycle, but your behavior on the day your personal stash was stolen seemed very suspicious." He gestured to the people sitting behind him. "In fact, I am sure that every single one of your peers present here today would agree." He knew they didn't, and most assuredly were so convinced he was a criminal that they probably hadn't been suspicious at all... up until now. Rare is the man or woman who finds out he or she should have caught unto something and later admits his or her ignorance. *They're already changing what they thought they believed into something that suits my line of reasoning, just to convince themselves they weren't wrong about it all,* Baour thought.

Baour noticed the innkeeper's hesitation, even though she tried to hide it. "What kind of behavior looked suspicious to you, then, necromancer?" It was meant to sound defiant, but it didn't.

"Ah! It pleases me that you ask this question, Mildrieda! Since you did, please allow me to present the answer. On the day of the theft – twenty-nine sleep-cycles ago, if I'm not mistaken – you and I were the only ones present in The Black Stallion. That is what you are saying, right?"

"Of course it is."

"As for you husband... You told us that he left Barnsby after your son was executed, a broken man."

"You heard right."

"You also said that you vowed to always remain faithful."

"I did. We just lost our son, and even though my husband needs time for himself right now, I'm not going to lose him too."

"Your patience is admirable." Mildrieda's lower lip dropped a little. She tried to hide it, but Baour caught the movement and smiled. He added, "One could say it is even wondrous."

"A vow made in front of Gealius is never meant be broken, mage! But what does that have to do with the theft?"

"Again, I am glad that you are showing me the way, good innkeeper! Your generous help is much appreciated! But you are right; I was digressing. Back to the robbery, then! Since your husband has gone away for an indeterminate amount of time and I was your only guest, it makes sense that we were the only ones present. Which makes me wonder... the door was locked, the window could not open from the outside and there were no signs of forced entry. It was only logical that you would accuse me."

"It was!" Mildrieda proclaimed, straightening her back.

The necromancer stroked the long wavy hair that was resting over his right shoulder and threw it over his other side, pretending to do so casually. "That is why I was not at all angry at first. I thought that you would notify the other villagers and ask for a trial right then and there. After all, your ales and meads are so dear to you, and you love them more than the expensive imported wines you keep in your cellar." He turned to his spectators before swiveling back to face Mildrieda again and pointed upwards a few times to accentuate his words. "And there was even more reason to distrust me! You had found foreign coins where your stash used to be!"

"True!" Mildrieda shouted, excited now. She suddenly realized that Baour was incriminating himself. "Gold from Illexalluh!"

"Gold pieces minted in the faraway lands of Illexalluh!" Baour rephrased, artfully stressing key syllables. "The same coinage, I may add, that I also gave to Roaldus, the tailor! He stood here, only scant moments ago, testifying that I paid him with currency from that nation!" The wizard turned to face the stupefied villagers again. "I ask you, does that not incriminate me even more?" He gleefully waited until several heads began to nod, and then turned towards Mildrieda. "The evidence against me was overwhelming!"

"It was! It was!" Mildrieda agreed, almost jubilantly.

"You suspected me?"

"Yes, I did!" the woman protested.

"On a whim! Yet after you saw that I was still in my nightly attire and after noticing that a window on the upper floor was left open, you dropped your accusations."

"It seemed like another might have done it after all." The witness sounded softer and more reluctant now.

"But why?" Baour pushed. "I could have easily gone up to the upper floor, opened the window, climbed down, hid some bottles, climbed back up and repeated the whole process a few times until I had secured your entire stash. How did any of those elements convince you to stop your accusations?"

Mildrieda shrugged, feigning ignorance. "I guess I didn't think things through."

"Ah, but you did! You did! It is precisely because you had some time to think about it that you changed your mind, is it not?"

The silence that followed amused Baour.

"So, dear Mildrieda, I started thinking myself. Why did my sweet host drop the subject so soon, so easily? Was it because of my eloquence? Surely not! You had just woken me up and I still hadn't collected my thoughts. Was it because my stories entertained your guests? Most assuredly not! After all, you said yourself that you were hesitant to grant me a room at first and, even though it seemed like I was attracting even more customers, the atmosphere was not the same anymore. The benefits you were hoping to reap would soon be lost if I were discovered to be a thief. Most people flock to the Black Stallion because of your own mixtures. Losing them would be bad for business, since – as you pointed out yourself – the good people of Barnsby all make their own drinks. It would only be a matter of time before your old customers found a nice welcoming host willing to share his alcohol with them. Maybe it was because you had grown fond of me? Nothing in your deposition seems to indicate that. A lack of tenacity, perhaps? I sincerely doubt that a woman who is willing to follow me around for almost an entire moon-cycle and who runs an inn all by herself after losing both her son and – in a certain sense – her husband would be lacking that trait.

No, not a single explanation I could come up with made much sense. Until I realized you were expecting a visit that very wake-cycle. But you never told me what the name of your guest was. Even while testifying, you did not mention whom you were talking about. This shadow, this mystery man... he was there in the inn, was he not? Waiting for you to make sweet love to him! That is why you went to the cellar. Not to check up on your supplies, but to get him a drink."

"That's absurd!" Mildrieda shouted. "Even if it were true, I would have known if this supposed lover had taken something that was mine!"

"Excellent remark, Mildrieda! Obviously, you want to clarify this strange situation as eagerly as I do... as we all do. Of course, I did take that possibility into account. It took me a while to figure it out, since the answer is built on several hypotheses I was not able to verify at first. You told us you got up early that wake-cycle to grab some ale. Which means you were sleeping before, probably with your lover in the same bed. But you also said that after you started suspecting me, you slid the bed towards the wall nearest to the stairs. Which is peculiar, since your inn is quite old. It exudes coziness and warmth and character, but the wood moans and croaks. Almost anyone would have heard me open a window and climb out of it. Except for deep sleepers, that is. When I realized this simple fact, I started to walk around at night more often, but you never came looking for me. I am sure you asked your guest not to come over for a while so I could not find you both together, but he must have been there during the night of the theft, drinking from your body. It was only two sleep-cycles after I first came in to rent a room, so you probably did not think about the possible obstacles to your romance at first. Or maybe you didn't have time to warn your lover not to come over for a while."

"That's conjecture! You've presenting no more evidence of this supposed affair than you presented of your innocence!"

"Again, you are the beacon that lights my way! You are correct. There was not enough evidence, so I wanted to elaborate on my hypothesis first. Who could this man be? A lover who cannot be trusted, of course. A lover who would let you break your vows. Men are men, though, so it would make no sense to distrust an able-bodied male companion just because he was following his instincts. But maybe there is someone who would normally care deep about the vows made to the Seraphalim Gealius. Someone who cannot be trusted; not if he lets you try to hide from Gealius's Sight in the hopes that your carelessness will not be noticed. Someone who has either traveled to Illexalluh in the past – or who recently received coinage from those lands as payment for a service or a product. Like Realdus, perhaps? Maybe he mentioned having received money from that nation just so you could ambush me with your testimony? Or mayhap we are talking about somebody else entirely..."

"He's lying!" Mildrieda shouted at the villagers, but she sounded too distraught to pose as an innocent victim. She fixed her eyes on Baour and gnawed at her underlip. "And even if I was wrong to accuse you at first, even if I have a lover, it wouldn't change the fact that you were talking to a dead person!"

Baour nodded enthusiastically. "Indeed! Indeed! This, too, is a subject we will have to examine! But you are not completely correct. You see, all of these events are connected, intertwined…"

Baour's eyes widened as he dropped to his knees, coming down hard on the marbled floor. Blood dripped out of his mouth. He clutched his stomach, but the pain was coming from everywhere, spreading out over his entire body. It would soon paralyze him, he knew.

"So the necromancer is human after all!" Reaphrastus shouted as he slipped his second throwing knife out of his sleeve. He had fashioned the wood handle and knob himself, especially for the occasion, weighing the balance of his weapons carefully over the last couple of wake-cycles. The woodcarver had walked up to the back of the temple slowly, carefully, purposefully, just to have a clear shot at Baour. His first throw had been a hit and the blade was now lodged deep into the necromancer's back, near the upper spine.

Mildrieda quickly stepped aside, but almost nobody else moved. Reaphrastus felt intoxicated with hatred. Up until the trial, he had managed to convince himself nobody knew about how he treated his children, living in a constant state of denial, and when he heard Zeitas had been attacked, he was able to point the blame at Baour. During his testimony, his own son had accused his father of being a bad parent, while at the same time treating the man Reaphrastus hated the most as a best friend… as a lover, even. This man! This mage, whom other villagers claimed to be a 'poet,' a 'powerful wizard,' 'interesting,' 'entertaining,' while Reaphrastus had been a valued member of the community for so many years, without being showered in the compliments the necromancer had garnered within only moon-cycles!

Everything was revolving around him, vague and almost shapeless, except for the mage. He fixed on his target, readying the knife, bringing it to eye level. In what seemed like the distance, he could hear Matthayas shouting, "No, Dad! No!" He would not be deterred, though. Reaphrastus had been planning this carefully. A negligent parent? Never! He and his wife had raised both of their sons like he had been raised himself: with discipline and harsh punishment. To him, only Baour could be responsible for the illness that, as it turned out, was affecting the entire village!

While Matthayas, who had been sitting next to his girlfriend, a shy-looking, embarrassed Eaerae, was making his way to his father, the woodcarver aimed for Baour's back again. This time the dagger would kill the wizard!

Just before Reaphrastus could finish his throw, a hand grabbed his arm.

Therionald looked straight into the bearded man's eyes. "Stop it!"

Almost without thinking, Reaphrastus grabbed the priest's neck. His veins pulsed with rage, the anger coursing through his body like a warm stream of lava, burning him up from the inside out. Spit escaped from his mouth as he shouted, "Never! Step out of the way, cleric! That man insulted me and no one did anything about it!"

"Let go of my acolyte." Eldried didn't shout. The elder cleric sounded composed, calm, as he slowly but decidedly walked up to the rough-hewn villager. "I am warning you, Reaphrastus. You may be one of my flock, but I will let Gealius's anger rain down upon you if you hurt my priest!"

Baour's would-be killer looked over his shoulder. "It's not him I'm after, Eldried! I just wanted a clear shot at the mage!"

Therionald grabbed his assailant's arm with both hands. It was difficult to speak, but he tried nonetheless. "This man… deserves… a fair trial… just like everyone else!"

The cleric's voice was coarse and Eldried realized his acolyte might pass out soon. "I can't let you do this, Reaphrastus. I've seen you grow up to be strong and tireless, but this anger of yours… I can't let it burn this hot. Not if it starts to endanger others."

"You want to see him executed as badly as I do!" Zeitas's father screamed.

"If he is, indeed, guilty – and I think he is – he will be brought to justice."

"This… isn't… about justice… It's not even… about poor Zeitas. This… is about you!" Therionald added.

"He's right," his elder agreed. "Halt now or I will make you feel the power of the Seraphalim!"

Reaphrastus threw Therionald aside. The priest stumbled unto one of the benches, over the laps of several women who were sitting there, then fell to the floor before they could grab him. A stinging pain went through his body, forcing him to lie still.

Just before Eldried could finish his plea to Gealius, Ignetius jumped in front of him, running up to the woodcarver. His master stopped praying, lest he hurt the boy. In the split moment after Ignetius's intervention, Eldried understood. What if his youngest acolyte wasn't trying to help Therionald and Eldried? What if he purposefully came between his master and the woodcarver, hoping that Baour would be killed while pretending to want to stop his murderer? It all happened so fast… but not fast enough.

By the time Ignetius had reached Reaphrastus and Eldried had gathered his thoughts, the second knife flew through the air, only to abruptly change course. Jerkily but swiftly, the weapon turned around, moving towards its maker, but losing momentum along the way. It fell to the ground a scant four men's lengths from the villager, gliding over the floor for three lengths more until it stopped moving just before Reaphrastus's eyes. Ignetius hesitated for a moment, and then launched himself to the floor, using his own momentum to skid up to the weapon just as Reaphrastus was reaching for it. Most of the villagers weren't looking at them, though. They were watching Matthayas, whose eyes had gone black. His hair was standing up, seemingly electrified by the colors he had manipulated awkwardly to change the course of his father's knife. At that moment, his fellow villagers weren't asking themselves if Reaphrastus would be stopped. Instead, they were wondering if the young man had been trying to commit patricide, or if he had purposefully changed the trajectory of the knife so that it couldn't reach his father.

The confusion was all Ignetius needed to grab the knife before Reaphrastus could. The woodcarver didn't waste any time, however. While the young cleric was still on the ground, he planted one booted foot on Ignetius's back, smacking him against the floor, and used the leverage to launch himself forwards. Matthayas jumped in between his father and

Baour, forcing Eldried to break off his second prayer as well. It wasn't specific enough to accommodate for the new situation, so he would have to rephrase his demand to make sure the young man wouldn't be hurt.

"Out of my way, boy!" Reaphrastus ordered.

"I've done what you wanted for long enough, dad. I'm not gonna do so anymore."

"Damn you, kid!"

The woodcarver charged his own son, hoping that his speed and weight would be enough to knock aside his child.

Eldried had almost finished his third prayer when Ignetius got up and started running after the woodcarver, blocking the old priest's line of sight. He fought the urge to sigh or curse and started adding some more lynchpins.

Before Matthayas could manipulate the colors swirling around him again, his father connected with him. The brute mass knocked Baour's apprentice to the side, swirling around his own axis and smashing his leg and then his ribs against the corner of a bench. He could hear the bones crush from the impact and let out a pained scream.

The bull rush had slowed down Reaphrastus, though, giving Ignetius time to catch up. He jumped on the woodcarver's back, wrapping his legs around the man's chest. The stout villager started to grab the acolyte's shoulder, but stopped just in time when he heard the priest whisper in his ear. "Take it! Take it!" There it was, in Ignetius's hands – his dagger!

Reaphrastus wrested the weapon out of the feigning priest's hands. It wasn't at all difficult, but of course Ignetius had to pretend he was resisting. A simple elbow to the cleric's plexus solaris was enough to let the acolyte lose his grip and fall to the ground. He might have hurt his back, but the shrewd youngster knew exactly what he was going to do and landed on the ball of one foot and on one knee, using his hand to push himself up from the floor again in the hopes that he would still block Eldried's line of sight.

The necromancer in front of the woodcarver was sitting down, bent over, clutching his belly. It would be an easy kill.

"I'm sorry, Matthayas!" Baour screamed, surprised that he was still able to say something despite the blood that was filling his throat.

"Do it!" the boy shouted.

The necromancer wasn't sure he would have enough time to finish his preparations, but then, suddenly, a great light blinded him. It was as if the sun itself was manifesting inside of the temple, its great energy filling the entire hall effortlessly. Reaphrastus tried to shield his eyes with both arms, but it was too late. The light, diffuse at first, started to converge around Gealius's statue, forming a shaft of pure energy. As it sucked in the ambient light around it, the spear catapulted towards the woodcarver, passing through his head and dissipating almost instantly. The woodcarver screamed as his eyes melted away, the warm, sticky, candle-like liquid pouring over his cheeks.

Still he wouldn't give up. As his fellow villagers were recovering from the flash, he stumbled up to Baour and raised the knife. He was completely blind now, but the necromancer was sitting close by and Reaphrastus had fixed his exact location for long enough to know he probably wouldn't miss.

With the last of his strength Baour toppled over, falling onto his back. As he had quickly calculated, the knife that had impaled him now pointed straight between two steps, so that it wasn't pushed even deeper into his body. He felt it tug at him as he slid backwards and downwards a little bit. The pain almost incapacitated him. The necromancer didn't lose consciousness, though, and he tapped into his rapidly dwindling reservoir of willpower to fling his arms backwards, unleashing the ball of entropy he had been weaving in front of his belly while pretending to clutch his stomach. It was only the size of a marble, but the sphere ripped through the air easily and faster than any object subject to the normal laws of thermodynamics could fly, punching a clean hole through Reaphrastus's chest. The woodcarver fell down, gasping for air.

"Duck!" Matthayas had screamed at Ignetius before his master had unleashed the sphere of negative energy. His eyes were still dark and he had recovered from the flash fast enough to see the colors moving in front of the necromancer, understanding what the mage was trying to do before his father's eyes were struck by Gealius's answer to Eldried's prayer. The priest hadn't reacted in time, but Matthayas had recuperated enough to tackle the boy and bring him to the ground. As the dark sphere speeded past above their heads, making a sizzling noise as it destroyed the air it traveled through before cutting out a clean hole in the front temple door.

Matthayas flung his legs around Ignetius's waist to hold him down. He started to punch the boy he had just saved, first shattering his nose, and then breaking his jaw. "Damn you! Damn you!"

"Matthayas! Stop!" Eldried screamed.

The young man stopped hitting the acolyte. His eyes were still sore, but just like everyone else he could see well enough to distinguish the priest in the crowd. The blinding effect had only lasted a few heartbeats for everyone but Reaphrastus. "He helped dad! I know he did!"

"We can't know that for sure!" Eldried tried.

"I was only trying to help," Ignetius said, holding his bloodied, fractured nose. It had moved to the right of his face, disfiguring him completely.

"The hell you were!" Matthayas yelled.

"Matthayas! Listen to Eldried!" It was Baour, speaking through gritted teeth as he tried to stay as still as possible in order to avoid the knife getting thrust deeper into him.

The young man was crying now. "My father would've been harmless without that knife! Or at least not as dangerous! Maybe he wouldn't have had to die!"

"I am not sure," Eldried said softly as he walked up to Matthayas and Ignetius. "As much as I hate to admit it, everyone could see that Baour was only defending himself. There was no other choice." He looked at the necromancer. "You could have done something that wouldn't have destroyed my front doors, though."

"I didn't have much time to think," Baour groaned.

The old priest put a hand on Matthayas's shoulder. "Your... *master* did what he had to do."

"I know, Eldried, but only because dad had a weapon! I hated him, but..."

"But he was your father. I know. Still, he would have found another way, Matthayas. The mage is wounded. It wouldn't take much to kill him now. Maybe your father would have tried to push that one knife deeper inside of Baour's body." The priest turned his attention to Ignetius. "You. We will talk about this later. For now let your nose be a reminder of what you have done."

Eldried started to walk up to Baour. The mage was still lying there, on the steps leading up to the altar, his face distorted in an effort not to scream in pain.

"I will heal your wound, necromancer, but this is still a trial and you are still the accused. You are too dangerous, too powerful. It would be nigh impossible to execute a judgment, whatever it might be." He groaned as he slowly dropped down to one knee and cupped Baour's chin in one hand. "I shall remove the knife and close the wound, but not entirely." The priest looked over his shoulder. "Reald! Bind him! Tie up the necromancer so that he cannot move his hands anymore!"

"Uh... I have no rope," the barrister said, scratching his head. "And what about Reaphrastus? We can't leave him like this."

"I will take care of my father," Matthayas interjected. There wasn't much emotion left in his voice.

"Anyone?" Eldried asked loudly without looking at the villagers. "Is there anyone who has rope for me, or something else to help restrain the necromancer without my needing to leave the temple?"

No one answered.

"I'm sorry I have to do this," Eldried apologized to Baour.

"They have belts," the necromancer suggested. It was difficult to make coherent sentences, but he had to try. "And other things. You needn't..."

"You know full well they won't give up their own property."

"Then why ask?"

The elder priest bent down until his mouth was next to Baour's ears. "Because I had to. After they see this..."

"Don't do it, priest."

"You are guilty," Eldried whispered. "You said so yourself. Reaphrastus shouldn't have interfered, but unless you can convince us of your innocence I will see you burn."

"I did nothing wrong."

The cleric nodded resignedly, knowingly. "I know. That is the tragedy of it. In your own twisted mindset, according to your own worldview, you probably tried to do the right thing. Or do you think I haven't listened? You came here because of the illness, didn't you? You never brought it with you at all. Of that crime you aren't guilty."

"Then let... let me continue, Eldried."

"Rest assured, Baour. This trial will proceed. But not before I have neutralized the threat that you are."

"No!" Baour screamed. Matthayas, who had been walking to the front door, his father's body on his back, stopped and turned. Ignetius slowly got up. Between two benches, Therionald asked the people around him to lift him up so he could sit. Everywhere, eyes fixed on what was transpiring on the steps.

Baour tried to move his hands while Eldried was praying, but he was too weak. He had to watch how the Strands connected to his fingers started to move as Gealius tugged at them from his place near the Spider. Orange and white threads started to swirl around each other and he cried in agony as his fingers began to warp. All he could hear was the sickening sounds of bone fracturing, shattering, and contorting. For a moment, he was oblivious to the pain caused by the knife in his back, the nerves inside of his hands protesting against the horrendous torture they were being subjected to as the digits on both of his hands wrapped around each other in surrealistic angles.

In the crowd, Maerae fainted, as did several other villagers. Matthayas started to cry and a single tear appeared in Zeitas's bleak eyes. It was the first time he had shown any kind of real emotion since he had been brought to the temple.

"Master!" Matthayas shouted.

"Do not interfere!" Baour screamed as he tried to remain conscious. Slowly, the pain in his fingers started to subside somewhat and he became more aware of the weapon sticking into him again.

"It is done, necromancer," Eldried said. Even though the man had made him lose the use of his hands, Baour appreciated the fact that the priest didn't seem to be happy or relieved about it in any way.

"I am still bleeding."

"I will ask Gealius to heal you."

"It will test your faith."

Eldried pulled away his face, surprised. "What do you mean?" he asked, careful to maintain a low volume.

"You will only ask the Seraphalim to heal me because you hope he will not answer. But he will."

Eldried shook his head, and then realized he was doing so too obviously and stopped. "That's not..."

"Yes, it is. I am losing blood, priest. If you are going to do this, do it now!"

"Can you turn to your side?"

"I would eagerly do so if I still had hands to lean on! Or if their current predicament did not prohibit the flexing of my arms."

"Ignetius! Help me!"

Ignetius got up and waggled up to his superior.

"Help me turn the necromancer to his side."

"I'm not sure if I have the strength. I'm still in pain myself."

"He is hurting a lot more than you are. Now do as I say!"

"Do we turn him to his left or his right?"

"For the Spider's sake! I'm bleeding!"

"We turn him to the right."

"His right or our right?"

"Make up your minds!"

"His right."

Therionald took hold of Baour's right shoulder and pulled the necromancer towards him while Eldried was pushing. The mage screamed as the elder priest pulled out the knife in a single, swift motion.

Eldried started to pray again. Baour understood the words: *Gealii tervor, Gealii sintinor, Baouru singir dayudarda, tii reclimo.* Great Gealius, compassionate Gealius, I ask you to help this bleeding Baour. Almost immediately, Strands all around the necromancer were pulled together while the Seraphalim started to close the wound. Even while new skin was being grafted unto Baour's body, he winked at Therionald while he turned to his back and kicked his legs outward, thereby gaining the momentum necessary to stand up. Eldried followed suit, giving Baour the opportunity to whisper into the priest's ear, "If Gealius finds me guilty, how do you explain the fact that he has just healed me?"

Eldried shook his head insecurely. "He must want you to have this trial."

"Yes, but not out of fairness. You will have to face your own fate this cycle, priest."

Before Eldried could answer, the necromancer turned his attention towards the hall. A few men were helping Matthayas lay down his father's body by the temple door, ready to be taken away after the trial. He fixed his eyes on Roaldus. "It seems like I will need new clothes, tailor," he said, wryly. Then, to Therionald, "Pull these down. They're wet from my blood." The priest obliged and pulled down Baour's upper clothing from his shoulders, exposing his bare chest.

Again, the villagers began to murmur as they laid eyes on the necromancer's half-naked body.

There were scars everywhere. Ugly scars, left after being punctured, slashed, stitched, and bludgeoned, but even though the traces of old wounds would have caused a reaction from the Barnsby citizens anyway, it was something else that provoked the mutter.

The wounds seemed random and dispersed, but there was a semblance of a pattern as well. Not one in the traditional sense of the word, though. No human eyes could feasibly detect any logical link between the groupings of scar tissue, but on an almost subconscious level, every single soul present could sense that something was off. Something altogether unnatural, unexplainable. Something wondrous… or maybe dreadful. As if that wasn't enough, Baour also bore a strange birthmark: a claw, grabbing his right nipple, extending into something that looked like a dragon, covering most of his right flank, and even though it was just as black as the night, it didn't look unhealthy or dangerous at all. In fact, neither did the scars.

For a moment, Baour thought of Quarmel, the young mage who had always been dressed in green and whom he had helped in his misguided quest to recover the Gauntlet of Gasyldur, several year-cycles after the boy had put himself in a stasis field while the barbarians of D'Ryld were assaulting his college, slaughtering every single wizard present. Baour had gained many scars during his travels with Quarmel and the others, and he had come to love every single one of them, memorabilia to adventures past.

The mage was all-too aware of his imposing, charismatic presence. His slender but muscular chest, the fact that his upper clothes couldn't be drawn over his hands and were hanging loose over his back, his scars and birthmark: they all added to his aura of power. He would need it, because everyone had just seen that he was vulnerable, too. It suited him well. Reaphrastus had almost killed him, making him seem more human to the villagers, and Eldried had shown them that Gealius still cared for the necromancer, and that the priest was capable of doing horrendous things as well. Now if they only also understood that Ignetius had tried to help the woodcarver… Baour tried to abandon his current line of reasoning. He had to be careful, because a lot of the people in front of him would have rather seen Reaphrastus succeed.

"Mildrieda?" It sounded more like a command to come forth than like a question.

The innkeeper had been standing against the wall. She stepped back to the front, looking more uncomfortable than before.

"I will not take away more of your time than needed. As I said, I shall explain all soon, but I will need to know the name of your secret lover."

"I don't have a secret lover!" Mildrieda insisted.

"I am sure that, if we question enough people, we will be able to find out who he is, but time is not a commodity we have in abundance right now. Everyone is getting tired and hungry, the disease is spreading and I have already been attacked. It would do you honor to give us a name."

Mildrieda didn't answer.

"If it is your vow you are worrying about, I am sure Eldried will be able to tell you that Gealius does not care whether people know your missteps or not. He judges your actions. You have nothing to lose and the truth will come out anyway."

Mildrieda looked down at the floor. Baour was getting to her.

"Think about your son, innkeeper. He never fought his execution because he knew he had done what he was charged of. However insignificant his actions might have been, he was ready to die instead of lie or connive his way out of the situation."

"Don't talk to me about my son, necromancer!" Mildrieda said. "Especially not if you're trying to weasel your way out of a conviction."

"I have already admitted to my guilt, Mildrieda. Now the time has come for you to do the same."

"I vowed before Gealius!"

"Yes. That is why you do not trust your lover. A vow… it is sacred to him, is it not? To make a woman break a promise made before the Seraphalim… it would be a heinous deed." He turned around. "I know of only three people who are prime suspects, but Eldried rarely leaves his temple these days and people would probably have seen him walking through the streets. More importantly, Gealius still bestows his blessings on the old man. Surely the Seraphalim would not answer his prayers if he were consorting with a woman who had sworn a vow such as yours? Looking back on what has transpired during this past cycle, however, it is clear we cannot eliminate the two other suspects." Baour pulled his facial muscles into a sad expression, but even though he had just almost died and Eldried had taken away his ability to weave magic, he was smiling inwardly. "How is it, young Ignetius, that you would question the Sight? 'How are we to know this is for real,' you asked the good people present here when Matthayas manifested his gift. Yet anyone who has ever seen the Strands knows the Sight cannot be faked, even through magic. It is too pure, too primordial. That one question showed me that Gealius has not yet granted you the ability to see the Web."

"That's not true!" He was being tended to by Therionald, but his face was still disfigured and he sounded more nasal than before.

Eldried raised his hand in front of the boy. "Hush, Ignetius!" The cleric found Baour, shaking his head in sorrow. "It is true, necromancer. The youth has not been given the Sight yet. But you may be wrong about the reason. He is still learning. He might still..."

"That is entirely possible," Baour interjected. "Even though I highly doubt he will ever gain the favor of the Seraphalim. But there is another one. I call Therionald to testify!"

Chapter Ten
THE PRIEST THERIONALD DENOUNCES

"I can't speak for Ignetius or Eldried, but I, for one, still remember how Gealius called me the first time. I was still a kid and I was living in the great city of Dor'O'Led, in the Empire of Normar. I know none of you have ever crossed the Strait of Raanesh, so let me tell you about how wondrous a place the Emperor's capital is, so that you may understand me better. I know I've never talked about it much, but it's better to remain humble and refrain from boasting about your travels in an inn, like this necromancer here has done so many times during the past moon-cycles.

"Dor'O'Led is a harbor city, the biggest one on the Normarian coast, and the only one where great galleons are able to dock safely. Now, most harbors don't only reek of the sea and wet wood, but also of sweaty, unkempt sailors and rotting fish. Dor'O'Led is different, though. There is no decay in the air, no uncleanliness and no disease, but only pure air, salty and fresh, ripe fruits, and blossoming flowers. Scholars claim that the underwater plants near the shoreline filter the bad smells out of the sky, but the mages' college has always maintained that the city is constantly being purified through great spells woven over its streets and buildings ages ago.

"As I've told you before, Mildrieda, you probably wouldn't like Dor'O'Led, because more than any other city in the known world, it is shaped by magic. Nowhere else has the Spider allowed its Web to be changed so much, and nowhere else have people been so eager to see it spin its Strands. It's even rumored that the wizards there have found a way to trick the Spider into making more threads connected to Dor'O'Led than to this entire continent. Whether those tales or true or not, the harbor city is constantly evolving. One year-cycle, great minarets will be erected, sleek, white towers climbing up to the skies, while another year-cycle, the towers will be leveled and palatial buildings will take their place. Dor'O'Led is a city of inventions, but the apparatuses cranked out of the mages' college have nothing to do with the technology found elsewhere. It's one of the reasons why the emperor can stay in the capital without fear of ever being conquered. Many foreign engineers have studied the strange siege engines and weapons made in the city, yet no one has been able to understand how they work. Powerful wards protect the walls from harm, and the Empire of Normar might be viewed as the biggest threat known to the races of this world if not for the fact that people gifted with the Sight from all nations flock to the city. They are allowed to run for a seat on the Ruling Council after having stayed in the city for one full year-cycle. Most of them keep strong ties to their homes and, with so many foreign wizards acting as councilors, rulers from other empires, kingdoms, and theocracies are convinced that Normar will never try to invade another country. They may be right; no emperor has moved against one of his neighbors since Elyonrad the Cursed tried to subjugate the people from Ymred after being possessed by a demon.

"Walking through the beautifully paved streets of Dor'O'Led, signs of magic are everywhere. The street lighting switches on when the sun has gone to sleep and both moons shine down on the city without needing to be lit. Permanent manipulation of the Web makes sure one can hover up to the upper floor of a building – there are no stairs in the city at all – and the architecture is designed to be accessible from all three dimensions, while many buildings seem to defy the laws of nature.

"With twenty-five members in the ruling council, most of them wizards, a majority vote is only called on for the most important of decisions. The councilors only answer to the Emperor and they have a lot of liberty in pursuing their own projects. It's even reflected in the layout of the city. A street might lead to the imperial palace – but end in an artificial well the next wake-cycle. Chaos abounds. The architecture is always beautiful but extremely eclectic, and brightly colored inns might stand next to black towers. That's why artists often don't paint the entire city, but rather one or two buildings. Some visitors say the hodgepodge of different ideas and constructions hurts their eyes, but even *they* have to admit they've never seen edifices, colleges, monuments, temples, cathedrals, inns, shops, or manors as beautiful as the ones found within the confines of the city walls.

"Naturally, guides make good money in Dor'O'Led. They are some of the most well respected people in the city and the only ones – except for architects and mages – to be organized into a guild. They usually have the Sight as well. It would be difficult to navigate the place without seeing the Strands. All guild members wear the same costume: an expensive affair of yellow, black, and red. The official guides are pretty tough on non-members, not because they're scared of the competition, but because a lot of incompetent fools try to con visitors out of their money by claiming they can show them around. It needn't be said that those not familiar with the city invariably get lost… sometimes forever.

"In fact, there's an entire underclass of people who have wondered into the seedy parts of town, only to mingle with others who have lost their way as well. By the time they get out they're destitute, leaving them no other option than to turn back and spend the rest of their days in the underbelly of Dor'O'Led. It would probably be easy to help out the poor, but in truth the existence of a small group of beggars and criminals suits some of the council members just fine. Not that they have evil intent in mind, but it's easy to find relatively cheap work there, and poor men and women who are given jobs with reasonable pay often are so grateful that their loyalty is unwavering. Of course, the council does make sure all of the buildings are well taken care off, even if they are standing in districts mainly inhabited by beggars and thieves… which makes it even tougher for visitors to realize when they've ventured into a dangerous area. Many of them never get to see the more affluent citizens of Dor'O'Led anyway, since the rich rarely walk around on the ground level anymore. They can usually be found flying through the air or strolling through the raised walkways that connect different parts of the city.

"There are more than just humans in Dor'O'Led, of course. Most of the intelligent races have at least some presence in Dor'O'Led. The Sundarun carefully keep an eye on the mages' guild, in fear of the day that the magic taught at College Findalbur will someday put even their knowledge of the Web to shame, and the stout, stocky Gerlau send every engineer to the capital once, on a holy quest to understand the inner workings of the devices made there. It is said that the first Gerlau who figures out how the artifacts work will be elevated to sainthood, but I don't know of anyone who knows for sure.

"But the wondrous magic... it's not the main reason why Dor'O'Led attracts so many travelers. Most of them come to the city to find distraction. Every kind of entertainment can be found in the harbor and beyond, whether it be festivals featuring the best minstrels of Normar, energetic performances by the talking birds of Byrmur, who sometimes surprise their audience by eating one of the attendees alive, great halls filled with mysterious and addictive fae smoke, or magic arenas, where mages of different persuasions try to prove the superiority of their weaving methods by surprising, intimidating, wounding, or even killing each other. Yes, there's much decadence in that city, and that's where the priesthood comes in.

"You see, a lot of people think the citizens of Dor'O'Led engage in questionable activities because of their own depravity, but that's not necessarily true. The real reason is that most of them are afraid. Very afraid. They live in one of the most awe-inspiring cities imaginable, but many seers, academics, philosophers, and clerics believe the Spider does not take kindly to mortal beings who manipulate its Web in such overtly grandiose and all-encompassing manner, so the citizens of Dor'O'Led try to gamble, kiss, play, drink, eat, smoke, fight, and scheme their worries away. Sometimes, the city is only a bright veil covering dark happenings, but mostly the people there live every day like it might be their last, with a zest for life and a love for everything around them that is the envy of many other nations.

"Now, there's one other thing keeping the citizens of Dor'O'Led sane. The fear for retribution by the Spider has made them the most devout and faithful followers of the Seraphalim possible. There are shrines to all of the Seraphalim all over the city, even to ones almost no one has ever heard from before. Dor'O'Led is ripe with cults, but all of those exist in the margin. Only the official priesthood holds any true power, and even cultists eventually turn to true clerics when times are dire.

"Since magic is commonplace and since priests, mages, and guides make up about half of its population, Dor'O'Led was a fantastic place to grow up in as a kid. Both of my parents were merchants who never had the Sight, so I was even more in awe of the place than I would have been if I had been born into a magically inclined family. As much as my father and mother tried to convince me otherwise, I didn't want to become a merchant myself. I felt that my destiny lay elsewhere, but I had no idea what it was.

Not until the day my mother got stabbed.

"I was ten and the market was in full swing that day. As usual, my parents had asked me to help out at the booth. I had to polish the glassware and the trinkets made of precious metals to make sure everything looked pleasing to the eye while my father was off to the other end of the marketplace to get us something to eat. Didn't see the glare in that one customer's eyes. I still perfectly remember what he looked like, though: a gruff, muscular man who reeked of fish, with a long, yellow beard. He wore his sleeveless shirt casually, loosely, so that the many tattoos on his arms were clearly visible, intricate patterns of circles, lines, and squares. The customer wanted to buy a beautiful upside-down bottle made of colored glass my mom had made, but he only wanted to pay two claws for it. That's one-fifth of a paw, which is roughly equivalent to a standard gold piece. My mother didn't want to part with it for such a low price, though. It was worth one paw, maybe even more. She always could detect a tough customer when she saw one and I'm sure she knew she wouldn't be able to haggle up, so she just started to concentrate on other people standing in front of the booth. It only succeeded in making the man angry, though.

"I saw the glint of steel only moments before he lunged forward over the table and plunged the knife in my mother's throat. Still remember how I screamed, but… but I didn't dare to come closer. Blood was gushing from her neck, spraying the bottles, the glasses, the intricate crystal carvings and jade miniatures, the customers… and covering me. I can't describe the feeling of tasting your mother's blood in your mouth while getting drenched in her bodily fluids. It was horrible.

"The man escaped, of course. There simply were too many people present. If only a few men had been standing nearby, they would probably have tried to stop my mother's attacker, either through brute force or through magic, but having a lot of people around often isn't a blessing. They will look at the assault, convinced that someone else will intervene. After all, there're so many innocent bystanders… certainly someone will step in? Why risk your own life if the situation can be resolved by another? Unfortunately, if everything thinks like that, nothing gets done. By trying to maximize their own profit, people often minimize the group's profit, and that's exactly what happened. To this day I wonder if I could have saved her if I had reacted in time. Maybe I could've contained the bleeding somewhat… I don't know.

"In any case, by the time dad got back, he had to fight himself a way through the crowd. Now that the man who had tried to kill my mother was gone, two women stepped in, trying to save mom with their healing skills, but they only managed to stabilize her somewhat. With my dad leading the way through the market square, we carried mom to the nearest temple. I was hardly aware of what was happening around me. All of my senses had gone numb and I didn't even notice the blood sticking to my clothes anymore. Everything seemed to happen too fast to take in. I can only remember my mother gurgling, trying to tell us something, but she was unable to make herself understood. It is a horrible thing to see one of your own parents and not only realize that she will probably die, but at the same time see the frustration on her face as she understands she won't be able to give that last piece of advice, shake off the terrible secret that has been burdening her for so many year-cycles, or at least say her final goodbyes.

"Our hurried trip to the temple has become a collage of random fragments in my mind. People either running up to us and slowing our advance or moving aside to let us through, screams, taking the wrong turn a few times, panic, finding the hovering platform to the temple proper, going up… It was all very chaotic, very disjointed.

"My mother was still alive when we finally reached the temple porch. It loomed high above the lower levels of the city, a huge, five-tiered construction abruptly diminishing in size and topped with ninety-six statues, with a magnificent entrance piercing the eastern wall. Five priests were already waiting for us there, as if they knew we were coming. Four of them quickly wrapped my mother in a thin sheet made of a white fabric I hadn't seen before while the fifth one tried to calm us down and started to ask my dad some questions. What had happened? Was there a particular Seraphalim he wanted the cleric to pray to? Had he or my mother done anything that might have angered the Seraphalim in the past? Did they regularly donate coin to the temple? The list of questions seemed to go on and on. Maybe the man just wanted to distract us, or maybe they were too used to getting in people the Seraphalim won't help, but I'm sure his fellow adepts were trying to help my mother without waiting for the answers. Or, at least, I think they were. I *wanted* to look at the priest who was talking to us, just because I was afraid of what I would see if I looked at my mom instead, so I didn't avert my eyes even once.

"It was as if time was passing by slowly, now… until I could hear one of the clerics attending to my mom that say she couldn't be saved. 'Dormand won't help her,' he said. 'And neither will Syglund, Torlun, Ainea, Lemia, or Lyibertis.'

"'I have tried, too,' the second cleric said, 'but Immyl, Sachrid, and Gealius aren't answering.'

"One by one, the priests started to name the Seraphalim who wouldn't help my dying mother. By the time the fourth one had finished, my father had dropped to his knees, weeping. He begged them to try again, but they wouldn't. Dad offered them crystal and gemstones, then coin and trinkets, but they just shook their heads and even while my father was trying to convince them, I could hear mom gasp for air one final time. It was a loud gurgle, summarizing all of her dying fears in a single sound, heavy and deep, wrought with helplessness and sadness. I will never forget that sound again. I still hear it during each sleep-cycle, far away and yet so close…

"My… my father was struck with grief. He screamed and lashed at the priests without thinking, his arms flailing wildly. There was insanity in his eyes, and hatred. Just as he charged one of the clerics, the man stepped aside. My father stumbled and fell off the porch, hitting his head in the process. It's the only relief I have. I know he was unconscious during his fall, at least fifty-five stories down.

"I was alone now. Both of my parents had died within moments of each other. These days I find comfort in the knowledge that they would probably have wanted to leave life together. The priests took me in, caring for me as if I was their own. During the first three moon-cycles there, I was impossible to handle, prone to bouts of rage, defiant, angry at the world.

But after I found a place inside of me to store my grief, I began to realize that, in a certain sense, I was living my dream. I was to be educated as a priest! When I finally came to terms with what had happened to my parents, I could only feel gratitude. My father hadn't thought about me when he attacked the clerics, but the priests had been good to me. They had tried everything they could, prayed to every Seraphalim they knew could manipulate the Strands necessary to close my mother's wounds in a fevered attempt to save her life, treated me as if I were their long-lost son. I was in debt to them, as I was in debt to the Seraphalim who allowed me to become their faithful servant.

"Even though the priests treated me like a family member, I never felt completely at home, up there in the Dor'O'Led temple. I was too young to inherit my parents' house, which was now owned by the city council, but according to Normarian law, I was still allowed to use it as I wished, and after I turned fourteen and became an adult, I left the temple to live where I had spent most of my childhood. But it didn't feel the same. Memories of the past were still haunting me and I associated every stone, every wood panel, and every corner with things that had happened back when my parents were alive. I had taken up the study of linguistics while staying in the temple and the decision to continue to learn languages and then leave Dor'O'Led, spreading the word of the Seraphalim as a traveling priest, was an easy one. Living with all of those memories made me a stronger man, too, and by the time I left the capital at age nineteen, I was a very different person.

"I didn't only visit many cities, but hamlets, villages, and small towns as well. I met nomads and strange races, learned how to speak even more languages, and taught people about the Seraphalim. It was a rewarding experience to share my knowledge, but after traveling around for several year-cycles, the constant journeying started to wear me down. I needed some time to rest, but most of the places I got to know were in need of guidance. Sometimes there simply weren't enough priests in the temples to address everyone's needs, while some places didn't even have temples and others were teeming with violence and lawlessness. I always stayed long enough to make a difference, then grabbed my bags and moved on.

"One fateful wake-cycle, I reached Barnsby. I was heading up to Cadelberas and I wanted to stop here to get some sleep and supplies. Eldried showed me around and made me feel at home right away. It quite possibly was the first time I had felt that way since I was ten. So I decided to stay, at least for a while. You have a great village full of interesting people, one that would be the envy of many if Barnsby were better known. I was glad to be here and I truly appreciate that you accepted me as one of your own so quickly.

"And then people started to get sick.

"It all started about two and a half moon-cycles ago, one moon-cycle after I came to Barnsby. Roaldus was still in Greensdale at that time. At first, we didn't think much of it. The symptoms didn't look like anything we normally worry about – headaches, a slightly lethargic feeling, sleepiness... nothing too unusual.

"Before the situation started to get worse, Merielda came to the temple. She told us that at least three people were suffering from an illness she couldn't quite figure out. The healer had already tried several methods to cure them, but nothing had worked. You all know their names: Faerae, Andil, and Restil. There didn't seem to be any connection between those three, but Merielda was sure they were definitely suffering from the same affliction. Now, priests have many tasks to take care of every wake-cycle, but when Merielda comes to us with such disturbing news, we make time to examine the sick. The pious Eldried usually takes cares of those who seem like they might be in danger of losing their lives, so it was up to Ignetius and me to find out what was going on.

"We asked all of the necessary questions, checked every body part completely, but there was nothing to find. As far as we could determine, Restil, Andil, and Faerae were just suffering from a rare kind of cold. Also, Restil's spouse had already visited that unholy witch, who had given her potions that seemed to take the edge off the symptoms.

"So we sent them back to their homes.

"Only sixteen or seventeen sleep-cycles later, we heard that a stranger had come to town. He was staying at the witch's place and those who had seen him told us he was a man who was gifted with an imposing presence. It didn't take long to find out his name was Baour. A strange name, for sure; one never used in these lands. I've come from afar, but even in the great city of Dor'O'Led, I've never heard of a single Baour. Naturally, we wanted to meet this foreigner, but we didn't feel any sense of urgency.

"Not until Rimled – Faerae's father – came to us. He was very anxious. Scared, even. His daughter had developed brown spots on her arms and breasts, and she felt more fatigued than before.

"The disease had worsened on the wake-cycle Baour had first been spotted strolling through the woods by Reginae.

"Eldried was busy cleaning the temple hall, so Ignetius and I convened and talked about recent events. We decided that Baour's arrival coinciding with the sudden worsening of the illness might be too much of a coincidence. We started talking to some of you. As Mildrieda testified, Baour had quickly become the number one item of interest in our village, and we made sure to stop by the Black Stallion every cycle, just to catch up on what people had been saying. Call it gossip, if you will, but even the foundations of gossip often rest on a bed of truth. At that point, there wasn't a lot of real information to be gleaned, though. Only a few people had already seen Baour and no one had already talked to him, so we only heard tall tales, far-fetched hypotheses, and pure conjecture.

"Back in the temple, we told Eldried about Baour, but our elder was still busy. Even though he listened to us, he had so many things left to do that he asked us to take care of the current situation ourselves. It was a normal thing to ask, so we complied.

"The next wake-cycle, Faerae died, and Andil and Restil were now showing black blotches all over their bodies. We asked all family members to handle them with care and not touch their bodies too much, but we didn't feel the need to institute a quarantine.

"In some nations people are still ignorant of the fact that diseases can be carried by touching someone who's been inflicted, or by inhaling tainted air, but those lands are few and far between. Ever since the first magician unraveled the structure of the Web, we have known how illness passes from one person to another. Only in places where the Sight is extremely uncommon do healers remain ignorant of this fact. The thing is, Faerae was a young girl, who never had anything to do with Andil or Restil, both of whom lived far away from each other. As most of you know, Andil had a farm on the outskirts of Barnsby and rarely ventured out into the village proper, while Restil was part of the Black Stallion furniture just as much as the tables and the stools are. No one in his or her vicinity had become sick either, so we didn't think the disease was being spread in any normal way.

"I admit... asking you all to refrain from touching the sick was more a way to make you feel like we knew what was happening, like we could feasibly control the disease, than it was a precaution based on empirical evidence. We weren't going to take any chances, either, and even though we thought closing off entire buildings would be a bit too far, we figured that banning physical contact would be far easier to implement.

"Soon after the news of Faerae's death had reached the temple, Eldried called Ignetius and me to his chambers. He was angry, and rightly so. We hadn't told him that we had been unable to determine what kind of disease our three patients were afflicted with, and we hadn't yet informed him of what was happening to Andil and Restil. We were wrong not to do so, and I would like to offer all of you our most sincere apologies. Within the walls of his small room, Eldried shouted at us, accusing us of being incompetent, ignorant, and foolish. We bowed and accepted his criticisms like the clerics of true faith we are.

"Unfortunately, Eldried soon discovered that informing him sooner wouldn't have made a difference. Before bringing Faerae's body to the Layn Hills, he examined her, using the full extent of the Sight and the powers granted to him by great Gealius. After doing so, he didn't waste any time and visited the homes of Andil and Restil on that very sleep-cycle, even though we had all just traveled to the burial mounds and back. You haven't been the same since, wise Eldried. Just like Ignetius and me before, our spiritual father was forced to come to the same conclusion as we. There was no way to cure our patients.

"Back in the temple, my younger colleague and I were already firmly asleep when Eldried came barging in. He was upset and worried and he commanded us to get up and walk along the temple walls ten times... on our knees, with our hands behind our heads. It was a just punishment, but after our atonement, Eldried didn't raise his voice at us again until this trial.

"After we woke up, we heard that both Andil and Restil had died as well. It was a sad cycle, but most of us never thought that other people would die soon, as well. So when the market opened one sleep-cycle later, those who had not been friends to the deceased, and those who were not part of their families, weren't burdened by the unfortunate events that had just transpired anymore. You just got up, ate, drank, and started to work, just you normally would have. And who can blame you?

"Of course, we did stay vigilant. We figured that Baour might accompany the old woman to the market and as soon as we found out he had done so, we rushed to the witch's booth. The mage was already gone, but my fellow acolyte and I questioned the hag as thoroughly as possible.

She wasn't able to tell us much, though, only that Baour was staying at her cottage, that he hailed from faraway lands, and that he was an extremely gifted person. It was quite obvious that the witch was in awe of the man.

"As if the string of deaths wasn't enough, ghostweed started to disappear everywhere. I was the first of us priests to notice something was amiss. Just like Eldried, I like to wander around in the forest sometimes. Back in Dor'O'Led, we didn't have big woods. The city is built on a shoreline and surrounded mostly by rolling hills covered with tall, dry grass and bushes, but wood usually needs to be imported from elsewhere. During my travels, I've seen many forests, but most aren't as beautiful as this one is. I know you all don't like to travel far, but if one follows the Lorenlon for a while, one can see – and even *feel* – how the trees gradually get bigger, the bushes livelier, the animal life more plentiful, and the colors more vibrant. It's because of the Sundarun influence, of course. I've never dared to tread foot on their lands, but they are reputed to be primordial, with trees that pierce the clouds and flowers capable of producing the most fantastic scents up to several moon-cycles after being plucked.

"While walking through the forest, it was obvious to me that something was amiss. It took a closer look before I realized what exactly. Ghostweed isn't exactly plentiful, but it grows in plain sight, under the deddallis, so it's easy to see when it's been harvested. I'm not an herbalist, but during the priest seminar I had learned about ghostweed, as its uses can be important to those serving the Seraphalim. It's one of the few plants I easily recognize, and its disappearance concerned me a great deal.

"When I told Eldried about it, he didn't seem at all concerned, though, so I decided to not pursue the subject any further. After all, maybe some kids who really liked the shape of the plant were collecting it, or maybe someone who doesn't know much about herbs had made a soup out of it. I did ask around in the inn, and I did talk to some of you after service, but no one seemed to know anything, and I wasn't about to visit the witch just to ask for her insights.

"Soon, other things took my mind off the missing ghostweed: Lorelei and Vigilius were taken ill and, eventually, the colors in the forest dulled, Mildrieda was robbed, and Zeitas was attacked by a gorogon. It was all a bit much. More of you flocked to this temple than ever before, but we just couldn't do much to help you. We were just as mystified as any of you when the colors of the forest lost their vibrancy, we were unable to halt the progress of the disease that was killing both young Lorelei and stout Vigilius. We didn't know Reaphrastus would let Zeitas play unattended in an area known to be frequented by child-eating monsters.

"As attendance grew, so did your protests. We all understand why you are so angry, we know that you wanted answers soon and we think it's normal that you want us to take up our responsibility. But all of these strange occurrences... we haven't been able to find an explanation, either. Not yet. There hasn't even been time to search for the truth behind one mystery, as another one presented itself so soon. It's been hectic and I understand that you're all scared, but I'm sure Gealius will eventually show us the way.

"We are concerned, though. Concerned about the unexplainable things that have been happening and concerned about your piety. 'Why would Gealius let anybody do this to us,' you ask. 'Has he abandoned us?' you want to know. 'Please heal my child before she dies,' you beg. 'Kill the necromancer!' you demand. You want us to bring back the colors to the forest faster than they're starting to reappear, you fear that our impuissance might mean that Gealius has left us, and you vent your anger at us because you're powerless. Yet you all realize that we are this village's last, best hope.

"And now, during this trial, you have seen Gealius's power! He has shed his light on us and he has struck a man who would have violated Divine Law blind! For make no mistake – killing someone in a temple without having been ordered to do so by higher powers is not a crime that is subject to the King's Law, but to the laws governing even the Seraphalim themselves! So you know Gealius is still watching over us, and if he cannot help, it must mean that he does not deem us worthy! Such is the way of the Seraphalim.

"I implore you, please stay calm! It is my belief that Gealius is showing us the way on this cycle. He has made the man next to me stumble. Do not forget there's a reason why Baour is standing here! Maybe we can't prove he has anything to do with the illness. Maybe we can't know if he is the one who took the ghostweed, but you all heard Mildrieda's testimony! Baour was overheard talking to the dead! A most heinous crime indeed, *and* one punishable under Divine Law. A crime, no less, he admits to having committed! If you find him guilty and the disease that we supposedly carry with us disappears, we will know for sure if the necromancer was responsible for that terrible ailment, as well. Even if he claims otherwise!

"It should not matter to any of you that us executing the necromancer might also diminish our chances of being cured. If he knows how to remove the disease, he might take that knowledge to the grave and then we will all die for sure, but how small a price that is to pay if it means we have enforced the laws set by the Seraphalim and given to us through priests of generations past! Priests who have long since died, but who have left written records of their conversations with the beings of the Web!

"Let us not forget that Baour is not being charged with any crime except conferring with the dead! Yes, we may suspect him of being guilty of so much more, and we have heard testimony covering many things, but in truth this trial could have been much shorter if we witnesses hadn't digressed so much. The witch used it as a forum to voice her frustrations and as a means to be punished for the vile deeds that were gnawing at the last vestiges of whatever conscience she might have had. Roaldus, you told us about your own suspicions and about strange goings-on in Greensdale that might be connected to Baour, but don't you think the memory of what happened in the city is so much of a burden that you tried to ease your mind by talking about it in great detail? Matthayas, your testimony was one of youthful brashness. As you get older, you will realize that Barnsby is a great place to live. Your father is still laying there, a cold reminder of what ignorance and hatred can do to a man, but also a sad example of what can happen if a son uses a trial to come to terms with his own unhappy childhood instead of first ripening to the age of wisdom. And you, Mildrieda, you were tying to tell us you aren't to blame for letting Baour stay in town.

Maybe you want to be a heroine. Maybe you are. But at least you've given the most pertinent testimony so far. The testimony on which I will elaborate now – but not before admitting that I, too, am to blame. This was the first time I told you about Dor'O'Led and about how I became a priest in this much detail. I hope it'll make it easier for you to understand who I am and where I'm coming from... and why I sincerely believe that Gealius's will is far more important than what might happen to us. Our lives be damned and forfeit should we ignore Divine Law, however unimportant the accusation might seem in face of recent revelations.

"When Mildrieda came knocking at the temple doors, the sun hadn't yet appeared on the horizon. Ignetius and Eldried were still sleeping, but they later told me that they were easily roused by the noise she was making, beating her hands, feet, and even shoulders against the entrance as if she had gone insane. I know because I was taking an evening stroll around the temple, like I also do many an early morning, to meditate on the coming cycle. I sprinted to the front porch, rounding the corner just as Ignetius opened the door, with Eldried close behind him. Indeed, it looked like the innkeeper had lost her mind. Her eyes were wide open, but unfocused, wildly flicking left, right, up, and down. She spit as she spoke and she made big hand gestures. Her language was garbled and chaotic. It was almost impossible to make sense of what she was saying, so we sat her down on one of the benches here until she had relaxed enough before asking to tell us what had happened.

"As soon as Mildrieda was finished, Eldried, Ignetius, and I left. We let Mildrieda stay in the temple, running outside without needing to exchange a single word. It was only while we were running through the streets that we decided on going to Vigilius's house instead of to the inn. After all, Baour might still have been there. As it turned out, he wasn't. The door was still locked as well and for a moment we doubted Mildrieda's words. Eldried switched to the Sight and immediately noticed someone had manipulated some Strands in order to pry open the door. Apparently, Baour had corroded the lock mechanism just enough for someone with some lock-picking skills to open it easily, and without leaving visible traces. Inside, we only found Vigilius's body, covered in festering black spots. As I said, the necromancer was nowhere to be seen, but it we knew it would be easy to confirm his presence. Either we would be able to still see at least some of the Strands connected to his spirit lingering about, or the necromancer would have used ghostweed, rendering us unable to reconstruct what had happened on a mystical level.

"We didn't see it at first, but then I pulled away the sheets that had covered poor Vigilius and there it was: ghostweed! Obviously, the necromancer didn't have enough time to apply it subtly, but he did sprinkle a liberal amount of the plant over the body. He had enchanted it, too, because there were no spirit Strands still visible.

"Strangely, Baour hadn't covered his tracks. With his command of entropy, it wouldn't have surprised me if he had put in the effort to undo his lingering presence, but Eldried could detect certain... anomalies in the web that quickly led us to the Black Stallion. The door was unlocked, so we just opened it and climbed the stairs to Baour's room. We were all very much agitated and prepared for anything. Clearly, Baour was a skilled magician, and we weren't going to lose any of our number. Too many citizens had died already. There was light burning inside of Baour's room, and we could hear the floor moan and croak, so we knew he was present.

"I barged in first, with Eldried just behind me, already uttering some prayers to Gealius, and Ignetius a close third. I'm not sure what we expected. A magical deathtrap, perhaps, or a fierce magician who had prepared the necessary spells in order to pummel us into submission – or maybe even annihilate us. Instead, we found the necromancer standing in his room, wearing his full attire. He was holding a bag, as if he was ready to leave. Baour... he just stood there, gently bowing as we violated his quarters.

"The mage welcomed us and told us that he was ready to accompany us to the temple, so that – how did he say it? – 'justice could be dealt fairly and swiftly.' Even when we said he was accused of communing with the dead, he just nodded and told us that the assumption was grounded in the truth! He even assured us that he was willing to spend one or more cycles in a closed-off cell, as long as we promised to start with a trial as soon as possible!

"We were... surprised, to say the least, but Baour kept his word. He just accompanied us, without resisting, but without saying anything more, either.

"And that's how we've all come to be here today. We brought Vigilius to the Layn Hills, Reald was willing to act as a barrister, we made sure you all knew when the trial started, and now we've been in this temple hall for such a long time that I'm sure everyone wants to finish this and go home. There's a young man here who needs to bury his father, an even younger boy who seems to be incapable of mourning, but who urgently needs the attention of a healer, and a disease possibly spreading between us. We're all hungry, we're thirsty, and we need closure.

"That is my statement, necromancer. That's what happened.

Chapter Eleven

THE CROSS-EXAMINATION OF THE ACOLYTE THERIONALD

Baour bowed, but the pain of realization hit him when he wanted to spread his arms, only to remember his hands were fused together in an inhuman lump of molten flesh. He threw his shoulders up for a moment to let his sleeves cover his outer appendages, and then managed to pull off a smile, even though his back wound hadn't been healed completely.

"*Tulunil graticibo, Therionald-i,*" the necromancer said, gently.

Therionald looked at the stunned people in front of him. "Don't worry. The necromancer just greeted me in Normarian. It meant 'Thank you for your testimony, honorable Therionald.' Nothing more."

"Indeed," the mage agreed, "but before we start this cross-examination, there is another thing on my mind. Reald, honorable Eldried... would it be possible to grant an exemption to these trial rules and let young Matthayas carry his father's body outside? Look at the young man! He has been distraught since the incident, as is his prerogative, and he cannot be expected to sit idly by, waiting until these proceedings end, before he can remove his dead family member from these hallowed temple halls."

Reald looked at Eldried, who stood up. "I am sorry, Baour, but Divine Law is clear on this matter."

"So the Seraphalim have written down what to do after a melee during a trial, in the event of one or more fighters dying? I highly doubt that Divine Law would be that specific!"

Eldried wanted to answer, but it was Therionald who did so first. "You know full well it isn't, necromancer, as you also know that the Seraphalim never passed down any written works. They speak through our prophets and seers."

Baour nodded. "There is no debate on the matter. Many of those gifted with the Sight have examined the claims of the seers who pass down Divine Law, and every single time they have confirmed seeing the Strands of the Seraphalim, always connected to their prophets. And yet... my knowledge of temple texts may be faulty, but I cannot remember ever having lain eyes on a scroll, book, or other text stating literally that the dead are not to be removed after an... *incident* during a trial. In fact, does Divine Law not state that the deceased have to be entombed as soon as possible?"

"Admittedly, the writings are incomplete on that subject, but they're incomplete on any possible matter," Therionald started saying. This time, Eldried interfered.

"That is not an accurate statement, acolyte! Our religious texts aren't faulty."

"Forgive me, honorable Eldried, but I only said they are incomplete."

Eldried looked at his disciple as if he wanted to mentally burn a hole through Therionald's head and, for a moment, the younger priest thought Gealius might actually grant his elder's wish. Nothing happened, though.

"By all means, let us settle this dispute between priests," Baour interjected. "These very temple walls hold the library. Why not quickly go through the manuscripts and settle this dispute before it can escalate?"

"That's a good idea," Therionald agreed.

"It is not!" Baour was glad to see the elder priest was having difficulty to contain his anger. "There are thousands of texts on the library level..."

"And obviously you know every one of them by heart!" the necromancer pretended to believe.

"Obviously not!"

Baour faked surprise. "Then how can you know this specific situation is provided for under Divine Law? Do *you* know, barrister Reald?"

"I..." Reald shook his head.

"I suppose we can let someone carry Reaphrastus outside," Eldried agreed. *He's got it now,* Baour thought. *The longer he lets me challenge the validity of his rulings, the weaker their case against me becomes. You shouldn't have asked Gealius to do this to my hands, priest. I was going to show you mercy, but before this trial is over, you will have lost all authority!*

Matthayas – still teary-eyed but more composed than could be expected of a sixteen-year old man who had just lost his father – kneeled down to lift Reaphrastus's body from the ground.

"Halt!" Eldried shouted, much to the consternation of some of the villagers. "Not you. Someone else will carry your father outside."

"Are you charging my apprentice with a crime?" Baour chose his words carefully.

"I may be," Eldried answered. "After all, how are we to know Matthayas didn't engage in the same repugnant acts you are responsible for? As you said, he is your apprentice!"

Baour scanned the hall quickly, almost unnoticeably, before responding. He knew the disarming young man was liked a great deal amongst his community, despite of his brashness and oftentimes less than gallant behavior. Many of the Barnsby men and women were reacting as he thought they would: with disbelief and maybe even a little disgust, the young ones more so than their elders.

"No accusation of that ilk has been raised during any of the testimonies, priest, and I will call no one else to the stand."

Eldried frowned. "No one else?"

"You know that your guilt has been proven?" Reald asked, almost as if he were embarrassed to say so. "The testimonies have not been shown to be false."

"On the contrary," Baour said, cheerfully. "I am certain that Therionald's testimony has shown Divine Law will not apply here today!"

Again, disbelief, then silence, as if everyone present could feel the tension mount to near-insupportable levels, as if they could feel something in the air.

It was Eldried who broke the silence with a round of applause.

"Bravo, necromancer! Such impudence might gain you some time, but the end result will be the same."

"Hardly, old Eldried. I still have to question this last witness of mine. You would do better to reserve final judgement until you have heard his answers." He nodded at Matthayas. "What about Reaphrastus, Eldried?"

"I said he can be taken outside. Dorek, Bildar? Would you…?"

At the back of the temple hall, two burly men got to their feet. Their obvious hesitance changed to eagerness almost instantly as they realized this was their chance to get out of the temple, at least for a moment. Matthayas stepped back as Dorek slipped his arms underneath Reaphrastus's armpits and Bildar took hold of the woodcarver's feet.

Most of the assembled villagers watched as the corpse was being carried out. Baour, never one to miss an opportunity, knew he had to start off his next remark with exactly the correct intonation in order to capitalize on the drama and make sure he grabbed everyone's attention again. "Honorable Eldried," he said, feigning a sudden flash of insight in the pronunciation of just a single name, "now that I think of it…" The necromancer paused, showing his best pondering facial expression. "Now that I think of it… if you are not able to find a legal text referring to a sad situation such as this one, are you positive you will find such a text on the subject I am being charged of?"

This time, the old priest made no effort to hide his anger, nor would he have been able to, as his face turned red almost instantly. "Insolent! What performance are you trying for, Baour? Divine Law is clear on this! *Thou shalt not commune with the dead*!"

"And I suppose it is also clear on what the word 'commune' means, precisely?"

"Of course!"

"Reald?"

"Uh… I am more intimately familiar with the King's Law. The priests are responsible for…"

"Naturally, and since Divine Law apparently makes no room for interpretation, Eldried most assuredly has the tome describing the specifics of the offense I am being charged of labelled, with its location carefully registered?"

"It is there!" Eldried shouted.

"Good. I am, of course, a gentleman and, even though you are apparently unable to procure the writings I ask for, I believe you. Why would I not? During my conversations in the Black Stallion, I was very much pleased to hear these good villagers have also always believed you in the past. Zerezsta, for example, Roaldus's beautiful wife, who obeyed your commands when her father died. A very popular man in Barnsby. She wanted to leave his body in the bed for a full cycle, so that the men and women who had known him could pay their respects, but she agreed on burying him here only a little while after he died. Or Aulea, who has not been following Maerae's… *guidance* on a whim, but because you told her she should be inspired by Maerae's devout way of living after she accidentally stumbled at the altar while she was being given her sacraments. Surely the text stating that such an accident is an offense to the Seraphalim must be found in this library of yours as well? Let us not forget Esmeralda, either, whose name Matthayas pronounced several times without being struck down by Gealius. Mayhap I should continue? I also had an interesting conversation with..."

"Stop, necromancer!" Eldried shouted. Next to Baour, Therionald's face had become pale, while nearer to the elder priest, young Ignetius was still trying to figure out what had just happened. "Stop! I know full well what you are doing, but the scrolls and books you speak of do exist!"

"As I said, elder. I did affirm those texts must be real. If not, what a travesty this trial would be, no?"

"Everyone here understands you were implying otherwise!"

"I was? In that case, I should again offer my sincerest apologies. I merely wanted to cite some examples of people I admire for adhering to your tenets so unwaveringly, so... unquestioningly."

"There! You're doing it again! Don't you all see? He wants you to doubt the words of the Seraphalim!"

"I would never want anyone to do such a thing!" Baour exclaimed, as if he were offended. "Of course, as you said yourself mere heartbeats ago, it is not the Seraphalim who write these religious texts of yours, but seers and prophets. Or scribes who listen to these seers and prophets and then transcribe their words diligently and accurately. Well... more or less accurately, I suppose."

Eldried looked at Reald and pointed towards Baour. "Shut his mouth!"

The barrister shyly turned towards Baour. "You should probably begin your testimony."

"I will, thank you for trying to speed up this trial, dear Reald! You are right: we were getting lost in irrelevant dialogue-"

"That was not a dialogue, necromancer! It was a monologue!" Eldried yelled.

"I am most sorry it appeared that way. I have nothing but the greatest respect for your viewpoints, honorable Eldried, and I know all of the people gathered here today feel exactly the same way. If nothing else, I greatly admire them for the trust they put. You are, after all, one of the only villagers in Barnsby who can read and write, so it is not like they can examine the documents your laws are—"

"If you continue this, I shall charge you of blasphemy as well!"

"We should have killed him!" Ignetius suddenly shouted. Everyone looked at the boy in disbelief. Eldried sighed and rubbed his temples with both hands, shaking his head. "What did I say?" the young priest asked his elder, this time in a slightly softer voice.

"Continue already, mage," Eldried said to Baour, sounding weaker and less assured than before.

"Much obliged. Please forgive me for digressing, priest Therionald. You *are* a priest, yes?"

"Of course I am."

"I am truly sorry for asking."

"This is a trial. I am a witness. You can ask me anything you want."

"Ah, those words lighten the heavy burden that was resting on my shoulders! Since you give me permission, I shall not refrain from posing questions I might not have asked otherwise, for fear of hurting your reputation or standing in this village."

"What do you mean, necromancer?"

"Of course I shall explain myself. It occurs to me that both you and Mildrieda, whom apparently you have a lot in common with, are very eager to help me during these troubled times, so I shall continue as fastidiously as possible." Baour wanted to rub his chin and pretend to think for a while, but since his current predicament rendered such a gesture impossible, he chose to squint his eyes instead. "You told us you have received your education as a priest in Dor'O'Led?"

"I have, indeed."

"The most magical of human cities! No description would do it justice, though you have put in an excellent effort. I am sure the good villagers here appreciated the time you spent on telling them about the wonders of the Normarian capital."

"I hope they did."

"Of course. Now, in such a mystical place, being endowed with the Sight is very common, is it not?"

"Yes."

"I believe the priests in that city will also only take in students who have the Gift?"

"True."

"So, priest Therionald, if you really became a priest there, that must mean you had the fortune of having the Sight as well, even though you were being groomed as a merchant?"

"Yes. As you correctly pointed out, the ability to see reality and weave magic are not uncommon there."

"It often passes down from son to father."

"It does."

"Your father was not so gifted, though?"

"He wasn't."

"And neither was your mother?"

"No, she couldn't see the Strands, either.

"What an amazing discovery it must have been, to find yourself in the temple accidentally, and, despite the tragic circumstances, discover your talent!"

"It was hard at first, but finding out about my real potential eased the pain somewhat."

"So it is your statement that you came to Barnsby a full priest, gifted with the Sight?"

"Clearly."

Baour tilted his face somewhat and stared at Therionald for a while before continuing. "Then I am afraid I find myself in the position to point at a strange inconsistency."

"What would that be?"

"Please bring the testimony of young Matthayas into memory. While my pupil was telling everyone here about the black coils he saw around his brother, Ignetius interrupted him, screaming – and I cite – 'Stop this charade! How are we to know this is for real!'"

"He did."

"How did I react?"

"You were surprised."

"Why?"

"You implied that no man, woman or animal could pretend being endowed with the Sight. No one is able to fake it."

"Which, of course, means Ignetius does not have the Sight, as Eldried so kindly confirmed. Now, I do not find this too curious, as the boy is still young and he obviously is too impatient to gain the favor of Gealius permanently. In that, your elder was not mistaken. It is something else that is bothering me.

"What is bothering you, necromancer?"

"Mildrieda, in her testimony, said the disease had been afflicting villagers before I came here. In fact, it all started after you first came to Barnsby – almost exactly a hundred and five sleep cycles ago, as I was able to figure out after talking to some of the good people of Barnsby in the Black Stallion – but before I even encountered Esmeralda."

"She also stated the disease got worse after you arrived."

"Yes! Do you not find that peculiar? What would I have to gain by worsening an illness that was already there? And how could I be so impatient? I had to realize it would be obvious I might be responsible."

"How can we know how the depraved mind of a necromancer works?"

"Indeed! Thank you for reminding everyone that they should not think they can comprehend my motives without me explaining them myself."

Therionald groaned.

"So, priest Therionald, you do not know what I would have to gain, but I admit that does not necessarily mean I am innocent. However, let us all continue to unravel this mystery! The honorable Eldried already mentioned the disease does not seem to be natural, correct?"

"Yes."

"Now, if it is not, would it be a stretch of the imagination to presume whoever – or whatever – *created* the illness might also be able to control its progress?"

"Uh… I guess it wouldn't be."

"Good. If the illness is both unnatural and man-made, that also explains why your elder has not been able to treat it, and why Roaldus told us the Sakhovan priests in Greensdale did not detect anything out of the ordinary when they examined the dead sailors. Obviously, all unnatural traces of the illness disappear once the victim is dead. As if it was *designed* to do so. Now try to imagine *you* are the one who made this disease!"

"I'm not!"

"It is just – how shall we put it – make-belief."

"Fair enough, necromancer."

"So, you are the disease monger. You obviously want people to die, but you make sure the progress is slow enough, so they cannot get too suspicious. Suddenly, a stranger arrives in town. He turns out to be a mage, as well! How convenient a coincidence! Would you not be inclined to have the disease progress faster, before the mage leaves again, in order to pin the blame on this foreigner?"

"I… guess that's what I would do, if the inner workings of my mind would have been corrupted."

"Good! Evidently, I am not accusing you, but let us talk some more about the Sight. You yourself testified that Merielda came to the temple one cycle, telling you three people were suffering from a disease she was unable to diagnose correctly. Both you and young Ignetius examined the sick, but at first you did not think your patients were suffering from anything more than a cold bug."

"True again."

"How can this be, Therionald? Do you not use the Sight when examining other people? How can it be that Matthayas and me can see these strange, unnatural black tendrils around everyone who is afflicted and you missed it? Ignetius does not have the Gift, so you cannot have depended on him to diagnose the disease!"

Therionald looked away.

"I... didn't know Ignetius doesn't have the Sight."

"That may be, but still! Why did you not stop Ignetius from making a fool of himself when he thought Matthayas might be lying?"

"Hey, I'm not a fool!" the young boy screamed, holding his recently-healed nose, but Eldried stopped him from saying anything more by holding his hand in front of the youth's mouth.

"Eldried was faster," Therionald replied.

"You seem shaken, priest Therionald. Ashamed, even." The mage pointed at Reald, who stepped back almost unconsciously, surprised. "Use your Sight on Reald! What do you see?"

The cleric fixed the barrister, who immediately felt very uncomfortable indeed. "Black coils!" Therionald said. Reald grabbed hold of his own throat as if he wanted to puke. "Oh, no!"

"Where, Therionald? How do they cover him? Have they enveloped his entire body or just a limb?"

"They... they reach up to his neck!"

Baour swiveled around to face the benches. "Do they, Matthayas?"

"No, Lord, Baour," Matthayas answered from the other side of the hall. "They don't." Reald stumbled to the wall so he could lean on it with one hand, relieved but shaken.

"Do they, Eldried?" Baour now asked the elder priest, who didn't answer. "Do they, Eldried?" Baour repeated.

With all of the villagers watching their spiritual leader, Eldried shook his head slowly, reluctantly, sadly.

"Now tell us the truth, Therionald! You do not have the Sight, do you?"

"I... I used to! I used to have the Gift!"

Commotion everywhere. Baour took a moment to savor the occasion.

"One important question remains," he said. "Assuming that this time you are telling the truth, how did you lose the Sight?"

"I..."

"Eldried, did your disciple violate Divine Law? Or at least, do you know of such a violation?"

"No. No, I do not know of any transgression."

"That's not true!" Therionald suddenly shouted, surprising Eldried. "You do know! You've *always* known! Stop trying to protect me, please!"

Before the elder priest could answer, Baour stepped closer to his witness until their faces were almost touching. "You are Mildrieda's secret lover, are you not?"

Therionald fell to his knees and buried his face in his hands. Almost simultaneously, Mildrieda started crying. "It's true!" the cleric sobbed, "I am!" The other villagers reacted predictably: with a mixed sense of disbelief, surprise, anger, and curiosity.

"It must weigh heavily upon your conscience: a priest of Gealius who lets someone break her vow to the very same Seraphalim! But he stripped you of the Sight, correct?"

"He… he did! Gealius took it away! He punished me!"

"So it was you who was sleeping in the same inn as me! And it must have been you who stole Mildrieda's brews, paying for them with coinage you collected during your travels!"

Therionald righted his back and showed his face again. Tears were still rolling over his cheeks, but he managed to pull himself together nonetheless. "I was the one who stole your ales and mead, honey."

The innkeeper stopped weeping almost instantly and jumped up. "You bastard!" she screamed. "How could you?" She directed her next question at Eldried, "Can he be executed for that? Priests aren't supposed to steal, right?"

Baour didn't wait for anyone to react. "Therionald, tell us everything. Why would you steal your lover's brews?"

"I…"

"*Why*, priest?"

"I… I'm the murderer! I poisoned Mildrieda's drinks with a disease I had manufactured!"

This time, almost no one inside of the temple hall was able to remain calm, not even Therionald's fellow priests. People were screaming for Therionald to be executed, tortured, or worse, but their protests didn't take long to quiet down as a few villagers started to realize the priest might also know of a cure. Knowing whispers followed angry shouts and then silence, as Baour beckoned everyone to sit down. Even Reald seemed to have forgotten he was supposed to step in during times like this. He just sat himself down on the steps, near the temple wall.

As soon as the villager's rage seemed to have been contained, Baour turned towards Therionald again. The cleric looked beaten, powerless.

"So your testimony is that it was you who made all these well-meaning people sick?"

"Yes."

"Could you please repeat that answer? Louder, this time?"

"Yes!"

"Then it must have been you who plucked the ghostweed as well. You testified yourself that you know how to recognize it. You killed Ewella because she caught you. You are responsible for the dulling of the forest and, thus, in many ways for Esmeralda's desperate actions as well. Vigilius's spirit never felt Mildrieda's presence outside of his house while I was talking to him. He felt you! You weren't taking a stroll around the temple grounds. You had come back from the dying man instead, in the hopes of arriving there before me. You wanted to cover him in ghostweed before I would arrive, but you were too late. When you saw Mildrieda run towards this hall, you ran after her. Tell them why you did all these things, Therionald!"

"Because... because I knew you have the Sight! I couldn't risk you talking to the dead! They might have pointed you towards the drinks I had poisoned. The ghostweed made sure their spirits got bound in such a way they couldn't be contacted anymore!"

Baour shuffled even closer to the priest. He locked gazes with the man's trembling eyes, then, suddenly, swung his arms, hitting Therionald with the lump of flesh that had once been his hands. The priest toppled over to his side. Some villagers started to cheer. Others held their breath. Eldried jumped up, but didn't interfere. Violence wasn't allowed in the temple, but this was different. Here was a man who had betrayed Gealius himself, and he deserved punishment.

"Liar!" Baour shouted, furious.

"No!" Therionald wept. "I am not lying!"

"Yes, you are!" The necromancer knelt down until his face almost touched the priest's again. "Who are you protecting, priest?" He looked over his shoulder. "Mildrieda! How long have you been lovers?"

"Kill the son of a bitch!" the innkeeper shouted.

"Answer me, Mildrieda! How long!"

"It started only cycles after he arrived here," the woman finally answered.

Baour stood up and kicked Therionald in the stomach. "I asked you a question!" The priest lifted himself up on both hands, trying to change stance, but Baour kicked him again, this time against the chin. A thin line of blood appeared on Therionald's mouth as he fell backwards and the necromancer came to stand above him, each foot against one of the priest's flanks.

"One more time!" Baour shouted. "Who are you covering for? *You have lost the Sight! You cannot have made the disease! And you cannot have unleashed the properties of the ghostweed*! How can you manipulate Strands you are unable to see, let alone touch?"

"Enough!" Therionald pleaded. He wiped away the blood from his mouth and stroked his hand through his hair, oblivious of the fact that he drew a red streak through it in doing so. Without saying anything or looking up, the priest raised his arm slowly, as if he didn't want to do so at all. There were no options left, though. "Him," Therionald said, pointing one of his own. "*He* did it."

Chapter Twelve
THE WEB UNTANGLES

Amidst the chaos Ignetius looked at Baour with disbelief. The pain in his face was gone, thanks to Eldried's prayers, and the young acolyte felt as if everything had come crashing down around him. He imagined how the earth might open up, swallowing the villagers seated on the benches whole. He imagined screams and desperate cries for help, lightning bolts sizzling through the hall, igniting wood and melting metal, columns crumbling and fire erupting out of the ruptures below. He imagined everyone present being engulfed by fire and eaten alive by the flames. He could almost *feel* the smoke and the heat, *smell* the sweat and the burnt flesh, and *taste* the ashes in his mouth. But never – ever – could he have imagined his elder, Eldried, to be responsible of creating a disease and spreading it amongst his own flock.

The old priest was standing next to him, shouting, but his voice got drowned out in the angry screams of the mob around him. Even Ignetius wasn't able to make out the words that were coming out of Eldried's mouth, nor did he concern himself with what the cleric had to say anymore.

From his raised vantage point, Baour was still able to retain a good overview of what was happening. He nodded at Matthayas, who started to make his way towards the mage's general direction. This is what Baour and the young man had prepared for and Matthayas knew exactly what to do.

"Behind the altar!" the necromancer screamed at Therionald, who slowly got up as Baour slipped behind the altar and sat down with his back against the stone.

The acolyte came up next to him.

"Get down, Therionald!"

The priest complied.

"Eldried is too powerful." Baour raised his voice just enough to be heard, despite of the noise behind him. "You have to heal my hands. It's the only way."

The mage cursed as Reald, too, appeared, kneeling down.

"Get away, Reald! This is going to become too dangerous!"

The villager shook his head. "I can't!" he screamed, his face twisted in the agony of self-doubt. "Eldried may have poisoned us, you are still guilty of communing with the dead!"

"No!" Therionald shouted. "We can't find him guilty! There's no one left to dispense Divine Law anymore! Ignetius and me don't have the Gift, and Eldried just lost all authority! Divine Law is forfeit!"

"He's right," Baour said. "I can't be judged. But Eldried can. His crime is well-covered under the King's Law." He clumsily took hold of Reald's arm in support and looked the man in the eyes. "It is time to step up Reald. Today you will have to convict a priest. But first I need my hands back."

"H... How?" Reald asked, confused.

"Therionald will do it."

"But... he doesn't have the Sight anymore!"

The necromancer turned his face towards Therionald. "Pray! If Eldried is indeed guilty, Gealius may forgive you! Pray, Therionald! Ask absolution and let the Seraphalim grow my hands back!"

In the temple hall, Eldried had realized no one was able to understand what he was saying. Villagers were blocking his way out of the bench in both directions, so he set foot on an empty seat in front of him and pulled himself over to the next bench, and then the next one. Everywhere, people were tying to grab the old priest. Eldried fought of the hands and blocked the punches and kicks he received in the process with his own arms. One hit bruised his shoulder. Another hurt his right thigh. A third one knocked some of his teeth out; but he was still advancing towards the altar, fighting off dizziness and trying to get it together long enough to pray. Just as he was ready to complete an entire sentence, he felt himself being pulled up by an invisible force. Two hands managed to tear off part of his robe as he flew straight up to the temple ceiling, the sudden movement and pressure almost rendering him unconscious. He hit the marble tiles hard, part of the multi-colored mosaic breaking off and falling to the ground, where it momentarily caused panic amongst some of the villagers.

It was difficult to breathe and almost impossible to move. The force that was holding him up against the ceiling was powerful and full of anger, but Eldried knew that his Sight would not betray him. He saw many bluish Strands woven together into something that looked like a wall. A wall that was pushing him against the ceiling and that was connected to somebody down below through a channel of interlinked Strands.

On the floor, Matthayas was holding his hands high above his head, palms up, as if he was physically pushing Eldried himself. He was straining, pouring in every single ounce of energy he had left. Zeitas's brother didn't have any fine manipulation over the color he was using to hold the priest up and he had to keep everything together, lest the old man would be released from his grasp. *"I can just make him fall down,"* he had said to his master, Baour, only one sleep-cycle ago, but the necromancer had asked him not to do that. *"The villagers will want revenge. Besides, if you don't pin him down, he might be able to have Gealius save him,"* Baour had said.

Matthayas felt his control waver. Some of the color was dissipating, the force weakening, and he could feel his nose beginning to bleed. His ears were under a tremendous pressure and he felt like his head might explode. Above him, Eldried was saying something, but he was too high up for anyone to see his lips move. Matthayas expected the priest to counter his attack, somehow driving back the color, or maybe overwhelming the blue with other Strands, but instead Baour's apprentice suddenly noticed a surge of power, complementing the turquoise he was commanding and increasing both its volume and brightness into a whirling vortex. Eldried was drawing in even more Strands of the same color, combining them. But why? Just when Matthayas thought the priest's chest would collapse under the pressure, the roof burst open. Parts of the ceiling were thrown away from the temple as a hole of about twice Eldried's size appeared. The priest was whisked into the moonlit night.

"Curse his colors!" Baour spit, but he knew Eldried had made a crucial mistake as well. He started to concentrate on his hands again. Therionald was cupping them with his own, all the while whispering to an unseen force in the process. Slowly, the flesh that had been fused together started to warp. Some of the skin was peeling off, while part of it was melting, drops falling to the floor like hot wax. The priest was constantly moving his fingers, more like he was molding a form than weaving a fabric, but he made sure to stay in contact with Baour while doing so. Reald was watching the entire process in awe, so focused on what was happening behind the altar that he didn't care much about what his peers in the hall were doing.

"Reald," Baour started. He wanted to make sure he had the barrister's undivided attention, dropping the more formal speech. "I'll have to go after Eldried soon. I'm the only one who can stop him and find a cure to the illness. Can I be confident that you agree with me on this matter?"

"I don't know," Reald answered truthfully. "You still communed with the dead..."

"There's no one left who can act as a judge on the matter. Also, do you really think your Seraphalim would give Therionald's powers back and heal me if he thought me guilty?"

"I... suppose not."

"Good. You'll have to keep these men and women in check while I try to find the cleric. If anyone here has any questions, just bring the facts into memory."

"I don't understand. What facts?"

"It's simple. Of all the villagers in Barnsby, only Therionald, Roaldus, and Eldried could have been in Greensdale around the time the R'Lallon left."

"Left?"

"Of course. The sailors became sick during their journey, not upon returning. It's even more evidence that the sickness was manufactured and its duration can be altered. Those men hadn't decomposed yet when Roaldus saw them. He told us the Sakhovan priests preserve the dead, but they can't reverse the rotting that is already visible. I saw the bodies, Reald. It was the same disease. Which means that Eldried poisoned them with the illness before they left the Greensdale docks and set it to finally kill them shortly before arriving back."

"You... stole the bodies?"

"Of course I did. I came to Barnsby because I was tracking occurrences of the illness. I only offered T'Halek to buy the three bodies that showed symptoms, but he declined. I needed to know what evil I was combating, however, so I took the corpses out of the ship."

"How?"

"Magic."

"Ah, yes... of course."

"The R'Lallon must have been a test case of some kind. A preparation for what Eldried had in mind here."

"But why would he do such a thing?"

"I do not know, Reald. Perhaps he wanted to assert himself as the head of this temple. He must have thought the presence of a promising priest like Therionald was a threat to his status. Or maybe he wanted to strengthen your belief in Gealius. Or punish you. Either way, I think he would eventually have cured most of you, but who is to say who he would have picked to survive?"

"I see. And you eliminated Therionald and Roaldus as suspects because—"

"Because they do not possess the Sight."

"So the ghostweed..."

"It was meant to obscure what had happened from me. Ewella caught Eldried and probably tried to stop him, only to be killed, causing poor Esmeralda to go insane. After I leave, search the temple grounds. Check every possible corner. Turn over every bench, topple every statue, lift the mattresses, and tear open the cushions. You should eventually find the ghostweed. And you, Therionald... it wasn't wise to try to protect Eldried."

The priest didn't answer. He was still concentrating on Baour's appendages. The necromancer's hands were regaining their shape, with the fingers visible again. Therionald was still working on the nails and joints, but Gealius was obviously answering his prayers. Baour's hands had lost a little volume and they were bright red, as if they had just been burned, but he didn't really care about such an unimportant side effect at all.

"Don't forget to wait until everything else is done before you start work on the nerve endings," Baour said to the cleric. There was no time to talk to Therionald much, however, so he redirected his attention towards Reald. "Are you clear on everything?"

"I would be, mage... But there's one more thing that's bothering me. If I understand everything correctly, we were poisoned through Mildrieda's drinks."

"Most of you, but the disease is... *sticky*. That's why I wanted Matthayas to keep an eye on the girls. They bathed in the Lorenlon and the water is able to conduct some of the bad Strands, so that people living downstream might have become sick as well. What if the Sundarun had been inflicted? They have the Sight, so it would have been easy for them to track the source back to the village."

"That would have meant war!"

"It would have."

"Why didn't you do it yourself?"

"There were too many villagers for a single mage to keep an eye on. I wanted to be able to talk to one of the dead before whoever manufactured the disease would be able to sprinkle them with treated ghostweed, so I needed to know who was infected. Now, almost everybody is, but when I first came here, the disease hadn't spread yet."

"But how could the dead have helped you?"

Baour smiled. "Hindsight is always clearer. And I might have alerted the one who was responsible for all this if I had talked to a living person. If I learned one thing in the Black Stallion, it must be that the people here aren't exactly tight-lipped. Also, I didn't want to spread a panic... and the dead often know more than the living do, anyway."

"It all still doesn't change what's been bothering me."

"What is it?"

"Therionald, I am sorry, but Eldried almost never visited Mildrieda's inn. How could he—"

"Wait, barrister. I am certain Therionald will answer you. For now, let him finish this."

"Lord Baour!" It was Matthayas. The boy looked exhausted. He was bleeding out of his ears and mouth, and crimson waters were also slowly dripping out of his eyes. "I'm sorry, Lord Baour, I wasn't able to—"

"Do not worry, Matthayas. You did your part."

The young man looked puzzled. "But I—"

"You kept Eldried busy long enough. Therionald is now healing my hands and the old cleric had to use magic to get away."

"That means..."

"It does."

"What does it mean?" Reald wanted to know, but the priest interrupted him.

"Finished!" Therionald said under his breath. He looked drained, as well, but, unlike Matthayas, he wasn't bleeding.

The necromancer looked at his new hands. They felt strange and somewhat detached from him, as if he had been resting on them for a very long time. He moved his fingers, watching them closely. It was difficult to find the exact motions, but it would have to do.

Therionald rested his back on the altar. He looked over his shoulders and saw how most of the villagers had already gone outside. Others were scraping gold off the relics, climbing up the walls to get to the diamonds set in the statues, fighting each other, shouting, weeping, or doing any number of other things people do when they feel enraged, abandoned, and panicked at the same time. Several were watching the altar, waiting for what would happen, but too afraid to come nearer. He sighed. "I poisoned the alcohol, Reald."

"What?"

"I did. But I didn't know what I was doing. Eldried gave a flask of thick, clear liquid to me. He knew I visited the Black Stallion often, so he asked me if I could find a way to pour into her brews. I thought it was medicine, not poison."

"Medicine?"

"Yes. Something to stop the common cold bug. That's what he said."

"But why do it secretively?"

"Because so many villagers were going to the witch. Eldried wasn't sure if everyone would take the medicine. He said that if they found out they hadn't become sick for a while..."

"They would see Gealius holds far more power than a witch."

"Yes."

"How could you not have told us?" Matthayas wanted to know.

"I wasn't sure..."

"That's why he stole Meldrieda's ale and mead," Baour explained. "But to no avail..."

"Because I had lost the Sight. Try as I might, I couldn't find anything peculiar about the alcohol. Not in the usual fashion." Therionald bowed his head. "I shouldn't have lied..."

Reald put a hand on the priest's shoulder. "Don't worry. Your first instinct was to protect your elder. Everyone will understand that. Well, maybe not everyone, but still..."

"Are you alright?" Baour asked Matthayas. "You strained your abilities. It has wreaked havoc on your mind."

Matthayas dipped his fingers in the blood running down from out of his nose and looked at it. "I may be bleeding, but I don't feel like I'm going to die. Not anymore."

"Good. You'll be needed here. These people have to be calmed down. They cannot be allowed to leave Barnsby in any way. Not before I cure everyone. It will be easier to do so now that I know Eldried was the one who created the poison." Baour said, but there was no joy of any kind to be seen on his face. "Matthayas, we are going to need Zeitas."

Eldried cautiously navigated the entrance to the cavern. It was only a small space and most of it was lit adequately by the light of both moons, but he asked Gealius to shed more light into the natural corridor nonetheless. The light flickered in and out a few times before the cavern started to bask in an unearthly, yellow, hallowed glow. He could now clearly see the freshly dug grave holding Vigilius, the earth still meshed up and soft. Eldried knelt down and contemplated what to do next. There had been enough time to heal the wounds caused indirectly by Matthayas, but his body still bore some scratches and bruises. He hadn't asked Gealius to make those go away as well. The truth was that he wanted to feel the pain. It kept his thoughts focused and reminded him of what had to be done.

"Eldried?"

A voice from outside.

"Eldried?"

The old priest felt a cold running up and down his spine.

Again, "Eldried?"

What could he do?

"Eldried?" It was closer this time.

The voice sounded so sweet, so innocent...

"Eldried?" More urgent, now.

"Yes?" he finally answered.

"Eldried! Are you there?"

"I am inside." He turned around on his left knee, supporting himself with one hand on the ground and one on the other knee.

The torch threw a long shadow into the burial site; its light conflicting with the eerie shine Gealius had cast over the uneven walls of earth, rock, and dirt.

Zeitas stepped closer. His body was riddled with black spots, but the kid seemed to be more alive than during the entire trial. There was some life in his eyes, and his face bore an expression for the first time in a long while. The young boy looked concerned; caring, even.

"I have come for you, honorable Eldried."

The priest nodded. "Yes, yes! I am glad you came. Has the situation in the temple been resolved, then?"

Zeitas nodded.

"So my congregation stood up against the necromancer? They revolted?"

Again, a nod, as Zeitas moved closer to the priest, opening his arms wide. Eldried motioned the boy to stop. "I don't think I should touch you, dear Zeitas."

The boy stepped closer to the priest. He didn't seem to take heed of the old man's words.

"Please, stop!" Eldried tried. He felt bad for the boy, but if he got infected as well, all hope would be lost.

Zeitas kept on advancing.

"Stop!" Eldried screamed, desperate.

The boy accelerated and jumped at the priest, freezing up before he could reach Eldried.

The priest let go of the pommel, his dagger jutting out of the boy's chest. Only a little blood was dripping out of the wound, but Zeitas just kept looking at Eldried. Surprised, shocked, questioningly. The cleric began to cry as the kid slowly dropped to his knees, grasping at the pommel. Unable to get the blade out of his heart, he pushed himself to the nearest wall with his feet, kicking away some dirt in the process. Then, he finally became still.

"Excellent!"

Baour looked through the opening to the cavern and stepped inside. "You did well, priest. That was the last piece of evidence I needed. A cleric who would kill a sick boy with the ceremonial dagger he always keeps under his sleeve. No one will care about an adventurous, helpful mage who tried to save the entire village anymore. Only your name will be on the villagers' lips. The name of the priest who betrayed them. The name of Eldried, former servant to Gealius, a man turned evil and mean, a silent assassin and a murderer of children!"

"I curse your colors, mage!" Eldried fulminated.

Baour looked sad. "You didn't have to do what you did, Eldried. I have come to bring you to justice."

"Justice? What do you know about justice, necromancer? The word rings hollow to you, devoid of meaning as well as sound!"

"Oh, believe me, I know what justice is, and you are not the only one who will feel its sting this cycle."

"What do you mean?"

"You needn't know. As soon as death embraces you, you will find out you don't care anymore."

"It's not over yet, Baour!"

The necromancer looked Eldried in the eyes, puzzled. "Do you really think I came here for a mage battle? To test the power Gealius is still willing to grant you against my mastery of the Strands?"

"It's the only way you will be able to get rid of me!" Eldried shouted, only to be greeted by a painful sting through the inner part of his upper leg.

He screamed in agony, the pain spreading through his body almost instantly.

Zeitas was laughing like a kid usually does as he rubbed his hand over the part of the barbed knife that he had just stuck in Eldried's leg, soaking himself in the old man's life fluids. On any other occasion, his laugh could have been deemed charming.

"I told you, I am not going to start a mystic battle. I am very much disappointed that you would desecrate these sacred grounds, priest. Oh, and maybe you should know: Zeitas just struck a major artery. That is why you are losing so much blood, while you feel overcome with dizziness. You will lose consciousness soon."

Eldried coughed. He knew Baour was right. His strength was leaving him, sapped by the wound. "How... how does a child know how to target an artery?"

Baour shook his head in faked sadness. "Tss-tss-tss. Use the Sight, old one."

The priest's pupils dilated, becoming even blacker and bigger. "Oh, no... No..." He touched the boy's cheek softly, caressing it. "Poor Zeitas..." Then, to Baour, "How could you do this? How could you?"

"As you and all of the others pointed out so many times at the trial, I am still a necromancer," Baour said. "This *is* what I do. But if you ask me how I could kill the boy, just to animate his body: I couldn't."

"No!" Eldried shouted, followed by a whispered "Matthayas".

"Yes. His own brother. He obeys me now, Eldried, and he will never serve a Seraphalim again! Neither will any of the villagers. Their eyes have opened up now. As we speak, they are destroying your temple, deconstructing it stone by stone. It has been plundered, ransacked, and desecrated. Soon, it will disappear into oblivion. The people of Barnsby are free men now. This is what I want you to know before you die."

"You shouldn't..."

"Matthayas knew his brother was going to die soon. We both agreed this death was more... *merciful*. In fact, Therionald helped. He talked to the boy..."

"How did you...?"

"Find you? Simple. You were stupid, old Eldried. You used magic to get away from Matthayas. I knew you would try to get some space between us and you, but you were still wounded. The only way to move quickly was to ask Gealius for help. But you shouldn't have done that. I may not be a tracker and I am not specialized in seeing the Strands you might leave by foot, but through the air... Ah, I only had to switch to the Sight and follow the anomalies in the Web. But..." Baour looked around. "I would have found you anyway. It fits your character, coming to the grave of the last one who died, asking yourself where it all went wrong."

Zeitas – or at least, the undead creature that used to be Zeitas – started to lick at Eldried's wound, eagerly, hungrily. The priest gritted his teeth. He was too weak to even lift his hand now.

"The... villagers..."

"I have cured them of their absurd, blind faith in Gealius, now I will cure them of the disease. I will draw it out of them, one by one, if it is the last thing I do. I only regret so many have died. It took a long time to figure out these Strands of death, to comprehend how they get entangled with other threads, to *get* where they were coming from."

"So you..."

"I didn't lie during the trial, no. I can see you are losing your grasp on life, old man. Shall I prolong it or shall I ask death to come quicker? I have no interest in seeing you suffer."

Devoid of all strength, the priest just nodded. Baour looked at Zeitas. "Do it, boy."

Zeitas grasped the grip of the knife with both hands, leaning back as he used the entire mass of his small frame to pull it out of Eldried. The barbs ripped open the priest's flesh, exposing his muscle tissue and veins as blood came spewing out of his leg like a joyous fountain. Eldried was too weak to shout or cry and felt how two cold hands grabbed his neck from below.

Baour left the cavern while Zeitas was still strangling Eldried, even after the priest had drawn his final breath. He waved his hands and the burial site became dark again. Gealius's glow was doused forever.

Epilogue

Baour screamed. He savored the moment as immense joy took hold of his body. Trembling, he withdrew from his lover and rolled over to lay next to the man, who was just as naked – and just as sweaty – as he was. The necromancer sighed blissfully as he ran his fingers over his mate's back, some of the perspiration sticking to his fingers like mountain dew. Licking his hands slowly, he admired the beautiful body next to him one last time.

The man turned over to his side and ran his left hand through Baour's hair.

"I've always admired your hair. Ever since I met you in Greensdale."

The mage smiled. "I know. You've told me many times."

"You were great during the trial."

"And you, my friend, were brilliant," Baour said, meaning every word of it. "I told you, the best way to cover up the truth is to be honest. At least as much as possible. When man speaks of those things most would leave hidden under layers of secrecy and mystery, people will often believe those words without pursuing a more... *inquisitive* line of reasoning. Better yet, if he is able to imply those things he wants others to think, they will fool themselves into believing they found out the truth all by themselves. Follow before you lead, then take the reins and ride to whatever destination you have in mind. Be vague. Create the illusion of self-control, of self-determination. Say 'You are lying!' but do not say what he is lying about. Develop the skill to ask 'What do you think I am lying about?' but do not teach those you want to manipulate how to do that. Learn, but share only with those you care about."

"You taught me well, Baour."

The necromancer turned over to his side as well. He kissed his lover on the forehead and smiled. "I did not have to teach you."

Therionald frowned. "What do you mean?"

"You already knew – if not all, then most – of these things, lover. You were well-versed in the art of deception long before I met you."

The priest nodded. "I had to learn. I spent so many years in that rotten temple, raised by priests I hated, to serve Seraphalim I hated even more. They let my parents die, Baour. The clerics spent too much time asking too many questions – curse their colors – and the Seraphalim didn't bestow their healing powers on them. And was it really so difficult to calm down my dad?"

Therionald had balled his hands, releasing his anger again. Baour was used to it, and he knew how to end it, as well. "Hush," he whispered. "You have avenged them."

The priest relaxed. "I know. But it will never be enough, Baour. Never."

"That is what I'm afraid of."

"At least we share a common goal!" Therionald's eyes turned glazy as he lay down on his back again, wrapping both hands under his head. "We will take down those temples one by one, Baour."

"You are wrong, lover."

"What do you mean?"

"We do not share a common goal – nor a common ideal."

"How so?"

"You want vengeance, but your thirst for priestly blood will never be sated. I only want to let people think for themselves. Release them from the shackles of religion." He looked at the ceiling. "But they are there, Therionald. The Seraphalim. They are watching. I do not want people to turn away from them. I just want them to see their priestly rulers for what they are. Without taking lives, unless absolutely necessary."

Therionald shrugged. "It doesn't matter. The end result is similar."

"Wasn't it hard? Pretending to have to pray?"

"I got used to it."

"I doubt you would have been able to navigate your way to the temple without having the Sight."

"Of course. Most people in Dor'O'Led are gifted. I said so during the trial."

"The fact that you became a priest made sure they didn't think you might already have been a mage."

"It did. Roaldus almost spoiled it, though. At the altar."

"Don't worry about it. I just didn't know you would remember that you weren't supposed to be able to mold my hands the way you did, so I quickly made up a story."

"Yes!" Therionald laughed out loud. "What was it you said? 'Gealius may forgive you'? I almost burst out in laughter!"

"He never needed to forgive you."

"He never gave me any power, either. It was always me."

"And you never lost the Sight."

"Of course I didn't. But sometimes it was tough, lover. Especially those nights with Mildrieda." He put his hand on Baour's inner thigh. "Every time I made love to her, I thought of you."

"That was your own choosing, Therionald. You insisted on going to Barnsby before me."

"To gain their trust. To prepare. The illness here made everything a lot easier; though. It would have been far more difficult to oust Eldried if he hadn't been unable to cure the disease."

"It was easy setting everything up that way. We had room to maneuver. I didn't even have to use the fact that you had convinced Ignetius to bribe Roaldus."

"He needed to make mistakes, to be too aggressive. To go after you."

"Your assistance in the inn was crucial, as well. I stole Mildrieda's brew, you were waiting below."

"With the key."

"Did they find those bottles yet?"

"Yes. Near the temple grounds. Exactly where I hid them."

Baour stood up and poured in two glasses of wine. He gave one of the glasses to Therionald. "To your health."

"And to yours!" The priest swallowed everything at once. He looked through the window. "The wake-cycle is so much brighter now that Eldried is gone."

"That was unfortunate. As was Esmeralda's death."

"Unfortunate? He deserved it!"

"Only for accusing me and melding my hands together."

Therionald squinted. "I don't understand. He did unleash that terrible disease—"

Baour shook his head. "I am afraid you were involved too much with your role. You obviously weren't paying enough attention to the trial."

"What are you talking about?"

"I'm talking about the coins I gave to Roaldus. Where were they from again?"

"Byrmur, Thoufeldt, and Arrkon, I believe."

"Yes. And Illexalluh and Tormar and Ür'd. Do those cities not sound familiar to you?"

Therionald thought about it for a while. "I've been to Illexalluh," he finally said. "And to Byrmur and Arrkon."

"And Thoufeldt is a stop between those Illexalluh and Dor'O'Led," Baour said. "I have never been to Tormar and Ür'd, though. Got those while buying goods at the Dor'O'Led market."

"I'm still not sure what you are talking about."

"I was following a trail, Therionald. A trail of death. My friends in Dor'O'Led told me about some of the priests they knew in the city. They had died from a sickness that was impossible to identify. It had already spread amongst some of the populace, but it stopped spreading after a while. Just like that. I found strange, black Strands, and started to track them."

"And they led you to Eldried?"

"No, my friend. Eldried might have visited Greensdale sometimes, he never was in any of the other cities."

"So you knew."

"I suspected. You do pride yourself on being a 'travelling' priest, do you not?"

Therionald smiled. "Good! Good! No need for secrets anymore, then!"

"You should have known I would find out."

"Of course. But I figured it would take you longer."

"It almost did, until you made a few crucial mistakes."

"Which ones?" Therionald wanted to know, amused. "Tell me!"

"Well, you neglected to tell me Ignetius doesn't have the Sight. So why use ghostweed on the bodies? If Eldried had manufactured the disease, he would have no need to examine the dead, and there would be no sense in using the ghostweed to obscure my Sight, either."

"Excellent! Excellent! I hadn't thought of that."

"Also, you forgot about Ewella."

"How so?"

"You killed her when she caught you foraging for ghostweed. She must have understood what you were doing. But you forgot I brought her back from the dead. I talked to her, Therionald. I didn't just animate her for Esmeralda's sake."

"That makes sense, but why didn't you just tell me? I just needed to get to know you better before I told you everything. Now that we've been through so much together, I trust you more than ever."

"You shouldn't."

"I shouldn't?"

"I needed time to figure out the disease, Therionald, so as long as my other motives were being furthered, you served your purpose. But all those people… they didn't have to die.

"The inescapability of their deaths weakened the priests' power! They couldn't help them, so the trust the villagers had always put in them was wavering. It only needed a final push…"

"Things could have been handled differently. Ewella didn't have to die, my friend, and neither did Esmeralda or any of the others. I did what needed to be doing when the time came, but it was unnecessary and unwanted."

"It worked, though. It always works. Only, in the big cities, there are too many priests. I can only do so much there. But in villages such as these… The revolution will begin in small towns and hamlets, in farms and on the fields!"

"There will be no revolution, Therionald!"

"But you want it, too!"

"I told you, I want different things. I want to take on Divine Law and the absolute power some priests think they have. I want to take on what men make of the Seraphalim's wishes. I want to abolish blind faith in mortals and Seraphalim alike. I want to make people see that the beings they worship do not always care about them. I want to let them find faith inside of themselves instead of outside of themselves. But I do not want what you want. I do not crave revenge or death."

"You do not crave death? You're a necromancer!"

"Yes. But death is all around us. It does not need any help."

Therionald stood up and grabbed his robe. "Very well. This collaboration is finished, then." Baour saw Therionald's anger turn to sadness almost immediately. "I will miss you, friend."

"I did not say we will be apart."

"Again, you speak in riddles!" Therionald laughed. Then, he looked concerned. The cleric put one hand on his belly, then another as he started to cough. "What…"

The necromancer put his own glass of wine – still full – on the shelf next to the bed. "It is poison, my friend. Esmeralda taught me how to make it."

"But why…"

"Because you are a murderer. You killed because you wanted to. I only kill if there is no other way."

"We are the same…" Therionald toppled over as he started to throw up blood all over himself.

"You told us we will not be apart!"

"We won't. But your spirit will be shackled, Therionald. Already, the convulsions are starting. You will be dead soon."

"You... you are going to..."

"Animate you? Yes." Baour smiled. "I would miss my bed partner too much. Matthayas will be going to Greensdale with Eaerae soon. Poor boy. He will never be able to see the Strands, so I can't be his master, no matter how much he would have liked to be my apprentice. And Esmeralda was executed. Because of your own actions. I have a long trip ahead and I want a companion by my side. I just want a companion I can control."

"You're... evil!"

Baour smiled as he saw the Strands of entropy taking hold of Therionald, as if they were living, avenging angels. It was beautiful. He started to weave the threads he needed to animate the priest before any rotting might begin.

"I am, my dear Therionald, a necromancer."

About the Author

One could say Dirk Vandereyken is an early learner. He wrote his first fantasy novel at 11, got it published a scant three years later, started roleplaying at 9, became Regional Director for the RPGA at 15 and opened up his own practice in hypnotherapy at 20. Dirk is a multi-faceted kind of guy, who juggles being an author, a critic, an editor, and a journalist with acting, coaching, helping others as a psychotherapist and running his own aptly-named PR-team, Badass PR – all experiences that help him write his suspenseful, psychologically involved novels.

Also from BlackWyrm...

by Jason Walters

At the edge of the known world, two desperate armies struggle for the right to siege a city that has never been taken. Terrible magics are unleashed and the fate of empires hangs in the balance. Highdome and his crew of cutthroats, monsters, and mutants don't care. They just want to stay alive. But when sorcery backfires and the fury of the Vast White desert is unleashed, the men and women of the Red Regiment must look inside of themselves to find the strength to survive.
[Dark Military Fantasy, ages 14+]
JANUARY 2009

by Ian Harac

One FBI agent
One geekette
One dead munchkin
Parallel worlds galore
An interdimensional conspiracy.
When Matt Anders stumbles across the body of a dead munchkin in a suspect's apartment, a conspiracy begins to unravel that leads him on a reality-jumping adventure to the magical Land of Oz... and beyond!
[Snarky SciFi Thriller, ages 14+]
FEBRUARY 2009

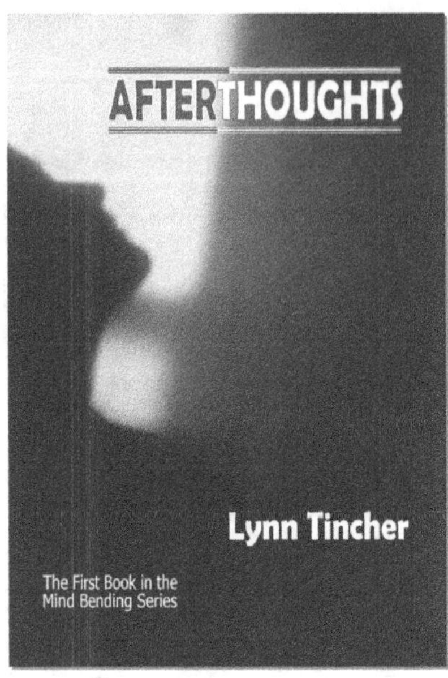

AFTERTHOUGHTS

by Lynn Tincher

Detective Paige Aldridge was found beaten and without any memories of the previous few months. When her nephew is found dead a year later, she begins to have terrifying flashbacks, plus visions of the murders of her own family! As her loved ones begin falling prey to a serial killer, Paige believes that she must be going mad. With her family dying around her and dark suspicions forming in her mind, Paige has to pull the pieces together before it's too late.
[Psychic Crime Thriller, ages 14+]
MARCH 2009

by Brad Parnell

Young Robert journeys to another world. There he comes of age amid a feuding government, grotesque monsters, an ancient ancestor ...and a couple of teenaged girls. With the help of a young wolf named Louie, Robert is introduced to the wonders and perils of a strange land called Gwerinatha.
[Allegoric Celtic Fantasy, ages 12+]
JULY 2009

www.BlackWyrm.com

www.ingramcontent.com/pod-product-compliance
Lightning Source LLC
LaVergne TN
LVHW020632100826
845148LV00012B/2149

* 9 7 8 0 9 8 2 0 0 6 7 2 6 *